THE HEAVEN OF FREEDOM

(A NOVEL)

SHAHID NASIM HYDER

Chennai • Bangalore

CLEVER FOX PUBLISHING
Chennai, India

Published by CLEVER FOX PUBLISHING 2025

ISBN: 978-93-6707-223-3

CONTENTS

SHAHID NASIM HYDER

Author's Note:-

Freedom without self-regulation is incomplete. This self-regulation we can learn by patience and a will to tame aggression. Taming aggression in the meantime is a difficult job as it would require plugging of the excess irritation. Irritation is vindicative as it inflames aggression and stifles self-regulation.

Bridling of aggression requires the activation of passive resistance. The passive resistance addresses not to the timid retreat from resistance but a calm bravery. Freedom is sure to be achieved bloodlessly through calm bravery as well but this calm bravery is hard to command and teach to the common mass. The raw and uncouth mass is likely to go berserk when freedom suddenly comes handy turning the mass vindicative. The principle of self-control then crumples down and hostility against the opponent goes berserk.

The realization of the true heaven of freedom as suggested in this novel lies in looking upon man and matter as not an aggressive avenger. This novel undertakes to examine possibilities of reaching the heaven of freedom via a non-aggressive calm bravery and for this the novelist examines Gandhi's principle of passive resistance as a weapon of resistance. But he regrets to note that the calm bravery of passive resistance meets disappointments. Different characters in different situations vent forth different reactions to the same goal of reaching the heaven of freedom and this becomes a delicious experience making this novel a non-conventional read full of doubts and thrill but evenly textured.

Martin Julius, an English forester, as a self-professed sentinel of the colonial power over India defends his version of heaven of freedom insisting upon maintaining the notorious arbitrary hold on the subject nation requiring him to do his maximum best to harness the Indians and keep them enthralled and humbled. He relentlessly breaks the spirit of the windy villagers by killing the Bonga Tigers, the reverential village deities and basks in the belief that he achieved his version of heaven of freedom. The humble villagers squirm in pain and shame but Martin counts it as his victory.

Contrarily his wife, Sophie Juliet, a self-proclaimed half-Indian owing to her birth and upbringing in India and nurturing a strong feel of affection for Indian freedom she without entering any bitter conflicts with her husband who was the opponent of Indian freedom, fights for Indian cause. This fight opens to her the avenues to her version of heaven of freedom as she thinks she can inculcate in the doubtful villagers a sense of trust but unfortunately, she achieves an adverse result. The warnings of her husband that she was a foreigner and would remain the same comes true. The villagers breach her faith and leave her disillusioned.

The other subsidiary characters, Shally Jaan and Salim Khan Bahadur, the two respectively timid characters not fitting in the frame of calm bravery are non-instrumental in contributing to the revolutionary mission. They respectively shying away from their responsibilities to boost the freedom struggle achieve their versions of heaven of freedom in retreat and hanging on to fantasy. Salim Khan declines the proposal of Sophie Martin to activate his channels of freedom resources. He withdraws from hot pursuit and Shally Jaan tugs upon her characteristic fantasy aero-dynamics.

The induction of the paranormal characters, The Bonga Tigers, in the novel remind us of the weak-intellect and the legacy of adoring the scary on the part of the villagers whose presence in the novel create impression that chaos too holds good in the human predicament. Sarita, Laxmi, Nirja Thakur, Ram Lal and Gobardhan along with Reshma and Rabbani meantime are the windy characters playing roles respectively to feed and push the plot leaving the readers bewitched. These windy characters operate loosely but work as the necessary ligament to give shape and size to the fictional texture.

No characters are regularized and the chaotic in the plot remains prominent validating the fact that too much of passive control over passion was likely to turn volcanic and blast.

As this novel is a large fictional narrative gyrating on the poetic axis the reader is solemnly requested to stick to the rhythmic motion of the novel for complete enjoyment of reading. Any arbitrary skipping of lines and passages would spoil the reading and curtail the joy of it.

Shahid Nasim Hyder
Author:
Death of a Hero
Tryst with Suicide
I Lost My Faith.

CHAPTER 1

WEARING THE BORROWED SKIN

The huge mansion, Hawa Mahal, a Gothic structure renowned for nothing particular was the residence of the zamindar of Candrapura estate in British India near Ranchi. Nothing was striking about the Chandrapura estate and the zamindar. Nothing was very particular except that a story was built around it, a tasty story that remained exempted from punches of the conflicts trying to invent the significance of freedom in different versions.

Salim Khan and his wife Shally and the secondary characters Martin Julius and Sophie Juliet all came face to face with one another, met tensions and escaped them as they could skip conflicts by devising means to quell conflicts. These characters were not the duplicate of each other. Their understanding of life and the handling of it too was not copy. They were consistent at what they were and were tolerant and interesting and manageable and individually complete in all respects. They did not overlap each other creating relational nuisances.

In Hawa Mahal the couple, Shally and Salim Khan was a grand pair living life on a slow pace. The pair became estranged in the passage of time from each other yet remained bound. Their estrangement mattered nothing substantial. Their marriage was not a horror and they were not given to reshuffle it. They were not romantically woven together nor sad in tussles as to them being together was no compulsion and remaining aloof no curse. They were the part of the story as the neutral cogs.

The British time known for its colonial oppression on the subject nation was a cool time to them. Salim Khan Bahadur had no grievances with Martin Julius, the typical English forester fostering love for holding control over the fellow people by threats.

The ongoing freedom struggle was a neutral influence upon Salim Bahadur as he had a nice digestion for conflicts. India then nurtured two types of people: the discontented ones and the smug fellows. Salim Khan belonged to the latter community, never indignant at what he was as he had no mission to fall out of the colonial coils.

He was indifferent to what bothered the opponents of the colonialism. He was reluctant to what was brewing in the minds of the sons of the soil, the revolutionaries. He did not look upon it as a subject of interest. He found himself properly settled in his nest, the Chandrapura estate that provided him with enough to sustain his life. The British masters were not his adversary and he was no foe to them.

He wielded no desire meanwhile to rule his tenants. He was a zamindar of a different version, an edited one not desirous to hold his tenants servile. It was not that he hated servility. It was that he hated being picked out as the opponent of servility. He loved withdrawal, a state of neutrality.

His tenants were no nuisances. They were not infected with the lust of freedom. They were lethargic fellow countrymen not affected by nationalism, copying their counterparts elsewhere in the British colonies. They did not know their history and had no urge to discover it. They were slow-witted snails, better prey to the predators rather than getting predatory themselves.

While the British India was replete with the revolutionary uprising, Chandrapura was calm and Salim-Salma duo were stable.

Nevertheless, they were vulnerable enough to build grounds for a story, 'My heaven of freedom,' Salim Khan said to himself secretly, 'lies in retreating from hot pursuit. I understand it is infamous and timidly but it gives me the sense of security. Everybody has the right to reach and fetch security as per his personal calculation. This would allot route to the heaven of freedom.'

He had not shared this to his wife. Shally who herself was a typically different version of character sticking to fantasy as release mechanism said, 'I have devoted my life to undertake to design escape that is marked by happy fantasy. The day dreaming is the marvel no monkeys and monsters would resort to. This is the grant of bestowal from God only to humans. I am allotted it amply.' Shally and Salim Khan were opposite to each other yet they were exempted from conjugal conflicts.

'Pain and wounds dissolve in due course of time leaving scars

Leaving people broken, tumbling, left afar

Nothing is in the hand of the poor man, the decision of destiny pre-determined

Marriages are made, lived and passed with care and fear implied

The rest that dangles in the memories are the memories

All finishes like stories finish to finish stories.'

The stories of Shally and Salim Khan Bahadur also finished leaving behind scars which would delete as stories of so many have been deleted but a question would hang out if the heaven of freedom was far more important than the freedom confirmed by dictates of fate.

'Freedom confirmed by the dictates of fate

Freedom written on the slate

Freedom that tasted monotonous, pale and sub-rate

was not the freedom leasing life of freeness to mate

Shally and Salim the fated duo would not take this confirmed freedom

Rebel they were not crude to mention

They smiled and backed out with whatever remnants of memory collections.'

The couple remained tagged together only to give the story necessary structural fabrications. Salim-Shally duo could never prove phenomenal in assisting the achievement of Indian freedom.

* * * * *

The tenants of Chandrapura estate were too crude for anything decent. They had distorted the name of Hawaii Quila to Hawa Mahal in order not to ridicule but only to sound it ridiculous. Salim Khan's father the Diwan of Dashrath estate had acquired the Chandrapura zamindari as a gift from Dashrath Nath for the latter's herbal treatment of his piles. The benefactor had applied a very simple trick to cure Dashrath Nath's piles by asking him to avoid spicy food and take instead lots of curd and honey and fibrous fruits for all his meals. This kept his bowels clear and his piles remained calm. This made the Diwan Dashrath happy with Nisar Khan and the former granted the zamindari as a reward and asked the latter to settle in the second mansion, Hawaii Quila, 'This Hawaii Mahal,' said Dashrath Nath, 'goes to you and you shall have it but I would request you not to rule the tenants like the British rule us. The colonial masters are not racially ours. They are the alien breed. We are not to them more than disposable stuffs. But our tenants are racially ours.

We cannot look upon them as disposable items.' These words developed a culture of soft handling on the part of Salim Bahadur. He maintained his soft-handling of his tenants as no counters to the British harshness. Salim Khan gave a rare expression of his credo in these crude lines:

'Control, clamping the soul, it is against the law of nature

We have no right to make soul stagger

No cause to wield power over it as if it were a matter

God has given us no right to do it

This is humanity, the real joy dispenser.'

The regime of Nisar Khan Bahadur ended in a tragedy as he fell prey to the bullet of an Angrez when Nisar Khan was trying to pacify the villagers fighting timidly with the administration to secure the Bonga Jungle for their benign guardian of it, the Bonga Tigers. The Bonga thenceforth became a myth.

'We gave the sacrifice of our father to the cause of peace and justice

We got the reward of death in return

But we are proud that we did not turn *satan*

It was no timidity, a meticulous sign of concern.'

'Regimes come and go, regime of the despotic rulers but what stabilizes in the memory is the goodness and sacrifice.' One night Salim Khan tried to narrate more about his father but Shally without showing disinterest she closed her eyes and pretended to sleep. The husband had full cause to get irritated but he was the progeny of the family which abhorred bitterness, 'Okey. Sleep Shally if you are sleepy. I will narrate the story sometime.' Salim Khan then lay beside her and not disturbing her sleep he kept his desire to share his story on hold, 'This lady is my fourth wife. This girl came in life via no matrimonial manipulation. I got her on the initiation from my side. Her mother was approached and she agreed to give her to me in Nikah because I had riches.'

Salim Khan saw the spider web spread across the walls meant to trap the prey. There was nothing unusual about it. He dragged his eyes from the scene of the spider dangling to tangle the little moth, 'I hate the predatory act. I hate the British for their predatory nature. I am not predatory.' Salim Khan then sighed with relief, 'I have never tried to let my tenants feel preyed upon. It might be un-fitting vis a vis the zamindari tradition but I am happy. I am a neutral zamindar, a weak authority. This is my limitation but also my redemption.'

He looked at his wife sleeping like an angel and pitying her he said that she was her fourth wife, 'Never my first choice, I have not been her choice as well. She lives absent from me, a pretty dislocated person in her fantasy.'

His thought line was cut as he witnessed Shally undergoing a visual ordeal. She was looking tormented. He wanted to touch her but refrained. It was his hesitation. He thanked his god that he had never been hard on her, 'No way being hard on a girl from the different family line. The Britishers have been hard on the people in their colonies, hard and un-feeling. They are so because they are ethnically different. I can understand the ache of it. I shall not let Shally suffer from my side. She is ethnically same as I am.'

The lady was half aware of it and half unaware but she was indebted to him for the relaxations in the conjugal spheres, 'We are different. I belong to my fantasy and you belong to the withdrawal. We are both on two bi-furcated lines yet tied by wedding. This is strange but not enough to abet irritation. Thanks god that we are not in conflicts.' She did not explain.

'I am really comfortable with withdrawal. I feel most harassed if I am sought to involve in troubles,' Salim Khan said without referring to the outstanding possible involvement in Indian freedom struggle. He asked her to bring a cup of hot tea.

He reverted to the memories of his first wife Rehana Sana, 'Her death was caused by the midwifery fault. Her labor pain had signaled something more drastic than the normal delivery pain. We had no proper doctor facility in Ranchi and operation was a taboo. The mid wife, the old hoary creature had guessed that the case was complicated. She suggested operation. But we had no ambulance and doctor and correct medical facilities. The delivery was delayed and the mother collapsed.' Salim Khan did not curse the British masters. He did not feel guilty as well for not having been able to save Rehana Sana.

Salim Khan had an urge to hold Shally and cry. He refrained. He had been timid at the display of raw passion. He had been timid even to open his tongue before Martin Julius. He despised conditions leading to arguments. He had his interpretation of his conditions in terms of what Gandhi professed i.e passivity, 'Gandhi's prime joy and concern is passivity. He does not let conflicts overtake actions. He resolves conflicts by recession and passive resistance.' Salim Khan was not a blind-folded follower of everything Gandhian. But he loved passivity in relations, 'No hostility, no tension. To me my Shally is not a prey.' He sighed deeply and dragged himself from physical touch with his wife, 'Treating somebody with care is bigger than treating the person with love. Gandhi treats people with care and respect and therefore Gandhi is more relevant in the turbulent British India. Gandhi will outlive death. He will survive the decay of fame.' Salim Khan uttered all this not as a hero. He only dispensed this feeling as a news piece

Suddenly he confessed, 'My Shall is my liability. I will treat her with care. She deserves it. I cannot humiliate her by mentioning Rehana Sana too much. This would hurt her. Hurting others is contrary to Gandhian principle.' Salim Khan felt big. He said that Gandhi is relevant, 'We can use Gandhi in keeping us calm and controlled.' He did not bother to explain it. He said again suddenly that he loved to withdraw from involvements and taking responsibilities and pressures. He felt a strong urge to touch Shally lustfully but he dreaded being snubbed. He squirmed in desire and strangulating it said to himself that he was not a conjugal-rapist.

* * * * *

In the bed at night Salim Khan lay beside her like a routine. She too followed the same. Both were good couple without any conjugal grievances. She was obedient as she had nothing to object him to. He was kind as he had not found her un-kind, 'We are the perfect portrait of a good couple,' said he absently and Shally absently talked of Gandhi and his freedom movement, 'I feel we are going to see a big upheaval in the future. These British powers would someday crumble. Gandhi and associate would cause the British Raj to go to hell.' In her tone was some irritation. He accosted her, 'Madam mark that the Gandhian code disapproves of irritation. We are not supposed to vent ire even against the apparent foe.' Salim Khan diverted his eyes from her taut bosom. He had never lusted for her body.

She knew that he was aroused. She knew he had the legitimate right on her. But she said that she was safe.

'Shall are you upset with me? I mean drawn from me?' asked Salim and then diverting his mind to the politics said that the advent of Gandhi on Indian national scene was a great hope blazer, 'Gandhi is a saint and his action and words resonate the noblest virtue.' He was not a staunch Gandhian and not at all maddened after him but he loved to mention Gandhi, 'Gandhi is a living saint, an angel of angels.'

Shally sighed and then suddenly she asked, 'Do you feel this our Gandhi is the right match against the formidable British? I fear that his passive resistance and moral-crutches are no counter match to the British. Gandhi sounds to me weak on the wake of the thumping might of the Angrez. These colonial masters are formidable manipulators of favor and loyalty of some vulnerable natives. The actual strength of the British lies in harnessing controls of mind. The Anglicized gentry educated in England and holding cream positions in British system will not they be used by the Angrez to stifle the voice for Indian independence?' Shally said all in reference to the critique of the existing apprehensions.

Salim Khan heard her. He did not feel guilty of being one of the many pegs as a zamindar with the British motives to lay control over his people and give proxy support, 'Yes you are right that the Angrez anywhere in their colonial domains select and fix the local power points to act as checkmates. The British are the rulers of the half world because of their manipulative powers.' Salim khan then smiled and removing the urge of desire sighed deeply, '*Begum*, dear lady I tell you that our great Gandhi has full understanding of the British manipulative strategy. He understands thoroughly well that his fight is two-directional. On the one side he has to diffuse the effects of the native proxy-throng and on the other the formidable Angrez. We cannot underestimate Gandhi and cannot overestimate the British.' Salim Khan wondered how he could make such a revealing critique.

* * * * *

The dawn in Hawa Mahal had its grace and color and while the sky of Chandrapura was wearing mellow color of the sun spreading rays shyly the distant horizon seemed like bowing to the earth, 'See there the bowing horizon as if drugged night over to embrace the earth,' she became poetic. She then touched him on his neck sliding herself away from him to mark distance. Salim Khan did not breach her transcendental arching. He let her follow her path. He was a genuine man of absolute reticence. He did not want to violate the code of reticence.

'We are bound by conjugal tie,' he said to her to make her feel the conjugal compulsion. But Shally remained absent and elevated, 'We belong to the puzzle of life that would not appreciate openings in matters of relationship. I believe that we are strangers within the captivity! We need decode this captivity.' Her words carried thickness of mystery and needed to be redefined, 'Your words fail me. I cannot decode them. You seem to be discontented. Are you upset with me here?' Salim Khan was too open.

She was scared. She cried, 'No sir. I understand my duty. I understand the weight of the conjugal knots.' Shally then lightly lifted from the bed and as a wind she drifted to the window trying to catch the views and meanings of life in the sky and clouds, 'I love the clouds. I love to watch the patterning battles of the clouds. I seek to catch the distant prince of charm there residing in the clouds. I belong to him. He is my silly soul mate, maybe like you can never perceive unless you come into my mental prison.' She confessed the languishment of her soul:

'The key to the heaven of freedom lies in pursuing the dream of dreams

The joy of this chase finds mooring in the faith of being un-seamed

Marriage and the compulsions of its bond

stifles the soul, restricts the flight, it frightens.'

For Shally marriage was a snatcher. She had no valid cause to feel abused in the marriage but she was. She felt like caught up and suffocating, 'Only if I could slide aside the chains. Only if I could decide my destiny. My existence has become a borrowed skin.' She was vague.

She was breathing heavily, in her eyes a scare of living was apparent, 'Sir *saheb* I dread being taken prisoner. I know the prisons would not break without fights.' She drifted from the personal woe to the national woe, 'The British people have made us prisoners.' Shally's eyes became wet. She whispered with pain, 'Sir *saheb* my greatest woe is that I cannot wish to rise and fight the British. I lack the necessary guts. But it is not my weakness. It is the essence of my being. I go for the freedom of choice. I hate confirmed freedom. I love freedom of choice.' Shally remained confusing. Salim Bahadur did not look at her with doubt. He knew that she was an escapist, a fleeter loving to shrink into her fantasy, 'She pines for freedom but not by struggles. She pines to catch it by fantasy.' Salim Bahadur then compared his wish for freedom with hers and sighed that he was scared of involvement and direct action for fear of detection and punishment, '*I am a withdrawer. I fear a proactive chase.*'

Shally diverted to Gandhi, 'He is a big topic today, a voice of Hindustan! But I have my feelings about him. Gandhi voice, does it hold the necessary bass to be heard? Do you think the British Raj will ever bother to hear it? I doubt. The British are the monarch of the world. Their sun does not set. The colonized subjects are without right means to get heard.'

'Then what? World over in the British colonies voices of protests are afloat.' Salim Khan informed.

'Good. But do we have in India the capacity to give protests a concrete shape?' Shally talked in whisper. She was used to talking important matters in whisper, 'My gut feeling says we are here too divided and outdated to voice protests.' She was referring to the divisions in India in the name of region, religion and accountability. She was also referring to the British capacity to keep Indians subtly divided in order to use them as weapons against themselves, 'I can understand that Gandhi has the idea of these internal fissures that is why he is trying to bring the common mass to his side. He is in the mean time trying to wake sense of dignity by churning among the Indians a sense of performance via suppression of selfishness and the violence.' Salim Khan tried to explain some aspects of Gandhian principles but he remained vague.

Shally did not ignore her husband though she did not agree. She was not a belligerent lady given to clashing on opinion. She said with a little unrest in her voice that she would rather go for fantasying in all matters including the desire for independence.

* * * * *

The sky overhead was full of silly clouds roaming about. The floating clouds were not meaningless vandals. She pointed to them, 'Catch the meaning in the movement of the clouds. Catch the meaning and joy of being free. There lies the key to the heaven of freedom.' Shally uttered the words in pain of the loss she suffered, 'I belong to that roaming transience.' She said it with eagerness to get free. She shook her arms severely. She sprained her arms. She sighed as she rubbed her hurting arm, 'I am like one tangled in the nets of life.' She whispered. She was in anguish.

Salim Khan wondered what really made her suffer. He wondered if he was the cause of her suffering. He said to himself that he had been soft to her not even demanding the conjugal privileges, 'I know she is frozen. She is not like the ordinary wife in the ordinary home. She is unique and enigmatic. Poor thing she is wedded to her dream prince. I am a usurper to her, a villain perhaps.' Salim Khan thought and thought and found no solution to her sufferings.

Shally then shrank into his arms, 'Hold me. Hold my bouncing life. My dreaming of the prince of the cloud is my trap.' Her words were vague. Salim Khan pitied her. He knew she a victim of her silly fantasy,

'*Shally I cannot understand your pain but I promise I will not add to* it.' He uttered the promise. She succumbed to the pressure of the promise, 'Ah! My great sir. I am no fit material for you. I am a waste of my birth not able to fulfill myself and you. I am sorry.' Shally finished the dialogue and asked him to carry her to the bed chamber.

* * * * *

Shally was the progeny of the Mughal lineage of Last King of Hindustan, the deposed and exiled King Bahadur Shah Zafar who at the time of his fall was hardly a Badshah in title holding no authority across the Red Fort. He was the saddest of the kings of Hindustan who witnessed the gradual decay of his power and rise of the British Crown.

It was 1857 when the Sepoy Mutiny under the waning Mughal power against the thumping British power had finished Bahadur Shah by letter and spirit and he had been deposed and deported to Rangoon as a punishment and shame to him. His Hindustan had been snatched. The British East India Company that had turned from trading to military powers had captured Hindustan without any resistance and shifted powers to the British Crown.

This little history had changed the fate of India and made it from a Mughal-ruled unrestful and loosely connected country to a slave nation under the British. It had changed the meaning of the heaven of freedom. It had altered the face of this meaning so Gandhi had emerged and his troops of the weaponless mass had emerged and a long battle of the non-violence had ensued to free India ultimately in 1947.

* * * * *

Shally Jaan was the daughter in the lineage of the royal Mughal breed whose mother was said to be the great-grand-daughter of the

Bahadur Shah Zafar, the last of the Mughal kings. Dildar Agha was her false name to escape detection and ongoing espionage of the Britishers given to wipe out the royal lineage after the notorious Mutiny, '*Gurria* you were my only hope and treasure when the British soldiers had plucked your *Abbu Jaan* and I had to escape the arresting via a crack in the house in Dilli. I was left alone, strolling about in utter hopelessness when a kind fellow coachman of the King's *darbar* took us to his home. He soon just got plucked away and we were again two hapless souls living in the ravaged Dilli.' The tale of grief told by her mother clung to Shally's soul tormenting her. Whenever she met the Angrez anywhere they looked like pink-face monkeys mimicking her and as by nature and inheritance she was not bitter she only sighed, 'These pink-face monkeys are our predators.' Shally Jaan knew she was genuine but she also knew she was no more an avenger.

She carried the teases of the past on her soul. She wore the thorn-cloak of it and for relief she clung to fantasy. After marriage with Salim Khan, she came to Ranchi. Her residence in Hawa Mahal became her final abode of compromise. She liked her husband and not liked him as well and for this she never felt guilty. Her dislike was not loaded repulsion, 'He is bound by chains of marriage and this chain I do not think is my chain. He is to me no foe and I am to him no foe. I do not treat me as a prisoner though his good behavior feels like imprisoning me.'

'Pining, reeling, falling, staggering.

I am a dream of the dream, crumbling between lines

I want to catch the sweet hymn

I am deserted, forlorn, down and lost

My dream prince come to salvage me from my slot!'

She pined for peace. Noise tortured her soul. Her soul was pure white. She loved white color. She loved White swan, swan airborne than the severe hawks in flight. She despised snatching, violence and the pride of the victory from dominance. Shally Jaan loved status quo. She said this made her feel strong like the diamond crystal that never further languished for change in its constituents. She liked the rippling streams rather than the roaring sea. She liked butterfly rather than the good-textured honey bees. She liked anything that looked humble, sober, noble and meek. She had inherited the regal calm of her mother blood that loved suffering and pain alike. She linked the pain to the child birth that to her was the wonder of wonders.

When she was a spinster, she shyly nurtured a dream of a prince charming of the cloud kingdom. She had named him '*Rahmania*' in a reverie when she was among potted flowering plants. She had felt like stolen, stolen from the bondage of reality; she had fallen out, fallen from the mountain height of confirmation down to non-confirmation; she had fallen enamored of herself and would love to tumble about in memory and desire, desire to escape and memory to cherish. Her *Rahmania* was a quixotic deceit of mind. She got to him for rehabilitation, 'Dear my prince of the dream come someday and let me touch you.'

Shally Jaan had no live will to get herself fulfilled. She desired only to loiter about in the haze of her fantasy. This was her folly and strength both:

'Dream and dreaming in dream

Funny crazy and yet not mean

I love to belong to this freedom

This strengthens me, gives me a hold

I would love to vibrate in the absent fold

I would love to play in the void clean

I do not know why I am what I mean.'

Shally had the illusion of hearing the whispers of her mother, Dildar Agha. It was auditory. She crouched into a bundle, her arms holding her arms. She hears the distant sound of the booming canons and the threatening thunder of an Angrez officer. She imagines her mother crying in fright and her *Abuu Janu* being dragged away. She became a picture of defeat, the defeat that carried the tongue of poetry. She sang the melancholic lines her mother used to sing when she fell prey to depression. She sang the lines of the *gazal,* Zafar Shah had composed during his exile in Rangoon. The lines of the Gazal were the bleeding tongue of the un-heard prayer and languishment. She recited the Gazal word by word trying to steal the pain of the lines and spread it like a sad sky over Hindustan.

'Na kisi ki aankhon ka noor hoon

Na kisi key dil ka qarar hoon

Jo kisi key kam na aa sakey

Main wo eka must-e-gubar hoon

Na to main kisi ka habib hoon

Na to main kisi ka raquib hoon

Jo bigar gaya wo Nasib hoon

Jo ujar gaya wo dayar hoon

Mera rang roop bigar gaya

Mera yaar mugh se bichar gaya

Jo chaman khizan se ujar gaya

Main usi ki faslebahar hoon

Aai fiteha koie iyea kiyoon

Koi Char phool charaey kiyun

Koi ia ke shamma jalaye kiun

Main vo Bekasi ka mazar hoon'

Trans: 'No darling I am to someone/no rest of heart/I am the wasted one /only a whirlpool in the vast

No darling I am to someone/none belonging to /I am the fate wretched/ I am the dwelling turned un-true

My looks got rotten/my dear one robbed away/the orchard torn by the gale/ I am the last breed of that glorious hell

O why somebody should reach with the flowers of tribute/ why should somebody lit the light of memory! I am lying here the hapless in the tomb weary.

Shally Jaan withered like the rose flower and began to crumple petal by petal. She sobbed like the oceans never sob and in her the zest for life got zeroed, 'I will give in. I will drop the soul of my body-weight. I will cling to my grand-pa and slink into his tomb taking the guilt of his exile upon me. She chanted the lines of Zafar Shah filling the universe with its resonance. It was the grief of a supreme king pining to lie in his Home Land but it was declined.

'Kitna badnasseb hai Zafar

Dafan hey liye do gaz zameen bhi na mili is

Koo-ye-yar mein.'

Trans: *How wretched is Zafar/For the rest he was denied two yards of mother's lap in the Home Land.*

Shally wept. She wept in torrents. She called her *Rehmania*, the dream prince to heal her pain. He did not hear her. *Rehmania* was a delusion. She sobbed and said that she was a prey to her fantasy. She did not hate her fantasy. She was not hateful. She had dignified royal blood. She cried with the memory of her mother to erase the pain.

'Living weak or strong with pain in the fate

I am the sad writ on the slate

My tongue is knotted

My life is blotted

I will try to hold the scattering soul

I will recount my role.'

The wild poetry held her and dropped her and she became a game on the bosom of surging emotions.

'Broken, trembling, demeaned

Fallen, un-supported, un-reclaimed

I am here the relic of the past

The remnant of the gone days

Save me if you want or let me be as I am

I am ready prey to be a sham.'

Her words hung around from the walls calling her in whispers. Shally felt defeated and then she gathered guts to rise and check if she was brave enough to face the defeats. She said that she would skip the falls.

She said that she would not give in. She made a lot of uproars validating her resolution, 'I am in the shelter seminary of a noble man. Salim Khan is a noble soul. He does not entrench upon me and get me trampled. He is true to his high blood line. Maybe he is not from the royal lineage but he is regal.'

She looked at his kurta hanging in the open sun. She felt like gathering and kissing it. The aroma of his scent he used was still clinging to the cloth, 'More than love, I respect you. I respect the way you respect me,' she said and felt reassured, 'I can trust him for the perpetuality of his honor he holds for me. Some people are born different. Salim Khan is different. His tie with me is not the tie of libidinal plugging.' Her eyes were wet with tears of gratitude, 'I can understand I do not satiate his nightly needs. But he never exerts pressure. He remains charged but he controls his passion. This sounds odd but this is the graceful truth about our relationship.'

She folded his kurta lovingly in the finest folds. It was an act of her displaying the care and value. Her dislike of him got deleted, 'Disliking somebody is a moral violence.' She could not explain this point and made a fleeting reference to Gandhi.

Shally heard somebody moving behind her. She thought it was her cat. But the size of movement was larger than a cat could produce. Reshma, the maid herself a nice -looking creature and full in youth and good in words was standing behind, 'Reshma I dislike your stealing gesture.' Shally chided her but her words were dressed in the nicety she had inherited, 'Sorry madam. I thought I would startle you.' Reshma sat beside her in the bed and began to press her leg.

'Sir Ji madam it has become more than two years since you married. You are still not expecting a baby.' The query was tasteless and not deserving straight answer. To divert her Shally took up the topic of Gandhi and Delhi politics and the relevance of British Raj. Shally talked vehemently on how the Gandhi reluctance of physical forces in the struggle for freedom would do meaningful services, 'I doubt him. He might prove irrelevant in the course of time.' Shally said all forcefully and countered herself in the same spirit, 'But no. Gandhi understands the ethics of struggles that would not commence from violent resistance. He is the votary of passive resistance, a difficult but substantially right tool to be applied against the formidable Britishers who are not totally brute. The Britishers allow justice to seek justice. They are good enough to sanction means and methods to the opponents to voice their resentments.'

Reshma did not enter upon the debate. She asked Shally to notice that her cat was pregnant, 'Can you see the heavy belly and the load of the baby kits.' The reference was boring but significant as the lady soon felt obliged to think of making a comfortable space for the cat. The cat became important and Reshma asked Shally Jaan to spare a space in the store room for the cat, 'Cats in any size and stature love to find out a safe, distant corner to breed. This is the nature of even the big cats.'

Soon the matter drifted to the Bonga cats, 'You know Bibi,' said Reshma, 'These villagers are heard to have developed an awe of two tigers. These animals due to old age and whatever have begun to ignore tough animals. Maybe their canines and lethal claws are too weak for hunting. Maybe these cats have turned lethargic and the villagers have begun to adore them. They are said to be starving till somebody from the village leaves something eatable somewhere in the forest.'

'It is strange and kind of the villagers but if they have begun to relate the cats to divinity, I think it is a folly. We cannot just raise deify the cats.' Shally waited for explanation tastelessly hearing anecdotes which did not suit intelligence, 'Okey. Reshma, I would like you not to get adrift to that folly. You are a bit better than the rustics. You can understand the difference between logicality and illogicality.'

The folded kurta fell from the hand of Shally and became dirty. The lady picked it and placed it on a rack, 'We are supposed to be careful. We are supposed to handle things carefully,' said the lady in reference to the general activities. In her mind the overwhelming question was that she was still trying to understand her husband. She was sure of his nobility but she was not sure of his biological potential. A stray thought of his male power infested her mind. She felt irritated. She thought of an exit, 'Reshma next day when you come here you must call Rabbani to meet me.'

* * * * *

Salim Khan was looking pensive. He was trying to hide something. He was trying to avoid eye contact with his wife. The lady could guess that he was upset. She asked the cause of his disturbance. The man did not answer straightway. She was not a common nagging wife. She let him plough through the tension. In the evening, he changed his clothes for white *kurta-pyjama*. He put on a round embroidered topee and humbly told that he was going.

'But where?' she demanded.

'Will be going to family graveyard.'

She could guess it would be his parents' death anniversary. But she knew it was not. She was then told that his former wife, Rehana Sana's death anniversary fell on that date, 'I do not know how of the three wives she was so dear to me. I miss her greatly.' Shally Jaan was not envious. She knew herself that she had a capacity to digest it. She looked into the sky and saw that the moon in the bright daylight was looking scrambling for space beyond the clouds. She smiled the palest smile she could ever smile.

'It is not against human nature. Love and attachment are not mathematical two plus two is four. It is free-lancing. Your attachment for Rehana must not seek explanation. In love attachment forgoes love. I appreciate your feelings.' Shally said very calmly. Salim Khan became excited, 'Salma you are superb, a really understanding one. I tell you honestly this Rehana was special.' Salim Khan caught her hand and kissed it, 'Will you come with me?'

'Why not? After all she too was my former relative.' Shally said she would change the dress. She was not angry. She was not upset. She was also not fighting ghost battles. She had not been designed to fight battles, 'I am not a common recalcitrant version of people.' She tried to find answer to it in her imagination of Gandhi and his passivity, 'Gandhi's passivity is his succor. I should appreciate it. If I build a battle field it would disturb my peace. I must abide in passivity.' Shally tried to cover her nice figure in her dupatta. She wondered if ever Salim Khan had appreciated her figure, 'Matter is not taking notice. Matter is the desire to take notice of my beauty. I am beautiful but not useful.'

The graveyard at the back of the huge Haveli was a vast land plot replete with wild vegetation. A care-taker was installed there to look after the necessary handling of the graves. The one tomb covered with a red sheet of cloth and giving smell of jog-stick was lying in question. The lady buried there had been Salim's favorite and in departure she had left deep pain to him. At the grave he babbled the necessary holy verse and at departure he suddenly flung to the leg side and embraced it passionately, 'You left me alone, forlorn. You went away leaving scars and teasing memories.' He cried and then sensing that his fourth wife was standing witness he stood guilty, 'Sorry Shall. Sorry for the embarrassment to you. I could not control my tears.' He apologized but Shally did not let him feel guilty, 'Saheb, love and affection are two different emotions and we cannot just juxtapose them. Your affection for the sleeping lady was testimony to your fidelity to her. Above all it was a matter of choice. Choice is not subject to interrogation. We have full right to pursue our choice. I think it is ethical and it should not suffer from hesitation.'

Throughout the day till night nothing remarkable happened. On bed time Salim was reaching her vicinity restlessly. He was purring like a pet cat and poking himself into her. It was not stark lust. It was a condition depicting his un-restfulness. She was shrinking. She had no abhorrence of him but his slinking to her was becoming abominable, 'Cannot we keep a distance. The body-touch sometimes gives me eerie feelings.' She wanted to say this but she refrained. He was not her choice. Her marriage with him was no connecting bridge.

Salim Khan was in need of an exit. He knew that sex would have pushed him to the exit. He tried overtly but she subtly declined. He was not angered. He knew that freedom of choice was primary. She was adrift to her fantasy, her *Rahmania* was peeping from the cloud bunches. She pined to hold him. But he was illusive. She found her deserted. Salim Khan was turning in his bed with aching heart.

The fellow Salim Bahadur tried to sneak into her limbs. She did not abhor the touch. She felt not martyred too. She had enough of the resilience to determine her domain, 'I can understand your state of mind. I should accordingly.' She gently dragged herself off, 'Sorry. Really sorry Shall. I was upset. I needed physical security.'

'Sorry sir. Very sorry that I am not emotionally fulfilling to you. You can have me but only my body will go to you not my soul.' Shally Jaan did not resist physically to salvage her. She had submitted herself to his control, 'Here I am to you but half only, half with my body given in and soul loitering aloft elsewhere.' Shally became no enigma.

'I can understand Shall. I can get it. I am no brute. I know I am not your choice so I am not a bridge to the bliss the heaven of freedom needs to connect to.' Salim Khan dragged himself away from Shally.

Shally sighed a sigh of relief, 'Sir *saheb* you are superb, an angel in human clothing.' She touched on his cheek. It was a sacred touch.

'Think sir, think of a possible reach to the blissful freedom. You will not find the freedom of bliss in the looted authority. You will have a sense of defeat in the victory of this version. Freedom of possession comes from dispossession and snapping of the bridle. We cannot pride in being hero by villainy.' She wanted to say something more but her thoughts snapped.

The night became a silent load on the soul. But they were not trampled. They both were qualified for dismissing the horrid. They had the inherent capacity to mean and value each other. They could recognize each other's will.

* * * * *

Khan Bahadur brought the album of his first marriage. It was a brightly hard bound book in which he had the photos of his first marriage, 'See this was my Rehana, the good lady whom I had loved secretly since my childhood and had won her hand by chance. This girl might have been married to a foreigner cousin of mine doing medical from England. But he declined this match on the plea that she would be a misfit in his Anglicized way of life. I got the chance as the disturbed family had nobody else me to handover this gem. I got this and became a winner.' He mentioned the secrets of his conjugal victory.

His face was lit with the light of bliss. He closed his eyes to display the soul's relief in facial features. Shally observed him and not hurting for his emotional reverie said that the real joy of being and belonging comes from this combination. She mentioned her experience of the bliss in her fantasying about her absent price, 'Again I would say that the key to the heaven of freedom lies in choice and its coming without hindrance. We are sometimes declined the chosen. We are sometimes handed over something else. We humans are unfortunate to be receiving many things unwarrantedly. Our irritations and the fouling of relation, I think proceed from these disparities. But we can save us from bitterness if we willingly sort out the un-wanted from the wanted and create conditions leading to compromise and acceptance.' Shally was no philosopher but her words carried a deep philosophy.

* * * * *

Reshma was pressing the legs of Shally Jaan. This was a scene of Friday, 5th March. After the Friday prayer Shally was lying on her bed and though from her mind the scene of the graveyard was deleted but she had the hangover of it, '*Bibi* I know I am so trifle a mouth to mention the demonstrative affection of Salim Khan Bahadur for Rehana Bibi but a stagnant question peeps out of the head asking why our *saheb* was so very molten there.' Shally heard the question and let it spill out of mind. But the echo of it was thick. Reshma had been a great gossiper. She had been the one who had been bringing news of the locality and the country and delivered it with added spices, 'I tell you Bibi ji this Bahadur Jaan is the adorer of his former Bibi.' Shally chided her. Her language added bitter words. The maid was scared. Silence fell between the two. The hands of the maid were getting loose on the legs of the Bibi.

To divert the mind of Shally the maid began tossing a couplet of Bahadur Shah in crooked Urdu that she had memorized from hearing it cite by Shally:

'*Kitna badnasseb hai Zafar*

Do Gaz zamin bhi na milee is ku-e-yar mein'

Trans: *How miserable is Zafar/ he failed to secure two -yard earth in his motherland.*

In a mad dance the images of Salim Khan's wet-eyed tribute in the graveyard rolled over aching Shally's soul. It was not revolting, not also the stagnation of being stagnant. It was the ache of the question asked in madness. She languished to diffuse the ache by recollecting her years old fantasy of her dream Prince, 'Come must my relentless foe. Leave me not in this abyss. I have been dismembered within my life-bag. You come, collect my parts, assemble them and make me regenerated.' She was crying in pain. Her long-cherished desire to remain neutral got swamped.

She had been left alone in her bed chamber. The maid having left her in a cruel torment with question on her existence had abandoned her. Her man was out to the town for last eight hours. Shally had never before felt so bereaved pining for emancipation.

She became a floating vagabond of an abstract quest to escape from her. She had been an escapist since she was only thirteen. Shally had chased a wrong dream of a wrong prince from the wrong world and had never felt guilty of it. In her guilt was not her halter. She knew that she was playing with storms. She also knew that her Prince of the dream was a volatile dream only but then she had been haunted by the graveyard punches and had become the victim of humiliation. It was not clear if it was humiliation inciting her to react. She wanted to react. She wanted to get enraged. She wanted to feel that she had been hurt. But reason downed on her and in a brave gusto of confession she cleared her doubts. She said that she was not a victim of humiliation and that choice of freedom marked the contents of life.

She called her prince desperately and her eyes became torrential rain. She was left alone with her crying and languishment. In her world of the loss the only helping occasion used to be the entry of an abstract exit route: this was her prince of the fantasy, 'My man, he left me trampled under the load that he belonged in soul to Rehana.' She was not jealous at all. She wanted an exit. She slipped to the margin of poetry and caught its neck. The poetry made her unhinged and brilliantly mad, 'Come you my heart's quest. Come down to my domain my prince and salvage me. I am direly in the cockpit of dread.' She was caught in the cages of questions and was trembling with fright and pain. She groped through the catastrophe to rediscover herself. But she was lost and the loss was inclement, 'I will break the walls of rules. I shall crush the silence of my existence. I shall squeeze the universe into a ball and kick it. I want answer. I want answer to my question as to why I am alive.'

She had become mad with no reason. On her the weight of courage to come up and the load of chaos to carry her burden had become a callous punishment, 'We all are bound severely to dream fetters. We are under the command of a dynamic mind. This our restless mind captures images and clings to them. Shally, too captures the shady dream! I am after this delusive invasion of images.' Shally Jaan laughed to hoot herself and then she recovered the sense, 'No, passivity calls upon our not going erratic. I love Gandhi. I love his face. I love his credo of the violence swallowed!'

Reshma had returned like a ghost and was sitting beside the Bibi. The lady of the house needed a somebody around to reassure her, 'I fear you are tormented by some dream. Is it a hero from your Dilli?' Reshma caught her hand eagerly.

'No hero from Dilli. No corporeal prince at all! This is a dream prince, the marginal poetry. I have nurtured a false dream of a wrong man.' Shally looked blank in the eyes. She became uncertain of herself. She felt like crying but she did not cry.

'Then what?' supported the maid, 'Then nothing untoward. We are permitted by our heart to dream a dream and try to make it turn true.' Reshma wanted to elicit the full details. The lady became relaxed, 'But no,' said Shally, 'Never have I cherished the dream to get it turn true.

My prince was my liquid dream, a living illusion only! He was a surreal imagination. It existed in my dream.' Shally Jaan was not confiding the secret. The maid became an intruder. She culled some information and was ready to make a gossip of it, 'Then Bibi ji did not you think of eloping with the dream prince?' It was a cruel question. Shally looked at the maid with disgust.

Shally heard peacocks crying. It awoke her from the trance. She could see the doves in the guava tree sitting morose. Her mind became fogged. Shally had olfactory hallucination of the same attar that had been sprayed upon the white sheet to cover Rehana's tomb. She felt like visioning a girl in the mourning cloak floating past her. It was the ghost of Rehana, 'Rehana do not desert your earthly abode,' cried Shally Jaan. Her face was an open book of horror. Reshma shook Shally by her body, 'Bibi ji please come back.' Shally returned from the trance, 'What happened?' Shally cried. Reshma had held the Bibi tight and lady Shally was struggling to extricate herself, 'Leave me *badmash*, rogue! Do not suffocate me.'

The maid was confused. She looked askance upon the lady and doubted if she was possessed. She preferred to stick there but not to disturb the lady.

Shally recovered from the attack. She felt like trembling, 'Reshma, bring me a glass of water,' the lady was sweating. She was looking tired. She said to herself that she was a ghost dreamer, 'I shall save me,' said she and wondered how she would save her.

* * * * *

CHAPTER 2

MARTIN BANGALOW

Salim Khan was summoned by Martin Julius to his Bungalow. Martin was the forester and the forest was his hang up. He felt like belonging to it as the bull belongs to the cow. Martin was rough and ruthless about his handling of the forest issues. He had never felt aligned with the forest. The forest was to him a raw mystery. He had heard of the Bonga tigers and had felt repulsed at it. He had heard of the silly Bonga cats whom the uncouth villagers had begun to adore and this had made him angry. Rabbani Shadman, the coachman had been informing more and more about the villagers and their silly Bongas and Martin had been disgusted, 'Shut up Rabboon!' Martin chided the coachman, 'Shit with your stupid Bongas. Shit with the villagers given to allotting name and position to the beasts!' Rabbani was afraid to mention the Bongas, 'Sir *saheb,*' he said in whispers, 'to the rustics the Bongas are their divine guardians.' Martin laughed then ordered him to go to Salim Khan.

Salim Khan casually asked his wife if she would like to have an outing expecting her not to join him. But strangely the lady agreed, 'Where shall we go?' asked the lady. Salim Khan who generally visited Martin in his *kurta-pyjama* on that day he chose his finest *Khadi-shirwani* and *Khadi-pyjama*. He waited for her as she changed her dress and did necessary make-up.

Shally Jaan a nice-looking lady, fair and slim and very graceful did not need any make up but as she was going to meet Sophie mem, the wife of Mr. Martin, she felt like having a competition with Juliet Martin,

'These English mems pink in skin and tall and looking special I would feel humbled if I do not wear more powder on the face. It is the inferiority complex we Indians are accustomed to and I am no exception.' Shally took more time to dress up as she was becoming more conscious of her blouse and saree, 'These gents of the Gora people are lechers.' This was her bias and misinformation. She reprimanded herself and correcting her said that Martin Saheb might not be a lecher. She then asked her husband if Martin was a lecher and on being told nothing she said that the pink-monkey face was not a lecher.

To secure her figure beneath the loud extra of the cloth she looked at the mirror last time and wondered that she was brown and doubted if it was her real complexion. Her saree became her obsession and in her mind Martin bobbed up and down like some floater. Her khadi saree was biting her soft skin. She thought reluctantly of the growing infection of khadi clothes among the Indians, 'I do not think it is necessary to wear coarse khadi and testify the following to Gandhi. This old half-clad fellow is a distinguisher. He wants to stand out prominent. He wears the half-cloth to harass the sense of English decency. Gandhi deliberately wears half-cloth to place psychological pressure on the English counterpart. His insistence on khadi is also a pressure tactic. He is a shrewd *vakil* and from looks to clothing he uses not logic only psychology to keep the opponent under pressure. It is his way of unaggressive demonstration of victimhood! Okey but the world knows this Gandhi is not a bluff. His energy and genuineness are beyond challenge.' Shally Jaan wondered how she could successfully refer to the Gandhi phenomena, 'Gandhi is a magician. He will change the game. He will eliminate the pink-face English and get us freedom.' She did not know why she was getting excited and if this excitement had a substance. She felt soon that Salim Khan was looking worried. She did not ask him the reason of his worries and concluded regarding the Gandhi phenomena vis a vis the Britons, 'These pink-face will someday leave, I tell this Gandhi will make them quit. Gandhi is powerful because of his soul force.'

* * * * *

The Buggy was moving to Martin Bungalow, the huge building that spread awe and authority. No common Indian had an access to it. The villagers of Chandrapura had no business with the Martin forester except that they had a cold conflict with him regarding the Bonga Jungle and the Bonga Tigers roaming the jungle. Sarita, Laxmi, Ram Lal, Gobardhan and all slew of the villagers were sure that the Martin forester was inclement in matters of the Bongas and the villagers' utmost love of the Bongas.

Salim Khan knew about this conflict and had been ignoring the villagers regarding it. He ignored it because he had the idea of the overwhelming powers of Martin behind him. He also knew that he was zero in matters of conflicting with Martin, the chief Forest Conservator, 'We have no cause to defy the forester. He is powerful,' said Salim Bahadur to himself and felt uncomfortable about the title Bahadur. He stirred on the seat and literally squeezed into the frame of Shally. He felt guilty as if he were trespassing on her inner solitude, 'Sorry,' said he and feeling awkward for diversion he recalled Rehana Sana and then the Indian political scenario, 'We are going to meet lots of battles. Yes, big battles of words and conferences and this our Gandhi will tackle those inflammations with his passive resistance. He is typical. He is a juggler of a new version. I do not doubt his potential. I doubt only my potential. I would confess I shall remain aloof as I dread involvements. I will withdraw.' Salim Bahadur felt cowering within and hiding his face in cowardice said that all are not Gandhis, bold but not rashly daring, 'I, at least am not rashly daring to run behind Gandhi and get noticed. I am sorry, yes sorry and I tell this is not treason. This is my way to keep myself safe from the English vengeance. I see in it my version of heaven of freedom. Our Gandhi is truly brave and my comparison with him is not justified.' His assessment of Gandhi had a universal validity and his confession about his timidity was also universally demeaning.

The lady Shally drifted in her fantasy as the baggy was running, 'My stupid romances about the prince of the clouds! I have cherished him as an escape route. He is quixotic.' Then she admitted, 'I am doing wrong to Salim Khan. The poor fellow is being put to injustice.' She was not passing through an ordeal of conflicts. She was only in a muddle. She then felt overwhelmed with gratitude to Salim Bahadur as she thought she was being tolerated, 'Others would have thrown me out of the bond.' She felt indebted to him. She stealthily looked at him and discovered that he was a handsome man in grey hair. She bit on her lips to contain pain. Her eyes became wet. She breathed deeply. She felt the skin of her man rubbing against her. She fell out of the present pressure. Her past began to haunt her. Her Mughal-legacy became her haunter, 'My past is my tormentor. I am not there but I feel I am knotted there!'

'The cruel past, past of my birth and lineage

I am a victim in the present

A victim of memory and desire

I suffer from the pinches of the lost time

This is my binder, my tormentor

O that I would slip free, get an exit!

But no, no more it is possible unless I quit it.'

She bowed her head and looking at the fleeting legs of the pony said to herself that the animal was quitting the past unrepenting. She heard the thumping hoof-sound and said that the past is capable of dissolving in the past, 'Let it remain a history. Let my Mughal-past remain a history.

I am not now a part of it. I am now the story of my present with Salim Bahadur.' In her mind Gandhi popped up like a little joker. She could not adjust her with the potential Gandhi vis a vis the formidable Angrez. 'He is fighting for freedom and teaching us the meaning of aspiring for freedom.'

The bumpy ride on the Buggy became hard on her bottom, 'Whatever our impression of the *Firangees*, the English they are hard to others but to us these Martins are friendly' she said suddenly to herself, 'I have heard from Reshma that the Lady Martin is a different Angrez. She is not snobbish. She is not arrogant.'

Salma suddenly became sad. She sighed hugely. The nature's melancholy became poetry in her soul. The clouds in the horizon and the sky bowing to the earth seemed wedded together.

'We are living specimen of huge mood swing

Like the face of the clouds changing masks

We are the denizens of the world on a flux

We would cry this moment and laugh then after

I belong to this wavering, floating surge

This makes me funny and sore merge.'

Shally sighed to commemorate the Death anniversary of Bahadur Shah Zafar, 'You know ji, last Monday it was the Death Anniversary of our great-great grandfather. The poor man who belonged to Hindustan by birth and soul had to die in exile. His last wish of being assigned to the soil of the Home was left unfulfilled. I do not know what politics and cruelty on the part of the English made him die in exile in Rangoon.'

'This Zafar Shah was exiled symbolically to exile the Mughals from the Indian mind. The Britishers wanted to prove to the indigenous people that the regime change was full and final and that they had to learn to live under the control of the Crown.' Salim Khan explained the exile of Bahadur Shah Zafar.

Shally told her husband that in Martin Bungalow she would like to sit with Sophie Mem. She also told that Sophie Julius was reported to have a soft heart, 'You do not know one thing about Juliet Sophie. She is by blood an English but by upbringing she is Indian. Her father was a practicing doctor in the remote parts of Ranchi.' Salim Khan gave history of Sophie's background and her schooling, 'The poor lady would have been aligned to us far more candidly but for her husband, Mr. Martin.'

Then Khan Bahadur mentioned that the detachment of the Angrez with the Indians had a valid clue in their scare of the foreignness, 'These Angrez over our head are actually in virtual exile. They have been deputed in India here and there on key posts strategically to keep the Crown intact. Poor guys they are banished ones! Poor Angrez they would have been comfortably in their England, seven seas afar but their pressure to manage the British colony they are here. They are the nostalgia patients, patients of the teasing memories of their Home Land. That is why they are alienated. That is why they are hostile. That is why they are arrogant and angry.'

'But I see your Martin is not visibly hostile to you. He seems attached to you.' Shally Jaan flung a question.

'His seeming attachment is business. His seeming in-hostility is business. He feels he is handling the sparse populace via me. He looks upon me as a bridler of the Chandrapura estate and its people. Martin is not totally good to me. He is good only to his convictions. He wants the Crown to continue.' Salim Khan talked reluctantly.

'You mean you are his chessboard and he is the master player. Martin seeks your proxy support to control the Indians via the villagers.' Shally talked interrogatively.

Salim Khan then explained the English plans, 'The handful of the English in Hindustan are on a mission to keep Hindustan stitched together and rule. They cannot afford to be very friendly with the natives as they are faced with a diversely populated community ethically as well as ethnically mismatched. These Indians are hostile to the rulers. The British know it and to maintain a hold over the diverse Indians the British adopt a psychological whip. This is arrogance and a stark reluctance. The British snobbery is a part of their demonstrative superiority. They cannot afford to connect. The British fear connection. They stay aloof and harsh. This makes them lonely. Poor creatures they are like circus tigers always seething with anger. They evade touches. To them the Hindustanis are sub-humans, half devil, half child. I tell these English mems are lonelier than their male counterparts. Why? These creatures cut off from the outer world are fed with panic contents about something drastic and incontrollable brewing up outside. In panic anybody would act more vengefully. The English women carry this panic. This panic makes them dissociated and lonely and ever anxious to get released from their virtual fencing.' Salim Khan had been in touch with Juliet Martin and had developed a soft corner for her. He was a mute admirer of the lady.

'This I can understand,' said Shally unaware of Salim Khan's soft feeling about Juliet Martin, 'Poor creature, the foreign rulers anywhere in their settlements and colonies are tormented souls. They might have control over the subject people but they are poor people alienated severely. The Angrez are virtually imprisoned in their self-created detention centers! Their female folks I feel have worst time living in virtual starvation of human contacts in the lack of socializing. They are more under shackles than us. Our slavery is situational slavery but theirs is spiritual one.' Shally sighed and pictured herself tagged to the spiritual slavery. She looked at her man and discovered genuinely that the Khan was handsome despite grey hair. She then noted that she was not happy. She said to herself that her happiness was not staked, 'He is nobly distant to me, a morning star.

I have no grievances with him. He is tagged to me and I hanging around him. In between him and me the joint is a bad welding.'

Shally felt lonely. She pined to reach out to her prince charming. She stretched her arms thirstily. Salim Khan noticed it, 'What happened? Are you feeling congested under the arms?' He tried to take hold of her arms and ease the nerves, 'Nothing happened?' she said softly and extricating her arms she felt like she had saved herself from a catastrophe. The Khan did not take offence. He was a gentle man. Except for his demonstrative affection for his Rehana he had never shown any untoward attitude to her, 'You know dear Shall my weakness is my memory of Rehana. I tell you she was a wonderful creature, an angel, a thing of spiritual material. If you had met her, you too would have turned her fan. She was simply wonderful.' Salim Khan divulged his feelings not ruthlessly.

Shally shrank to the extreme and would have fallen off the carriage but then suddenly she gathered guts and sense and laughing at her folly she normalized. She did not approve him but did not also reproach. She said nothing in particular as inside her a storm was forming and un-forming making her feel awkward, 'Yes, we all have our secret attachments. This is natural. We cannot outright reject them. We are humans pursuing our choices. I too cherish one such a very smart dream. It is about a prince of the cloud kingdom. My Rehmania!' She finished the line. She clutched the nearest rod in the carriage to take support.

He took his pipe and tried to lit it but a bad wind extinguished the matches. He then referred to Gandhi, 'You know even this Gandhi is acting from the pressure of choice. He might have talked like other Congress leaders of the revolutionary group to snatch freedom by physical force. But Gandhi stuck to seclusion, a shy passive resistance. We would have a far better chance to survive bitterness by not trying to beat it by bitterness.'

* * * * *

The buggy reached the Martin Bungalow. But its main gate was locked from inside. Salim Khan was irritated to see it. He knocked on the metal door and from inside a sentry peeped through a window opening, '*Sahib* is out.' said the sentry, 'But where?' foolishly demanded Salim Khan, 'I have no idea,' said the sentry. Salim Khan felt humiliated and helpless. He smiled at his wife who looking away to the blank sky passed no comments, 'Mr. Martin summoned us and himself vanished,' babbled Salim Bahadur then correcting his tone said that he was not important enough to be received. Shally Jaan made no comments. She thought about her future with her husband and said that she would hang on to him as the English hang on the Indians, 'I feel sure the Gandhi motion will set the country astir.' There was nothing new about her guessing. The Buggy returned.

* * * * *

Chandrapura state was a sparsely populated pocket of three villages having nothing grand and striking. The villages suffocated with poverty, illiteracy, superstition and despair were figuratively the Hindustan of the British Raj marked by sullen lives in sullen despair.

The villagers were the suffering lot, un-sure of past and present and future but they had a zest for life. They had no idea of the background struggles of Gandhi to free India. They had nothing like a fire for freedom. Sarita, Laxmi, Nirja Thakur, Ram Lal and the silly Gobardhan along with many like-minded behind each other consisted of the community of the humble ones. They had nothing like violence as violence behaves. But they nurtured the hate of the Angrez as suited their circumstances. They were also afraid of the red-ace Angrez as was prevalent elsewhere. Sarita, Laxmi, Nirja Thakur, Gobardhan and others were not Gandhi- disciple in spirit but they had sneaking admiration for Gandhi, 'Our Gandhi is our Bonga, the savior. The Bonga tigers roam the jungle protecting us so the Gandhi does, guarding the boundary lines.' This was the statement of Ram Lal.

The villagers hated Martin Julius. They also dreaded him and would not like to face him. They hated this Angrez as the latter had passed orders that the grazers would not take their cattle into the jungle. The villagers had brought this order to the knowledge of Salim Bahadur but of no avail. The zamindar could not get the order repeal. Sarita, Laxmi and Nirja together sneered at their zamindar, 'Pulpy fellow this *shirvani*-wearing Bahadur is not *bahadur*, plucky. He is a Martin's spoon!'

Ram Lal when drunk, he became boisterous and would then facing the Bungalow spit on the sky. The spit dotting his face made him feel sticky on the skin. Wiping the spit with the reverse side of his palm he would then grunt, 'Yes time will come. *Azadi*, our cherished freedom will come. Our great Gandhi will bring a*zad*i.' He was not sure where from this freedom as a savior would come. Laxmi Surin and Sarita Dhan were his enemies taunting him, 'Good boozy hero of the wine we know when the *azadi* came it would take you to the heaven.' Ram Lal could not mean the allusion to heaven. He was irritated. He would then growl and quarrel, 'Shut your mouth ladies! I tell from my knowledge of Gandhi effect that Azadi is building.' Ram Lal then checked his passion and doubting his argument turned to go.

Laxmi and Sarita were envious of Martin Juliet because of her pink-white face and fine legs. These women used to talk in suppressed whispers that the Lady Martin was a red-face *bandariya,* a childless woman because she had a flat chest, 'How this pink- *bandariya* can have a baby when she lacks the female full breasts! Her man is also so thin always piping tobacco.'

Reshma Sagar, the maid of the Bangalow then once mentioned that Sophie Juliet was not a harmful thing, 'She is typically un-English. She talks of the Indians with sympathy. The pink-*bandariya* is not hostile. She also talks of our Bongas!'

'What do you mean?' demanded Laxmi and Sarita. She explained that they had heard from Reshma that the fair-leg lady Martin was born in India, 'Born in India? Then What?' shouted Laxmi.

'Idiot woman. Juliet was born in India out of illegitimate affairs. Her father was an Indian doctor but her mother now divorced and back to England she had an illicit relationship with her driver.' Laxmi pinched Sarita on the bottom. This was the ugliest lie that had no substance.

'Who gave you this news?' asked Sarita.

'*Behan,* sister I gathered the information from my sources. You know because of the Indian blood this lady Sophie has soft feelings about us. It is a case of happy hybridization! Do not you notice her facial features, the black eyes and her hair is not golden. Above all her tone and sympathy! She supports our belief in the Bongas and sometimes talks of Gandhi. She is not like other Angrez.'

'Gandhi? What do you say? This Gandhi is ours only. Gandhi the grand! Gandhi our Bhagwan! To the Angrez, Gandhi is an enemy. This Juliet lady must not be talking of Gandhi and if she may be talking of the old fellow it must be against him. We have heard from Ram Lal of our struggles for freedom. We have heard from Reshma too about Gandhi building freedom for us.' Sarita yawned and looked bored, 'Freedom and Gandhi and such big talks! We would remain the same in our plight, poor and suffering and after freedom is built the big ones in India would replace the white Angrez for the black Indians.' Sarita sounded hopeless.

Sarita's despair got diverted as she was haunted by the outstanding issue of what she would cook for the night meal. She asked Laxmi if she had some spare salt and red chili and Laxmi afraid that Sarita would not return them, she reversed it by asking to give her a loan of five rupee.

'If the Bongas are loving to Sophie and if she is inclined to us, we should respect her. But no. We are not ones to regard this lady. We are the haters of everything Angrez. Gandhi and his tension away we are always in the bad book with Martin forester, 'said Laxmi in the last. The matter about Gandhi and the Bonga tiger and everything else got meshed up and Sophie Juliet could not score points of favor, '*Behan* we natives in the colonial Raj are to suffer humiliation. Ours is the Hindustan a large prison house. Would that some Gandhi really come forth and take care of our grief and humiliations.' Laxmi concluded with a sigh as her mind hovered over the issue of next meal.

* * * * *

Gobardhan, the half devil a child had once brought a boo from the forest swearing that he had witnessed a long-tusked devil lurking about in the vicinity of the Bungalow. He was a nuisance fabricator. 'Shut up you, bottomless fool,' his mother Laxmi, kicked him and the boy giggling at the kick and sucking the pain howled and howled in imitation of the howling of the tusked devil, 'This way I heard the *bhoot*, devil. Yes, I was driving cattle back when I turned and saw the tusked-devil at my back and as I ran for life the devil flung back to hide behind the Bungalow. The Martin Bungalow is haunted. The Martins are the haunters!' Gobardhan created a sensation. The villagers chased him and pulled at his hair to tell more in details what he had encountered, 'It was getting dark and the cattle had begun to stampede,' Goberdhan began his lie, 'Then a tornado-like whirling dust storm rose from the Martin Bungalow side. I saw the demon, a tusked-headed something leading a body in its hands. The head was dripping with blood and the hand was shaking. I could not focus attention but whatever I gathered was horrible. The body was hanging from the sky down like a colossal beast. It was like some bat. It was like some phantom of the sky. I was terrified. I closed the eyes.' Govardhan Thakur was suffering from visual hallucination. His obsession of the Bungalow had made him spread this rumor.

Sarita and Nirja Thakur chided the urchin. They wanted to hush up this theory of Bungalow's haunting. They were trying to hush it up because they had a grudge of Luxmi Suren. Luxmi Suren had been a rival to them in many matters like in fruit gathering from the forest and grazing of her cattle. But Laxmi was not a cowering soul. She undertook the haunting theory of the Bungalow as a clue to prove the upper hands in matters of stunning the villagers. She knew that the villagers would love to get charmed by such sensational theory, 'Shut up. My gem of the child is not a tale-maker. He is telling just what he met. I would like to add that I too had once experienced something eerie about the bungalow when I wanted to steal in and spy on its inmates. I had felt as if a slap had fallen upon my cheek and I was dazed.' Laxmi had lied. She had never had guts to steal into the Bungalow boundary. No local had never had guts to transgress it.

Ram Lal shouted aloud then checking himself said that he had been several times round about the Martin's Dera but he had never encountered such horrid presences. The locals were aware of the bad temperament of Ram Lal and his drunkenness. Nobody dared to counter him. Then Ralm Lal himself referring to the death of the tigress admitted that Goberdhan Thakur was the first to bring the news, 'Yes I recall our pretty Devi Kirpani's body was detected by this Gobarwa.' Laxmi recalled that the dead body of the tigress was found bloated and half decayed nearby the pond. Her son had come running to tell the news. The villagers had cried together and carried the body on a cot and buried it near the Bungalow.

Andrew Morgan was the Angrez forester who was alleged to have poisoned the tigress. There was no proof of it but the villagers were sure that Andrew Morgan was the killer. Ever since the villagers had experienced many untoward happenings like shock wave, a rumbling sound from far off forest area, a bright winged-horse in the night sky, a scary howling coming from the mountain holes, a terrible rain leading to the rolling of a huge rock, on a few occasions cobras hissing and fighting and worst a glaring light flashing suddenly and dying out on the fourteenth of the moon night, 'There was *shakti*, celestial power in the tigress. The nice tigress was pregnant. It had been poisoned by deceit.'

The matter of the Bungalow and its haunting became news. That night the whole of the village sat inside the huts and let the wax-lamp lit. The eyes kept looking to the white glowing Bungalow. The moon lit night had made the Bungalow look like a ghost spreading its limbs. The front face of the Bungalow looked like an open jaw of a demon in torment. The villagers had peeped from the port-hole openings in the mud walls to spy on the changing face of the Bungalow. It seemed to move its body as per the imagination of the seer. The nervous villagers had been visioning shapes not tallying together, 'Yes,' confirmed the wisest Nirja Thakur, 'The Bungalow is the abode of dangerous shadows.' Dwarika Pahan was sizzled to the core on hearing this. He had no guts to confirm the verdict of Nirja Thakur. Dwarika had had a very scary encounters of the rustling passage of something behind the bushes as he was last Thursday returning from the jungle alone, 'There was something huge and yet invisible, a shadow of Devi Kirpani, I am sure seeking to take a prey for her unborn cubs. She was not growling. She did not want to take me a prey. She was just out in search of Andrew Morgan. I can tell that the cat was groaning with pain. The poison had given her a terrible death.'

They were hearing the cries of the owls and wails of the jackals. The hyenas were also howling as if to warn their children to hide in the den. The night soon fell dead spreading murkiest silence. The villagers were awake and their eyes straining through the portholes towards the

Bungalow, 'We shall remain awake whole night.' This was the instruction of Sarita Dhan. But she was the first to betray. She was sitting squatted and had closed her eyes to take a stealth nap. Nobody was there to shake her so she was snorting like a pig being slaughtered.

They heard the devil's cry. It was like hell cracking overhead. It was like hell being choked by hydraulic engines. The hearts in the cage-ribs got stifled to silence matching with the sizzling silence of the night. They were waiting for the day to breakout. But the night had worn the thickest pall of darkness. Nirja Thakur had nothing to imagine about the Angrez and the azadi stolen. Even the boozy fool of a man named Ram Lal had no story to tell about *azadi*. The question of *azadi* and the heaven of freedom had been adjourned. In the head of the villagers the scary fright of the haunted Bungalow had sat like a pest. Gobardhan Thakur had spread this boo and was himself sleeping well underneath the rug he had once picked from the garbage of the Bungalow. He was the villain of the story and was innocently sleeping to his heart's content.

The night continued to grow in volume and made the watchers weary and sleepy. Most of the people fell asleep including Ram Lal and Nirja Thakur. There was no sign of any scary return of the ghost. The Bungalow had been shrouded in darkness. Then suddenly the howling of the animals started as warning. The jackals were the first to warn then the wolves started the howling and in pitch dark Dwarika Pahan saw a huge shadow lurking about the Bungalow. The Bungalow seemed to have been devoured and a weird fright was spilled about. He ran into the hut of Laxmi Suren and literally pulling her hair awoke her in a panic, 'I saw. I saw the lurking shadow. It was half like death and half like devil.'

Many villagers awoke. Some showed as much courage as they stood up and peeped through the port-hole. But they could not catch the glimpse of the ghost. The Bungalow had mysteriously vanished. There was a colossal void in its place and the howling jackals were sounding like crying when animals are throttled, 'Shoooo!' the drunken Nirja planted his finger upon his lips, 'Wait and strain the head and you shall hear the squeaking of the rats.' This was preposterous. An angry hand gave him a slap, '*Harami,* bastard we were expecting the howling of the ghost but you heard the squeaking of rats!'

Matter did not cease there. Govardhan who was sleeping in his bed was babbling in a delirium. He was not audible. He seemed to shake from head to toe and her mother, Laxmi Suren was trying to control his convulsion. It was a terrible scene. The boy was passing the ordeal of a vision that had sleep and waking combined, 'My child,' Laxmi Surin fell upon the body of the boy. The impact of the fall was big. The boy woke up shouting. He was looking wild with dread. He was worth nothing to trust even if he was going to tell the barest truth. Then somebody gave him a handful of jaggery stone. The boy ate it greedily and then he was being asked again and again about his nightmare. Goberdhan looked blankly at faces and would lick his hand of the jaggery fluid and not tell what he saw in the nightmare. His eyes were rolling on the sockets and his face was clean of expression. All together cried that the boy had been possessed, 'Laxmi Surin on your boy the Devi Maata has descended.'

Morning came and the mystery of the Bungalow got wiped by daylight. The glaring June sun became cruelly hot. Its direct rays began to parch whatever was in the open, the cattle and the vegetation. Mercy came in the form of the dark clouds from behind the jungle and soon the village was having a freshening bath of the rain, 'Strange,' said Laxmi, 'Really unexpected,' said Nirja Thakur and Goberdhan ran into the rain followed by Laxmi and Sarita and Dwarika including the drunk Ram Lal, 'We are freed, freed from the horror grip on our mind. We are freed from the shadow of the night. O that we really are freed! O that Gandhi won.' Nirja sounded weird. He had caught his head and was looking like a buffalo carried by the nose rein.

The whole village was dancing a weird nuisance dance. But their tongues were knotted lest they go noisy. In their world their terror of the Bungalow had made a coil of horror sit on their psyche.

The horror of the villagers was the embodiment of the horror and hate of the Angrez. Whatever shadowy and scary lurked in the vision of the rustics was the sum total of their hate and horror of the Angrez. To the villagers the Angrez were the zombies! The villagers were the illiterate and demeaned creature so they reeled via hate and horror spree. Gandhi was only an image worth being heard but not worth being understood. Sarita, Laxmi, Nirja and Dwarika had clubbed their hate of the Martins and the Angrez anywhere and Gandhi was ousted, 'Silly talk Gandhi giving non-violence a weaponry status! Silly to believe that the violence inside would be assuaged! Gandhi may be a saint but he cannot make saint of the common mass.' This was the statement of the boozy Ram Lal. Ram Lal was heard and not heard as the villagers together felt inside their heart the distinction between violence and non-violence was zeroed.

* * * * *

Chandrapura was ever at the verge of something eerie to happen on it. One day as the evening was sinking behind the mountain and as murky silence of the day was falling prey to the night the mountain began to growl and howl and the sky over it looked like possessed. A huge wailing began in the mountain and then rumbling rain shower invaded the world of Chandrapura. The rain had thickened licking away visibility then from the mountain *a big boulder got dislodged and swept down in the landslide*. It was violence, violence of the nature giving clue to the fact that nature hid violence in its bosom. The rolling boulder as it fell gave the sound of slaughtering devils in a massacre. It was the testimony to the hibernated violence taking manifestation.

Nirja Thakur held his breath. Laxmi Surin too held her breath. Gobardhan became dumb. The eyes could see the boulder roll down like rumbling fury through its falls as if it were possessed, 'Bonga Bhagwan,' cried Nirja. His tongue got knotted, 'Yes, the fall of the rock is a sign of curse on the Bungalow from our Bongas! Would that the Bungalow get demolished. Would that the Bonga rage befall the Bungalow.' The villagers together chanted strange *mantra, verse.* They linked the fall of the boulder to the curse of the Bongas befalling the Martin Dera because of the poisoning of the tigress.

But the violence of the boulder was restricted to a degree. It hit the western part of the Bungalow with care. It landed at the feet of the hoary Bunyan tree as if beseeching forgiveness. Except for a portion of horse stable and a few potted plants the boulder did not attack the Martin's main building. The Martins were left safe. Their god had saved them. The boulder had patiently embraced the trunk of the huge Bunyan tree as if apologizing. The villagers could not get their vengeance fulfilled. They remained as much the evil wishing creatures as they were born. 'Our Bongas they did not take a full revenge!' said Sarita and Laxmi endorsed her, 'Our wish to see the Dera demolished remained un-fulfilled. Violence hibernating in the nature took charge but then the god disposed it.'

All the souls in the village, children, adult and the old bones together rushed in a mass to the Bungalow. It was not like the stampeded rush of the saviors. It was the stampeded rush of the villagers to check maximum damage to the Bungalow. But the god is a neutral party in human affairs. His will and that of the human never synchronize. The Bungalow was safe. The inmates in the Bungalow were safe. The Bongas had not taken a full revenge.

The pain of un-detected clutch on the soul that the villagers suffered was the culprit behind their ill-will. The villagers carried hate as the weapon against the Martins as the latter had been unjust not allowing the villagers to graze their cattle in the jungle. The villagers had other misgivings fostering their hate of Martin forester. Andrew Morgan had poisoned their Kirpani tigress. Andrew was the friend of Martin so the latter was foe to the villagers. Above all the villagers were voiceless and would not have guts to vent their ire openly. Their heart was volcanized. Inside them violence was hibernating. They were too illiterate to catch the message of Gandhi as to how to palliate the violence. Gandhi to them was only a juggler fascinating them and not training them in learning forgiveness, peace and reconciliation.

The villagers were pushing to the Bungalow. They had a wish to see it get demolished. This was wrong from Gandhian perspective. The Gandhi doctrine on it was clear that nobody should wish ill for even the enemies. The Angrez people were the enemies. The villagers were pushing to the bungalow to see it demolished. But the God of the universe was kind to the Martins. The boulder had tugged against the Banyan tree, the Budha icon of Peace.

The villagers had crossed miles through the tortuous passages to see the plight of the Bungalow. It was a celebratory run to the site of catastrophe to see the catastrophe and feel nakedly glad, 'Yes, yes let the rock trample the couple, trample their legs and heads and I will be so happy that I will offer four kilos of the rice to Kirpani Devi.' This was Sarita and followed by her, Laxmi was to offer the five kilos of rice and dal and then soon the entire village was out with the promises of offerings.

'Why for such celebratory offers? Why to be mean and feeling triumphant over the casualties in the Bungalow? Is it what our Gandhi teaches? Is it justified and divinely endorsed?' shouted Ram Lal. He was not drunk. He was sober and not drunk talking like a divinely inspired saint. He became to the villagers a creature of traitoring ferments. Laxmi wished to hit him on his face so did Sarita and the rest of the villagers felt like out-casting him. Ram Lal realized that he was talking contrary to the sentiment of the mass. He tied his words into a bundle and swallowed them like the snake swallows the live rat.

Dwarika Pahan took guts to support the thesis of Ram Lal. But he was disputed by silent hate of the mass. He heard a growling volley of abuses flinging upon him. Laxmi was abusing him. He saw Sarita sneering. He found himself caught amid hostile faces. He sighed and correcting his tone said that the British people should have treated them in a better way. He failed to continue. He said, 'Okey Laxmi and Sarita. I withdraw my words. I know our hate of the Bungalow inmates is right. Freedom and the feel of freedom we have been denied. We are enthralled for centuries. Our Gandhi has read the pain of this slavery. He is fighting for right and dignity. Alas! Alas! Only the good god will bring us the freedom. Our Bonga will it not contribute to the opening of gate to the heaven of freedom?' Dwarika Pahan then hid behind Ram Lal. He feared Sarita would scratch on his face. But Sarita's violence got reined in. She feared the physical strength of Dwarika.

The Bungalow was standing lofty. Its loftiness spoke volumes of arrogance, 'There in the Bungalow hides the culprit who had destroyed our Devi Kirpani, our village deity. Our tigress was pregnant. The Martin people killed her. They killed her because they knew we loved her and tugged our faith on her.' Ram Lal corrected them, 'I tell you it was an another Angrez, one Andrew Morgan. He had killed our Devi Kirpani to prove that he was mighty.'

Nobody among the villagers shouted at him. They were near the Bungalow and they feared detection. But Sarita punched Dwarika Pahan with the hateful words 'Might! Showing might on the innocent tigress was no testimony to bravery. Andrew Morgan will suffer disease for the killing. Our Bongas will take revenge. Our great male Bongas, we shall someday see them come forward and take revenge. The poor Bongas have been left mate-less.'

'I agree,' said Ram Lal, 'I admit that it was cruel of the Angrez fellow but here in the Bungalow lives the Martins. The culprit Andrew is elsewhere. These Martins were not the killers. Our Gandhi does not endorse any punishment in proxy term.' Ram Lal was heard with care. Even Goberdhan heard him and pulling on the hand of Laxmi he mumbled something.

He had again witnessed a shadow in the sky of the Bungalow. He had seen a winged horse floating over the Bungalow suggesting something. The boy shouted hoarsely. He was a patient of some mental error. He was having hallucinatory encounters. Ram Lal till then the lead voice slapped the boy on his cheek and the boy infuriated took a big stone to pelt it on the offender. But his mother stopped him, 'Gobardhan, stop.' The mother shouted and the boy dropped the stone. From his eyes the horse vanished. He looked stupid as stupid as the one bereft of judgment. Gobardhan was ignored as the mob was on a flux to the Bungalow to check whether the Bungalow had been demolished. They wished the Bungalow got demolished. Poor guys they hated the Angrez there. But they feared them too. Their fright of them was the fright of the English boo.

The drama and the scene ceased for a while as the villagers could see that Rabbani Shadman was running from Bungalow side to them with his shirt hurling in his hand. This was an indication of warning, nobody was capable of discerning it.

Rabbani Shadman reached the villagers and warning them not to march to the bungalow said that the Bungalow had been attacked and the forester was sure the boulder was rolled over by some culprits, 'I was in the Bungalow. I saw the scene. The Martins are safe but infuriated. He has sent call of distress to the higher authorities. He is sure it was the act of insurgency. I am sure he would take severe action.' Rabbani was surrounded by the crowd and Ram Lal who was talking Gandhi and morality became upset. He was sure the action would lead to thunder raids and arresting and would lead to penal vengeance. He tried to open his tongue but his tongue got knotted. Every heart was throttled on the information of the infuriation of Martin, 'What shall we do?' cried Sarita as she clutched Gobardhan into her bosom as if she were his mother. Laxmi was so havocked that she clung to Ram Lal and begged him of something to do. Ram Lal instead of consoling the woman found her warm flesh sensual and he clutched her breasts greedily moaning with orgasmic frenzy. The woman tried to disentangle herself but the male body tangling the legs into her legs literally dashed her on the ground and vomited the orgasmic shot.

Rabbani attacked Ram Lal with kicks and fists and injured him. The woman not wet inside had been wetted on her saree by the discharge of the hungry man. She was crying, 'My honor! My virginity!' she cried and hitting on the face and chest of Ram Lal she made hell fall.

'Stop this nuisance,' shouted Rabbani, 'Make sure how you all will save yourself from the crack down. You all will be charged of the insurgency and thrown into the jail.'

Panic caught the villagers. They became timid. The villagers began to run helter-skelter not knowing how foolishly they had ganged together and had been half-way to the cursed Bungalow to see the destruction of the Martins. Their ill-will vaporized. Their hate got paralyzed as panic mounted higher. They became the picture of phantom violence.

'Okey we will turn Gandhian, taking weapon of non-violence, we shall together form a wall of defense with folded hands and would not let us lift even by their mounted soldiers.' This Rabbani heard Dwarika Pahan whisper then Pahan asked all the villagers to lie down and wait for the crack down, 'We shall not resist the arresting. We shall fight the arresting by soul-force. We shall wear the skin and courage of our great Gandhi and shall give us a collective support offering everybody first before everybody next.' This was a confusing strategy not going to succeed when the real crack down would take place but for the time being the strategy was soothing enough, 'Then shall we sit here and wait for the crack down?' asked Sarita. Laxmi suggested they should move to the nearby Bunyan tree and its shade would give adequate protection, 'It is a Buddha banyan tree. It will give protection.'

Rabbani took the lead and posing him to be a Gandhi he climbed the thickest branch of the tree and from there he hung down like a huge bat. He looked like one hanged. Rabbani was shouting hoarsely to have courage and face the crack down without panic, 'Our great Gandhi asks us to fight threats by soul- force, not surrendering at all but also not getting aggressive. Gandhi ji asks us to turn brave on the wake of attacks without fighting back physically. Gandhi holds this will make the oppressor soft.' Rabbani had placed himself on the highest branch of Banyan tree feeling secure against the raids and delivering moral sermons. Sarita sensed this cheating of Rabbani and shouting names upon him she demanded him to climb down and face the English when they cracked down. Laxmi Suren too admonished him for his cowardice. Rabbani Shadman would not get down as he knew the only possible escape from the baton beating and boot kicking would come when he hid himself in the banyan tree.

Ram Lal replacing Rabbani took the lead and offering him to face the first blows said aloud, 'Up with our innocent struggle. Zindabad!' His wine in his head failed to concentrate. He failed to say whatever proper slogan he wanted to shout. Laxmi took the lead, '*Yaroo*! We are innocent. We have no bad intention. If we were wishing the Martins to ruin, we were not wrong. They and their community have usurped our freedom. Our great Gandhi says we have been made slave in our own mother land. Gandhi asks to fight. Our means to fight is restricted. We can fight only by hating the Angrez.' Laxmi herself did not know from where she gathered guts to talk in high pitch without sense.

The villagers stayed till noon under the banyan tree waiting for any crack down. But there were no raids coming. The Martins were nowhere visible leading an avengers' army. Sarita laughed, 'Foolish fellows we were waiting for a crackdown without reason. These Martins are not going to do it.'

Rabbani heard it and he shouting at Sarita said that he had heard Mr. Martin to call the higher authorities mentioning the slide of the rock.

Nobody heard Rabbani. Laxmi and Sarita, Nirja Thakur and Dwarika Pahan all together waited there willingly to suffer the crack down but not receiving one they and others began to retreat like the ghosts in the children's book.

The Bungalow was standing un-touched the same lofty structure where the Martins lived and the villagers were thinning out in twos and threes as Rabbani, the horror monger was clambering down the Banyan tree afraid of a fall, 'God willing this Bungalow will someday demolish,' said Laxmi and Sarita not hearing her said nothing particular. Gobardhan looked back to the Bungalow trying to vision the floating horse but in the glaring June sunlight he was not successful. He doubted if he was ever hallucinating. The retreating legs were hurt but not baton-beaten. They were lucky that their Bongas had saved them. They were angry and afraid and in this muddling state they returned un-punished. The whole village returned home weary and buzzing in the mind that they had been left unpunished because of the Bongas.

* * * * *

CHAPTER 3

SOPHIE MEM

Sophie Juliet, a kind lady of high moral contents and a votary of justice was the wife of Mr. Martin. She was not his shadow, the carbon copy of Martin Julius attitude to the Indians. She was an English by genes but by birth and upbringing she was an Indian. She had been born in British India. She had liking for Gandhi. She had not met Gandhi but she felt she had his influences. About her husband she held she was not his copy at all, 'I am no way his copy. I cannot copy him. I should not. My birth and upbringing restrict me. I am not against him. I am pro myself. I am half Indian.'

Sophie was an angel living in the heaven of her imagination believing in the heaven where freedom was the natural gift. She was a supporter of the Hindustani causes. She had been hearing of the Gandhian struggles. She had been reading articles on Gandhi and from Gandhi and had been convinced that he was fighting for not only political freedom but the spiritual freedom that would make every individual religious in the true sense. He was to her the votary of everything that fell to the bracket of truthfulness, 'Passive resistance, the soul's force to fight against the tyrants. The denial of aggressiveness in matters of resistance! These all sound marvelous. I wonder how and why Gandhi does not prefer the weaponing of gun and instead he prefers the weaponing of voice. I like his looks and half-clad tall, thin figure that does not impress but seems to invoke respect.'

This Sophie had once noted in her diary, 'This man is rightly the Mahatma, a great soul! Gandhi is the correct man here to resist with his tools of passive resistance the British.' She used to remember her mother in England talking of justice and mercy, 'All tyrannies die out. All tyrants get wiped out of mind. Only the just lives eternally. We have to agree that life runs on the fuel of justice not on the ignition from violence.' Sophie sighed deep and said, 'Gandhi is that power-house of justice, a legend in the world of the aggressors to teach non-violence. I admire him, I adore the naked-fakir.'

In pursuance of the development in Chandrapura recently she had been convinced by her maid, Reshma Sagar that the boulder had dislodged due to loose soil, 'Madam ji it was not an act of evil hands.' Sophie wondered as to how a boulder of that size could just dislodge and slip. But she was not wont to getting prejudiced, 'Okey. Okey but this rolling of the boulder should not have happened. It was contrary to what Gandhi pleads.'

She was told a lie that the villagers had rushed to the Bungalow in good faith, 'Laxmi, Sarita, Nirja Thakur and Dwarika Pahan I tell you were running anxiously to the Bungalow for rescue.' Sophie was not a simpleton. She knew Reshma was fabricating a lie. But she did not refute.

Sophie Juliet was a born angel looking upon occasion to forgive people. She forgave Reshma for her blunt lies of the villagers' good intention, 'Good that the mobbing villagers ran for our rescue.' Reshma noted that Sophie mem was avoiding to encounter her eyes, 'Not that much good mem. I can understand that some of the villagers would have felt relief if they had found the Bungalow harmed but Laxmi and Sarita and Nirja Thakur would have been sad.' Sophie gave a little slap on the glowing cheeks of Reshma. Reshma Sagar was her favorite maid. Sophie liked Reshma for her spicy talks and gossips. Sophie asked Reshma to stop lying, 'Reshma I can guess the right from wrong.' This was in reference to the actual intention of the villagers, 'Reshma, I am not un-aware of the development. I can see that the villagers are desperate and angry and these guys would have done us a big wrong if they had got the chance.' Sophie's statement had no resentment. It was as pure as the holy verse, 'I wonder why these villagers do not get together and take violent turns. Is it due to Gandhi influence? But no. Gandhi to them is nothing. If they do not talk violence this is due to the scare of the Angrez.'

* * * * *

One day Reshma after finishing the kitchen chores sat beside Sophie Juliet on the sofa. Sophie was looking absent from her. She was looking anxious too, 'Reshma sometimes I feel lonely. However, I want to connect to the people here but I am not accepted in the circuit.' Sophie asked for a cup of hot tea, 'Lemon tea and some toasts.'

Reshma said, 'Madam ji connecting to people in a foreign land is a task.' Reshma uttered this line and apologized, 'I do not mean that you are not acceptable because you are an outsider.' Reshma began to press legs of Sophie, 'You are wrong Reshma. Wrong technically. I am no total foreigner. I am by birth a Hindustani, only in genes I am outsider. I was born in a small village hardly known to outer world. I was born in Torpa in Khunti where my papa was a doctor. If birth endorses nationality, I am an Indian.'

The discourse did not shake Reshma Sagar. She looked gravely at the lady and finding her so English-like, pink-white, her body texture so slim and the facial features resembling not the Indians Sophie was not insider, 'You are great that you consider yourself as an Indian.' Reshma remarked detestably. Sophie Juliet could guess from Reshma's tone that the girl was lying, 'Okey. No problem whether I am accepted or not I owe my indebtedness to Hindustan. I love this country and would love to do something meaningful when I get the chance.' This confession made her feel secured and made Reshma tearful, 'Sophie mam I wish you are not disappointed.'

The lady then patted on the back of Reshma and said in whispers,'Sagar my feeling of loneliness gets quelled when I feel I belong here. Am I not rightful to feel connected here? My birth and papa's love for this country, get me bound to this country. He remained till the last a devout medical practitioner in the rural blocks around Ranchi. You know he sacrificed his marriage for this. My mom left my dad because she wanted him to shift to Delhi or Calcutta. But he would not hear her till she left him forever. She sailed home to England. I was only ten years and my dad had to raise me single hand.' Sophie divulged the information.

Sophie Juliet finished the line and stood up. She was looking restless. She had been hearing sound coming from the forest, something like the witches wailing, 'Reshma do you think this forest is haunted?' This was a silly query. Reshma described many fake and true stories about the headless bodies strolling through the nearby burning-ghat and ghouls dancing in the moonless night. Sophie heard the stories with interest and felt thrilled.

'Mam, I tell you we Indians however qualified we have half of our minds accepting the *otherness of life*. There is a rumor that a shadow has been lurking about around the Bungalow. Yes, you would experience the pressure of it in the mid night. You can check it. I tell you when the moon is in its death phase a shadow larger than we can imagine lurking about as if seeking blood. It is thirsty. It might be hungry. It might be restless. It comes from behind the forest core and spreads into a gossamer of angry prayer.'

Reshma became confused how to explain. Sophie did not seem interested. She had her English blood. Sophie chided her, 'Nonsense!

I do not like to hear your scary tales.' Sophie dismissed Reshma. But Reshma was adamant to tell something odd. She began, 'Mam you know the Muslim people on death bury their bodies. But the spirit I tell does not get buried. It remains un-lodged. It remains restless and desperate. Then many of them congregate into a single frame. This roams about and hits the eyes.' She stopped apologizing that she could not explain. Sophie laughed and said ironically on her behalf that the assembled spirits would then get ghostly, 'They would tumble and rumble and would float overhead the Bungalow to frighten the inmates. This is stark folly. I have never faced anything untoward. I will not believe in your theory.' Reshma asked her madam to shut her eyes and feel. She asked her to shed her feeling of being in the human body. She asked her to spread her limbs and let her catch the sensation of *otherness*. She asked Sophie then to hold her breath and feel like dead, 'This will prepare you to apprehend the shadows. From your head to the toe you would have an eerie sensation, sensation of cold fingers all over. This is the picture of the ghost sharing its existence with you. We have the Bonga feeling over our skin this way. The Devi Kirpani, the dead tigress would make her presence registered by way of this eeriness.' Sophie laughed and Reshma too laughed and as they were laughing their eyes became wet. It was the eclectic moment to experience *the otherness* of something scary.

'Reshma, I do not believe in your Halloween phenomena. But I believe in the hankering of the soul for release from bondage to freedom. Each soul in its magnificent state seeks freedom, freedom that fulfills. When in bondage the soul languishes for release. This I term as the hankering for reaching the heaven of freedom.'

Sophie sounded too esoteric for the plain Reshma to comprehend her. Reshma looked around and catching sight of a tiny robin bird she asked if ever the bird should be kept in the cage. Sophie in a poetic flux said that she would release the caged bird, 'Any version of life tiny or human size I would see it released from behind the bars.' There was nothing more than poetic in her words. But Sophie meant it, 'To me life is a precious treasure not to be kept in the chest.' She took a crumb of bread and flung it to the direction of the robin bird. The poor creature not sensing good intent got scared. It flew away with a little tweeting sound leaving a blank behind, 'There in the scare of the bird and its sneaking flight lies the key-meaning of what I mean by the heaven of freedom. This key when snatched it makes soul oppressed. I refer to this torment. Dear I refer to this anguish.'

* * * * *

Reshma was back to another gossip related to Shally Jaan, 'This Shally thing you know mam is as fair of skin as you are. I wonder if Shally Bibi is somewhere your descendant?' This was an absurd question but this was enough to raise curiosity in Sophie to see Shally in person.

'No mam you cannot meet her. Her pardah and I think her reluctance to come out of her cloistered world and then her dislike of contacting the *firangees*!' Reshma swallowed the last line but Sophie had caught the term '*Firangee*', 'What this *Firangee* stands for?' demanded Sophie, 'I do not know but they also call you English people Goras and Red-faced monkeys.'

Sophie Juliet was a liberal lady. She was not made piqued. She admitted that in a country where the natives were ruled by foreigners, they were likely to vent ire by calling names and swearing upon the foreigners, 'No problem I will someday call your Shally Bibi and make friends with her. I will make her shed her biases. She will find me pleasant. You know I feel very lonely here. I need a companion. I will ask your Shally Bibi to become my companion.' Sophie Juliet told her mind. The maid did not notice that the mem was really a lonely person. She said that it would be difficult to get Shally Bibi here and more difficult to get her for your friend.

'Why difficult? Is she unsociable?' Sophie asked.

'Yes mam. I think she is scared of coming in touch with anything alien. But if you have guts, you can fetch attention of her man, Salim Bahadur.' Reshma introduced Salim to her. Sophie felt a sizzling ripple running through her body, 'Okey then how does he look?' It was an odd query. Reshma said that he looked more handsome and tall and more impressive than her man, 'He is a Khan of the Afghani blood. People say his ancestors migrated hundred years ago from Iran border. He is a Kurdish.'

'Okey. I would someday approach him. I like meeting people. I like people with such fascinating background.'

Reshma was then dismissed to finish the remaining domestic duty.

Sophie roamed through the adjoining garden and reached the site of the accident. She was horrified to notice that the boulder had destroyed part of stable and it was just the grace of the god that the horses were out on patrolling, 'God really exists. He saves the lives. If the horses had been there, they must have been injured. Animals or humans anything injured horrify me.' She checked the site and noticed that the boulder had been checked by the trunk of the Buddha banyan tree, 'It is the living miracle,' she said and walking to the spot over which the boulder had rolled noticed that many of her favorite flowering plants had been crushed, 'God decides the happenings.' She closed her eyes and tried to vision her god, 'Everybody in the intense moment of prayer seeks to vision God. My god is without form and figure but I sometimes pine to give Him a shape and touch Him.' She laughed at her folly to vision God like the pagan natives who create impersonated gods.

'These natives are pagans, curious fellows and irregular in the rational thinking. They allow their imagination to supersede the reason. They cannot be justified for their folly but I appreciate that they seek to recognize the mystic in nature and give them ample significance. This I would grant as the freedom of choice. I have no virtual right to spite them. Every sane mind has this natural right to freedom. I have heard of the poisoning of the tigress. I have heard of the locals crying for the tigress. I have also heard they have been calling the tigress Devi Kirpani. It sounds weird but it is not totally messy. These Hindustanis are the worshippers of chaos and this is their strength in recognizing the mystique of nature.'

Sophie mam then turned to her Bungalow and saw Rabbani standing at the main gate. She knew him by name. She was a typical English lady without the English snobbery. She was very much a Hindustani when she felt that the urgent need of the time was to hear the Hindustanis with attention, sympathy and affection.

'*Shally* mam,' Rabbani Shadman wished her in Muslim style. The good lady answered it in the best of the gesture but failed as she was not wont to it. She had folded her hands in the copy of those locals wishing Martin sahib in utter humility. She disliked people supplicating, 'This is like freedom of communication choked.'

'Well Rabbani,' she began, 'How is your *sahib*? Is he not one Salim Khan?' the inordinate mention of Salim Khan made Rabbani Sultan feel odd. In his opinion a lady had the right only to mention a lady, 'Do not ask about my *saheb.* He is a busy man. Recently he had been on a visit to your place along with Bibi ji but the Bungalow main gate was shut and the sentry had not opened the gate, 'My Khan *saheb* had come on the call from your *saheb.*'

She recalled it, 'Yes, I recall it. Actually, I was suddenly taken ill, my maternity problem. I had to rush to hospital.' Sophie explained.

Rabbani felt sizzled on his male spots and wished to clutch the lady into his bosom. He mentally ravished her unaware. His lustful eyes devoured her on the spot. The lady sensed his discomfiture but ignoring it she talked about Mrs. Salim and converged on Mr. Salim, 'Then when your *Saheb* would visit?' This was a query of no substance. The lady sensed her folly. She to divert asked if really the rolling of the boulder was human mischief. Rabbani did not answer it correctly, 'How I can mam? Martin *saheb* would know it better.'

'Your Martin *saheb is* angry and he might have brought troubles upon the villagers but for me. I pleaded him not to go that far. He agreed. But he is still very angry. He doubts it was an act of mischief.' Sophie was interested in the affairs of the natives, 'Rabban ji can you tell who this Gandhi is like? I wonder how any man can create such a magic drawing mass after mass of people to his stands. His passive resistance! It is a weapon of miracle making! How he can manage it and make the mass mesmerized! What a great feat!' Sophie was looking dissolved. On her pink cheeks the charm of youth had made her desirable. Rabbani not interested in her Gandhi was enthralled by her utter charms. He desired to take collect her in his sensuous arms and ravish her.

The lady sensed his sensuality. She was not offended. She knew the more the human male is mean the more he was likely to get sensual. Rabbani stole his eyes from her face and soon submissively dragged it to her feet. He became afraid of her reaction. The lady did not bother. She belonged to a different race. She ignored the lechery of the vision and laughing said that the Gandhi was a magician of words. This remark had no relevance. Rabbani dittoed it, 'Ji madam our Ghandhi is a juggler. He can build a big crowd and enchant it. I sometimes ago had seen him in Ranchi in a rally. He was a brisk man of big thin legs and agile gait.'

The lady heard the man with fleeting attention as her mind was back to the incidence of the boulder, 'How a huge boulder just rolled down!' she babbled, 'Madam ji the slide of the boulder was not a human mischief. I tell you behind it was something weird. The jungle is mysterious.' Sophie ignored him but loved to hear more about the haunting, 'You people are very loose of reason, very floppy in mind! Your villagers have been talking of Bongas and Devi Kirpani.' She did not emphasize on the existence of such and such shady beings. Rabbani's eyes strayed to her budding breasts. He wondered how the *roundening* of the breasts was maintained. His late wife had two huge sagging ones. He abhorred the sagging breasts.

Sophie Juliet then asked Rabbani to go. In her mind Salim Khan, Shally and Reshma became resounding obsessions. She felt very empty in her heart and also very lonely. She tried to divert her mind to her school days in India. She did not mention the name of the school but recalled well that her doctor father was posted in the remote area. She recalled difficult names of his postings like Simdegha and Khunti. The utterly jungle features of these posting places had hung up in her mind like cloudy memories. She was able to recall the kind expression of his father in his face. His father Jacson was very much a hybrid fellow living the life of the rustics and trying to speak Hindustani to his patients. His patients used to be very intimate with him. He never made them feel that he was a foreigner. He treated his patients more with the soft words than the tablets and syrups. In his time injection and antibiotics were rare. The patent products were hardly used. Instead, the compounders mixed drugs in red and yellow syrups. The patients with fever and dysentery and pneumonia were treated with the same version of yellow and red syrups. She laughed. She remembered her father narrating funny stories of his patients, 'These Hindustanis are very muddling creatures. They need more than love only pity. I would tell one thing about these pagan Hindustanis that they are so inclusive and non-conformist that they seek divine elements even in the rolling rocks. They are fantastically free of choice. Their faith in the power of God in the little things is their strength. We can only pity them if we want to dispute them.' Sophie had caught this phrase. She had been practicing it in her daily life, 'Pity is more godly-thing than love. Love is psychological but pity is human.' She did not explain this distinction.

* * * * *

Her mind was suddenly arrested. She remembered the days in her college when she was informed by her mate that in the college ground the police men were gathering. The principal of the college was in panic as he had been instructed to keep the students in check. There was a rumor that the Gandhian movement had penetrated into the Ranchi College Campus. Her college mates were secretly part of the Gandhian squad. But she was treated as an antagonist. She wondered why she was treated as an opponent, 'I can understand it. My friends doubt me because of my ethnicity.' Sophie once tried to explain her half-Indianness with Sulekha Dhan. Sulekha looked at her with doubt and smiled, 'Yes, yes dear you are India-born. You are like us. We honor you.' Sophie Juliet could sense the lie of Sulekha. She tried to take Sulekha in confidence but the latter sneaked away, 'I can understand that my friends would not accept my pleas. They distrust me. My half- Indianness does not confirm me.' But she was not discouraged, 'I do not need to prove my half-Indianness. This I am and this is my pride. I like Gandhi. I like his passivity-kits in all matters of relations and conducts.' Sophie consoled her and said that she was for freedom, freedom of choice and operation and conduct.

Sophie diverted her mind to the tragedy of her father's death. She recalled that on his death his hospital staff had gathered in the little house where her mother was crying, 'It was a miserable time for me. My papa's body was wrapped in the white sheet. He had died from heart attack. His treatment during those days was impossible in Ranchi due to the lack of expertise. I remember the death time of her father. His death was a sudden shock to me and my mother. His body had been brought on a bullock cart and entire hospital attendants had followed him.' Sophie recalled that she and her mother were the loneliest person in India. She was broken by the death of her father and would have returned to England with her mother. But fate had something else in reserve.

She met Mr. Martin then a young man with brown hair and blue eyes very much a material to get attracted to. He had been in the funeral and had since been around Sophie on different occasions. His presence had begun to notify his leanings, 'I was not very sure about him and myself and was sometimes in a confusion about the growing intimacy till it was too late. Martin Julius was a good name and his coat was good as also was good his tie. My mother had been fascinated with him. Her responses to him were far more intense than mine as I used to be shrinking from him when he tried to touch me physically. I remember his eyes seemed to carry mischief. I hated being touched. It would pollute me this I thought. But Martin covered me like a big shadow.'

Sophie Juliet stopped in the middle of the thought as she saw a koel bird cooing from beneath a thicket. The bird was scared of attack from the crows which had an enmity with it, 'I know the crow's anger is genuine. The koel bird steals the crow's nest. It leaves its eggs there and on hatching the koel chicks cleanse the nest of the crow's chicks. This is cruel but this is god's planning.' Sophie felt horrified at the behavior of the koel chicks. She wanted to escape this abhorring thought.

She jerked her neck and sprained it. She moved the neck softly hoping the sprain would go. Then in a dismal mood she allowed her mind to imagine a handsome young man called Salim Khan, the legal husband of Shally Jaan, 'Shally Jaan what a name! Her name carries hybrid overtone. But the name Shally sounds musical and English only 'Jaan' sounds like she comes of a Mughal breed. Well, I shall have a time to meet her. I would also check if her Salim Khan is as handsome as I hope he should be. My Martin is the stereotyped white and thin and gentle guy but not impressive. I like somebody who is different, different from the English physiology.'

Sophie laughed at her flight of imagination and felt dirty, 'I am betraying,' she charged herself. This thrilled her. This made her feel adventurous. She said in whispers, 'An English girl like me should not worry about propriety and norms. I belong to a different race, different attitude and trait.'

The harsh sound of the koel bird broke her reverie. She saw the bird rocketing into the next and next thickets with the poor crows failing to catch it, 'Bravo! My bird you will outfly. I love adventure and stealth.' Sophie concluded her thoughts and for diversion she tried to remember names of the villagers like Laxmi, Sarita, Nirja Thakur and the last name she forgot, 'Was it Gobardhan or Gobinda?' Sophie Juliet felt drawn to the villagers, felt like willing to support them. She knew that Mr. Martin would bring troubles to the villagers, 'But no. I will take care of them. I will convince Martin that the boulder rolled down because of loose soil.'

Sophie had an urge to take tea. She preferred lemon tea. The milk tea unsuited her bowels. She called Reshma. The maid brought two cups of the tea, 'Why two cups?' asked the lady knowing well that the second cup was for the maid. Sophie was unlike the English, not a snobbish creature. She loved to be normal. Her motto in life was inclusive. She was tolerant and she liked to copy her father. Her father was a very plain man of no arrogant ways. His skin color and even facial contours had changed. He resembled the locals. His loose tie and dirty shirt made him look like an English in the wrong body, 'I love the ways of my father. I love to follow his manners. He taught me two things: sympathy and kindness.'

Sophie finished her tea and asked Reshma to tell something new. Reshma told nothing new but initiated a talk leading to her pregnancy and the birth of a still born baby, 'Mam your baby was born still because of some evil influence.' Reshma put up the issue with such callous haste that Sophie Juliet was baffled, 'What!' she shouted. Reshma stuck to her point, 'Begum *sahiba*,' Reshma started, 'I am sure of what I say. Your baby was born whole, no fault at all. But it was still. So cute baby but still. I remember its face. The baby was as if smiling.' Sophie was saddened. She had a great desire to recall his baby. But she could not, 'Madam ji if you hear me, I would suggest you to take a local treatment. We commonly go for some mystic treatment in such cases. Molvi people become our outlets.'

'What is that?' asked Sophie without curiosity. Reshma was encouraged to describe the treatment. It sounded weird but interesting. It involved non-descript ingredients very much near to witchery, 'Tell in details.' Sophie paused. Reshma feeling jubilant undertook to mention methods and ingredients but she failed to convey meaning, 'Okey ji I will bring Rabbani to you. He knows the Molvi Saifoo in Simdegha. This Molvi is a god's man, so hoary and sacred. I will get you necessary blown water and amulets from him. Your womb carries evil shadows. The use of these stuffs will clear the shadow. You will have your cute baby.'

In a dream-like sequence Sophie had visuals of her bed-time acrobatics. She saw her in the sticky act thrown like the used toilet paper. She groaned in pain of the soul confessing bluntly that except for the vegetative filling of her interior the Martin thing had done her nothing marvelous. She recalled the kneading of her flesh and the torture and the spilling of his semen and the sudden completion of the act like the pigs climb at the back of the female and climb down to grope through the squalor. Sophie had had no orgasmic relief in the act. It was like the python coiling the python. She abhorred herself and her partner and not feeling salvaged she said to herself that the heaven gate of freedom was closed on her, 'My marriage, yes, my marriage it was a false beginning to a false end and in between I am not a victim of persecution but I am. I am singled out for a rare of the rarest persecution minus humiliation. I am a free slave to Martin sir whose nobility and racial tissues bind me though I think it is cheating. I live in an absent retreat of the defeat I belong. I cannot put it in words. It is a matter of experience, absolutely abstract devoid of a concrete exigency.' Her poetry in the prose became vague but she felt thrilled and verbally fulfilled, 'I know abstract thinking is not the wrecking of rationality. It has its significance. We humans are wont to catering to such a salvaging spree to keep us buoyed out of the mess.'

* * * * *

Sophie was an un-fulfilled wife of her husband Mr. Martin whose prima facie focus was on his duty, duty which he self-professedly claimed was to protect the Crown. He thought he carried his Queen's burden. He also thought that he was bound to support and promote the Crown. It was his fidelity and he was happy for it. He had no desire to get recognition for his duty unto his ruler.

Sophie was not secondary to him but he did not feel accountable to her emotion related to the Indian scenario. She had been resenting his untoward reactions to Gandhi, 'This Gandhi is a blank shot. He will not get what he dreams. We English are invincible.' Martin talked in disdain and Julee resenting said that he was mis-estimating Gandhi and associates, 'Gandhi is far above the physical powers of the English. He is shielded by his soul force, protected against our militancy by his will to fight by not enmity. He is typical an opponent. Quite new a foe to the Angrez. We are accustomed to using physical against the physical and Gandhi is spiritual, an adversary with smile on the face.' She paused then began. Sophie was herself not sure how she was evaluating Gandhi and enjoying the discourse, 'Our power is the stolen one. We steal the power of the Indians. We use Indians against Indians. This is immoral, a stark cheating. But Gandhi is contrary. He does not engage physical forces. He takes the weapon of the soul to fight the guns. He is unique, the votary of non-violence. He is para-natural in the corporeal world.'

Martin looked at her with awe and not feeling antagonized he patted on her back as the teacher would do to the taught. He opened his mouth wide and yawned falsely to trivialize her. He was not of trivializing nature but he was irritated to hear her elevate Gandhi, 'My obligation is my nation, the colonial power, its pride and expanse. I am most upset these days to see the wars breaking our guts. These nuisance demonstrations everywhere in our colonies, do you think we are going to stumble? God forbid if and when my country submits to pressure will it not be humiliating to me? I would rather die of shame. This would be a personal loss. I love my English nation madly.' His words fell flat on Sophie. She was not struggling to change his mind. She was not desirous to control his mind. She therefore ignored him. She pitied him for not having a capacity to estimate the Gandhi honestly.

'During the crisis time when our position and prestige world over is staked you know my entire energy and living elements get drained dear.' Martin continued, 'My anxiety is to pick and hold our national prestige. Long Live the Union Jack!' he paused then blasted, 'You are my necessity. I am your necessity. What hurts me most is that you are shrinking from me. I would be most lonely if you made me lonely.' Martin became emotional. He became hoarse in the throat, 'We are as the colonial power losing weight. This horrifies me. Then your Gandhi here and like him other domestic movements in our colonies are worrying me.' Martin patted on her cheeks. He lit his pipe. He inhaled smoke. He coughed spasmodically.

She was passing through an ordeal, 'He is my husband. He is definitely a husband by law but this does not suffice making me welded to him. He is on the wrong and this I abhor. Alas! Alas! I have become antagonized,' she sighed and looking at him with pity said that she could not rectify him, 'I can understand his position. I do understand mine. I respect him, more than respecting him I honor him. I cannot quarrel with him to get him to my point of views. Controlling others is ugly to me. I cannot try to control him.'

Silence fell in between. She suffered hoping that he might relent to her point of view. But she found he was rigid. She argued, 'We are here only the alien rulers, in control of this land externally. The English unlike the Mughals are not assimilated powers. We are the detached ones, only foreign rulers! We are subjected naturally to winding up of our tenure. We should note it and prepare for a congenial departure!' She sounded not harsh but she was not pleasant either, 'You are insulting me. You are sounding like threatening us. Our tenure is not winding up! We would be leaving India on our own conditions.' Martin looked away to the far sky seeming to measure distance. He became sad, very sad, 'We are losing controls and our colonies in Africa and Australia and elsewhere are receiving blows of the damned freedom movements. Freedom! Yes, freedom of people from the foreign yokes.' She heard him distantly. She bowed her head and said without guilty sense, 'We are suffering not the territorial loses. We had no moral right to seizes those lands. You are mistaken to treat it as your loss of prestige. We were just the usurpers. We had captured others' freedom.'

'Throwing nations into serfdom

Cutting skin by razor blade

Seeing the body writhe in pain

And feeling not shame

is shaming the concept of freedom

We English are committing it in evil name.'

Martin Julius squirmed in pain, 'Okey! Okey! My brave lady! But note we are here only the outsiders, their sworn enemies. We cannot turn insiders. Dear Ju note that when time comes these Hindustanis will retaliate. No Gandhi will save us. They will not let us go un-avenged.' Martin was trying to bring home the simple truth that her feelings for the Indians would pay her hard.

Sophie heard and un-heard him, 'Sir *saheb* I know only one thing that freedom to any nation should come and no nation is morally entitled to curb it.'

* * * * *

Martin had shot a peacock. The blue plumed bird was calling. The call was loud and ear piercing. He became excited and taking his gun he fired randomly. The poor bird fell from the tree bleeding from its little face.

Sophie Juliet sat stiff watching dazed at the dead bird. Martin strutted with wild pride and looking crazy with excitement said that he downed the bird.

'Nothing brave sir. Killing has become your habit.'

'No habit Ju. I killed it to kill my indwelling rage.' Martin gave a silly explanation.

'Sir ji saheb,' she felt like crying, 'Your gun is your savage partner in the brutality. Your gun is the replica of not strength. It has become your obsession. Where you seem, you are superior you use the gun.' Sophie could not check her tears. She wept hugely.

'Dear my love. Sorry. Really sorry. I was upset. I wanted to vent the passion.' Martin took away his eyes from the peacock. He could see that the bird was still brilliant and glorious at death.

'Dear Mart you know your English blood you are fouling it. I tell you your Christian blood is getting polluted. I expected you to revert to the Christ and save you from the pollution! But no. You are getting bloody.' Sophie still felt no hate for her man. She was convinced that her man was under the influence of vengeance syndrome.

Mr. Martin tried to explain. But his explanation was flimsy, 'Juliee I am not getting polluted. My Christ in me is as it is. I am only impelled to relocate myself and read the historic fact that we English are out on foreign adventure to raise our prestige and power. But sadly, I discover that our investments in the foreign lands are staked. We are being ditched. These revolutionaries in our colonies are creating nuisances. This has made me wary and so-called mean. We have acted from missionary zeal to execute the White Men's burden. You know it is our ingenuous wish to invest in the service of civilizing the barbaric race. We exert pressure and means toward it.'

'This White Man's bluff,' said Juliee strongly, 'I tell it is your arrogance Mart, not your inner Christ. You have defeated this Holy soul!' Sophie was arguing to evoke the Christ in him.

Martin did not quarrel. He to divert her pointed to a strange sound coming from the jungle.

'Do you mark that these jackals and hyenas and the damned wild beasts had been there but recently these creatures have really turned horrible, their howling I do not fear but it is frightening.'

'These animals are not simply howling. They are addressing you, addressing to convey a message.' Sophie could see that Mart was blank of expression.

A dull sound of something tumbling came from the corridor. It was shrill. Sophie was scared. Martin was startled. He strained his ears to catch the sound. He failed.

'Wait is it a common cat?' asked Martin.

'Maybe they are seeking to investigate on the poisoned tigress. That cruel Andrew Morgan he had by deceit killed the tigress. He had thrown poisoned meat on her path. The cat was pregnant. The villagers have been upset at her killing. They adore her as their deity of sort, some power deity; they call her Devi Kirpani.' Sophie was looking distressed.

Suddenly a thunder-fall of something filled the universe, 'I am sure it is someone from the villagers,' cried Martin. He caught the gun and rushed out.

'Your gun wielding,' she snubbed. She said sorry then continued solemnly, 'Your gun wielding craze is going to delete the Christian in you. I am proud of my Christianity that consists of bounty, charity and compassion. But gun and threatening and subduing someone is contrary to my nature. It is contrary to compassion the missionary lesson teaches.'

Mr. Martin rushed out to cover the phantom. He could encounter none. He was deluded. He returned sweating. Julee looked at him with pity. She could see for sure that Martin was in nervous panic. She did not blame him. She wished healing for him but she knew that he was infested with some phobia.

Sophie Juliet scooped into the limbs of Martin Julius. It was not like sex poking her. It was her sudden scare of the para-natural happenings, 'My lord, I tell we have had three miscarriages. The last one was quite un-warranted. Reshma talks of the lurking dark shadows. Reshma talks of a Molvi Saifoo and his blown water. She talks of the correction of the pregnancy by amulet wearing. I would like to try it. Who knows it will work?' She sounded irrelevant. Martin did not fret. He had tolerance for her. He had been noting her follies of late. He had been wondering why she had been talking of the Bonga tigers and their divine profile.

'Dear me, you are straying. You are getting un-hinged. Sometimes you refer to the silly Bongas and now a live Bonga Molvi. Please stay true to the English scientific temperament. Your contacts with Reshma and Rabbani and God know who has impaired your reasoning.' Martin rebuffed her then he feeling awkward apologized. His mind was trying to figure out the happenings outside. He was sure that something was intruding into the Bungalow, 'Dear my love please remain sane. I have been warning you not to be in contact with these duffers. You are getting spoilt. Molvi and his blown water, amulet and the relation of the biological faults to the mythical power, I tell you dear your head will rot. The Bonga follies I wonder how you can tolerate them?' Martin held her in his bosom to reassure her.

She briefly but sternly said that she needed the mystical treatment then she withdrew it. She said to him that her mother had been torturing her mind recently, 'I wonder if her marriage after the divorce from my papa survived. I recall that she was not my influence but she had a good thing in her that she preferred to leave India on the plea that she did not fit here.' Sophie bit her lips hard till it bled. Martin chided her then caressed her and asked if she was suffering from nostalgia. She said that she had no nostalgia, 'My England is this, India. I wonder why I cannot pull myself out of the illusion if I belonged here.'

'Okey! Okey! You will learn in course of time. You will have your shocks.' Martin pampered her as his fingers played with her black hair reminding of the oriental genes.

* * * * *

Months later Sophie Juliet not still bent upon shedding her fascination for Gandhi and Hindustan she sauntered to the Banyan tree, the giant Buddha tree that seemed to get activated. Its snake hanging roots seemed to wriggle in the hidden desire to take her into its laps. She could notice that the mysterious herons nestling in its lofty branches were attentive to hear a whisper. The sky far off in the firmament seemed attentive. The earth under her feet seemed to vibrate. She felt an auditory magic, 'Sophiea! Sophiea my child!' This was a whisper of a hoary mouth in the ancient cadence, 'You are Sophiea.' This was the final verdict.

'Why Sophiea?' demanded Sophie Juliet calmly and herself answered that she was born Indian that is why Sophiea, 'Okey! Okey! I would love to cloak myself in Sophiea self. It really enthuses me.'

The Banyan Buddha hailed her. The Buddha reminded her of the Bongas and the villagers. Sophia then corrected the stress pattern in the new name and without insisting on any phonetic correction agreed that she would call her Sophia.

She sat down under the tree and closing her eyes she imagined a Buddha of her choice wearing no hoary beards and gray locks. Her Buddha was a Gandhi wearing thin, enchanting smile on his toothless face, his body brown like the average Indians and his upper body naked while looking in no way a miserable pauper of intellect, 'My Buddha is my Gandhi; Gandhi of the crores of Indians tugging at him for freedom and release and an exit to the heaven of new making.'

* * * * *

Inside her womb something moved. She had missed her periods and had never known that it was the sign of a life sowing life inside. She was silly of the biological calculus. She was carrying her baby. This baby was vibrant and impish.

'Yes, my baby from Martin.' She wished she had not been impregnated that way. She wished she had been a WOMAN of some Khan, maybe Salim Khan. She felt unclean. She closed her eyes and eclipsed her thoughts, 'I am kidding myself. I am drifting to the wrong side. Am I a flirt?' Sophie left this question as a doubt and never gave it importance. She discovered that she had if not love for her man she had a caring heart.

The thought of the Bonga tigers overwhelmed her, 'These Bongas, are really they worth the deification? I will not add my remarks and would respect the villagers' belief. Is not India a muddle and these people bigger muddles. We English are too scientific to accept the shadowy though we would love to read thrillers and horror stories.' Sophie sat under the banyan tree and felt the Buddha of the tree protecting her. Her baby was kicking her belly. She laughed at Reshma's insistence on catching the Molvie Sophie for her pregnancy.

She shouted hosana. It was a wrong shout in the wrong time but she shouted hosana without calculation and care. She became wild and elemental and felt free, free from racial bracketing, 'I am no more the former self, a branded red-faced English monkey. I am no more the votary of the rationalism. I am no more a strict skeptic.' She laughed, 'Foolish or wise I am relieved from the unkind prison of distinction. These Indians are not harmless and meek. They are capable of avenging themselves. But no. I do not bother. I enjoy supporting the Indians. This is not due to any of my envies of Martin. I do not feel envied at him. He is right on his path and myself right on mine.' Sophia Juliet then lay upon the ground sprawling and sucking fresh air.'

* * * * *

Sophie returned to her Bangalow not clouded in the mind but very clear that she had completed the journey of transference, 'Sophia Begum! Yes, Sophia just adequately reshuffled in the spellings of my original name. This did a magic on me. I do not know what configural change it influenced but I feel I am restructured. The great thing happened on me. I am capable of feeling like Indians, seeing them as Indians and without hating the English I can see that the latter are distorted version of their hyped claims of superior race. A superior race is superior by deeds not talks.' She sat on the floor squatting like a rustic. This hurt her bottom. She wondered how the rustics could squat for hours, 'My life henceforth is devoted to atoning for the wrong of our ethnic brethren.' She heard this dialogue and felt thrilled and ashamed, 'We are born not to subordinate a nation.' This dialogue thrilled her and she wanted to add more of this intensity.

To compensate she recalled her college mate Rakesh Sharma, 'I could not adjust with his sudden recoil of whatever was building in me as regards intimacy or loyalty and soon I was evoked by my inner-self to check my advances. I withdrew from him and the guy vanished from around me on the pretext of studies abroad. He went to England. He never tried to connect with me. It was not his betrayal. It was a stark dismissal of a relationship on racial components. Poor guy!' Sophia concluded the tale with a hashtag. She did not feel lost. She did not also feel bereaved. She had guts enough to maintain necessary equanimity in the crisis. 'I am on the race to achieve freedom, an exit from the clutch. This is my right as a human character in my story. This is no added chapter in my story, an integral part of it.'

'Rakesh or the Khan, any Indian to me is

not important

Important is my floating belief that I carry Indian hue

This gives me strength to feel secure as the clue.'

Sophia Begum then looked at the photo frame of her wedding time. Martin was in his Nevy blue suit and her white gown was a match predicting confirmation. The frame had gathered dust. She picked it and softly wiped the dust with the loose end of her saree. She wondered the saree fabrics had done the cleaning perfectly. The pair photo became bright and clear, 'Marriages happen in resonance with the biological necessities. Marriages then grow and continue and despite whatever transformation my marriage will also grow and progress. I am not like my English guys to change partner. I do not like changing partner. I am very much strict in this regard, a monomaniac fellow. Martin is my final spouse. Martin is not otherwise matching my tastes and my caprices but he is noble and this alone is my hooking point.' Sophia said to herself that she had begun to acknowledge her Sophia-hood, 'We human beings are susceptible to adjustment; survival being our life-mission we love to stay calm and connected where we should have revolted. Martin is not my minus point. He is not my negator. But inside me the emergence of my second self is my second wedding to my Indian obligations. I will fight for the return of freedom to these Indians. But I am not going to disturb my relation with Martin though I will fight his ways that intervenes in the achievement of the path to heaven of freedom. I adore it as the prime right of all human of all race and ethnic configuration.' She was not agitated as she uttered these lines, 'My taste is different. His taste is different. Between us disparity sits aloud. He is a pure English, a complete outsider but I an insider by upbringing and contacts. In me the English is only limited to my genes.' She explained her position in different ways.

Sophie Juliet then had a little kick in her womb. It was the baby there. She fondled her belly and imagined with care that her baby would carry her features, her mind and nature and that it would succumb to the empathy she has for the foster land: India, 'I cannot totally eject myself from the fostering fold of India. I remember the little sensations of the *gol-gappa* and the *aalu-chat* at the gate of the school when with Reeta, Rakhi and Sulekha, I used to enjoy the fun time. I recall to my deep pain that these Reeta and Rakhi stuffs vanished from my contact line once they entered their early marriage.' She doubted if this vanishing was deliberate or accidental. She solaced that these girls did not abandon her, 'They must have lost my address. They must have become too busy with their children. They were my class fellows. We together used to steal into the adjoining mango orchard and steal the raw mango. Those were the silly days of childhood. Once I had been caught by the watchman but the fellow had released me as I was in panic and he was frightened of being located for harassing an English girl.'

Sophie Juliet was confounded why she had an advantage as an English girl. She was young and silly not ever regarding her as a superior race due to her ethnicity, 'That *Chacha* should have harassed me but instead he looked nervous and apologetic. He released his grip on my frock. I wonder if this concession was because of my color.' She did not ask Rekha about it but Rekha one day explained that the *Chacha* released her unpunished because she was an English, 'What connection with my ethnicity to my theft?' This was a direct question to which Rekha answered, 'Only that I had been like you a White girl! Being White is an advantage in Hindustan. We Brown race hate and awe the English at a time but would not dare offend openly.'

She had been hearing from Reshma Sagar and occasionally from Rabbani Shadman about the mass movement. She had been wondering how the Indian mass, men, women and even children had been incited to the cause of freedom, 'These guys, resourceless and seemingly weak are they fit material to collide with a colossal power: the English?' She admitted un-mistakenly that the national fire ignited would not extinguish, 'Only I doubt if after independence the English would remain safe. I also doubt about the total bridling of passion in the mass. It would burst out in wild fire. The back-lashes I mean the back-fire it will come.'

She was in college when she became convinced of the excesses of the British and began to support the Indians. But her support was not acknowledged by her college friends who doubted her because of her English genes, 'Yes, I will not be acknowledged but despite it I will enjoy supporting the Indian cause. It is my nature. It is in my blood from parental side. My papa, Joseph Paul was a humble doctor practicing in rural belts and my mother was not a hardliner as per her ethnicity. Gandhi is my man. He is the hero of whatever meagre he could do to protect the right to freedom. One day he will open the gate to freedom.'

* * * * *

Sophia was feeling blissfully heavy in her belly. It was her baby. She loved to carry the weight. She fell into a trance. She felt indebted to Martin, 'My Martin is my hero. He may be wrong to others but he is right to me. Alas! This is half justice. The full justice would have been there only if he had been a man with wide spectrum showing compassion universally' She then reverted to the thought about her pregnancy, 'It is God's grace that I got pregnant without whatever catalyst influences of that hoary Molvi Saifoo of Simdegah. I had been in Simdegah during my papa's service time. My Papa was a liberal English fellow aligned with the locals but I recall he was irritated from reference to Saifoo when his patients came to him with more complications due to Molvi materials. Most of his patients with tuberculosis and heart diseases came in the last stages and would reverentially refer to the treatment of the Saifoo Molvi by his blown water, fake herbs and spurious amulets.' Sophie felt relaxed that she had not permitted Reshma to bring spurious nuisance from the Molvi, 'We are the rational people. We should remain rational. Any stupidity does not suit our racial contour.'

She walked with care lest she should stumble. She was climbing the steps running to the main Bungalow. The courtyard below was a big space flanked with greenery. There she climbed down with care all the time wishing for somebody to support her. In usual days Reshma used to support her but on that fateful evening she had not called Reshma Sagar.

She was climbing the steps and her saree, definitely a villain was suddenly un-furled about her entangling her steps as if some evil hand was active and was going to punish Martin via the lady. She had a sudden blackening of consciousness, a reeling of head, a big error of calculation; she swooned; the body as if got flung; her steps lost control; she became a bundle of load on her and a savage hand as if jolted her; Sophie stumbled and her saree became the physical villain. A wrong step on the loose fabrics and she fell with a huge thud rolling down to the courtyard. A shriek of horror and pain and severe darkness spread over her eyes. She rolled down the stairs. Julee was bleeding and the case was a maternity emergency.

Mr. Martin was alarmed. She was bleeding profusely. In a state of dazed consciousness she called Devi Kirpani, the tigress. In a flash the scene shifted to the hallucination of the rolling boulder almost swallowing her. The broken wing of the stable seemed to turn into a jaw. Sophie Juliet was sinking gradually. Before her eyes the shadows of her past were clouding her intelligence. Soon came Rakesh Sharma in a flash and soon he vanished as Reshma came then the jubilant faces of Rekha, Rakhi and Sulekha came. All these faces were shrinking from her touch in horror and repugnance. Sophie's delirium continued as her body kept draining of blood.

She felt the strong hand of Martin underneath her belly trying to plug up the bleeding point. But of no use. She needed a correct medical aid and it was absent, 'I am dying,' she had the resonance of this alarm, 'My life is hung up,' vaguely her mind contemplated. Soon her hearing was blurred while she became a lost case of hope, 'I will die before seeing the freedom of Hindustan. It is not a matter of a country getting free. It is a matter of seeing freedom being achieved by a slave nation to give the natives a push to the heaven of freedom. I fail to elucidate the point.'

'Freedom, anybody's freedom robbed and declined

it is the most suffocating a feel un-refined.

I hate to pass this ordeal, hate being a party in it

The universal justice I seek an exit

I know I am nothing to add meaningfully

But I hope and pray in favor of the needy to achieve it successfully.'

Then suddenly she wished she had been born a total Indian. She looked at her facial features and felt disappointed, 'I know I am an English but Hindustan was my foster land. I am indebted to it. I should feel indebted.' The thought ripple in the mind came flickering.

Mr. Martin called Rabbani, the coachman. Luckily Rabbani heard his shout and he applying his good brain dispatched the panic-struck Reshma to Salim Khan.

The patient had been rushed by car to the nearest municipal hospital for first aid and from there the patient was motored to Ranchi District Hospital. The injection administered in the Municipal hospital had worked. The patient had stopped bleeding but she needed advance maternity treatment. In the District Hospital the male doctor was insufficient to conduct necessary maternity emergency. Sophie Juliet was for him an emergency case, 'Dr David,' shouted Martin the order, 'attend to my wife. If she needs operation conduct it.' The order was like a lightning thunder.

Dr Devid Panchanan, a local breed given to treatment of only the minor cases was quite baffled as to how he would handle this critical maternity case. He stammered and sought permission to manage an expert lady doctor from higher establishment, 'Damn your higher establishment. Damn your seeking a Lady hand. You are a doctor and you will have to treat her. Mind it any mishandling and you shall have the English rage.' This threatening made the doctor nervous. He was trembling in fear. Rabbani took guts to argue Martin, 'Sir *saheb* we are in the hospital. We are not supposed to frighten the doctor. After all he has to treat the patient. The patient is critical. We cannot afford to argue and threat the doctor.' This argument worked. Martin gave up. He held the hand of his wife and in a prayerful mode he addressed the doctor to do something immediately.

* * * * *

Salim Khan along with his wife came rushing to the ward and they found the lady in a critical condition, 'Martin ji why still no treatment has started?' shouted Salim Khan. He looked at her and felt like added to her. Her pale face, a thin smile of despair, a gesture of surrender made him drawn to the lady. He was overexcited seeming to cross limits, 'Poor lady she needs pillow under her head,' he talked in concerns. Mr. Martin still anxious to get the best treatment was not peeved at this excess. Shally Jaan was standing aloof bewildered not knowing why her man was over-excited.

Shally was not a common lady of common jealousy. But she disliked her husband's excitement, 'Sir let us shift her to another hospital.' This was a foolish counseling from Salim Khan. Martin grunted defiance. He had sensed the un-due leaning of the rival man to her, 'Shut up,' Martin shouted and literally shaking the doctor by his shoulder he told roughly, 'This David ji is handling her case.' The doctor was astounded. The doctor got activated. In him a sense of performance mounted high. He gathered the guts of a doctor in crisis and decided to perform necessary operation on the lady. It was risky but imperative. Mrs. Martin was pushed into the operation theatre headed by Salim Khan. Salim Khan's excitement peaked when his eyes got wet and his throat became hoarse, 'How this good lady met the accident?' It was a redundant query. Shally answered irritably, 'Accidents do not come foretelling!' Shally had no grudge as she had attributed the excitement of her man to his multiple female tastes. Shally looked upon Salim Bahadur with no suspicion.

Martin was muddled by what transpired. In his mind only one thing was tiding high and low that if something happened to her, he would suffer, 'Whatever more or less she is my companion of all time.' Then after his mind drifted to the very inordinate conflicts, 'O that we English had been just! Only if we had not looked upon this land with step-motherly eyes. Would that we had raised correct hospital and correct base for treatment. My Julee she needs the correct treatment.' Martin was looking aghast.

Salim Khan had placed his hand on the shoulder of Martin, 'In time of crisis let us pray to our god. Do not worry. This doctor will somehow handle the case.' His consoling did not console the husband. He was irritated, 'Okey thanks man. Well tell how you happened to learn about it?' Salim Khan narrated details.

* * * * *

'Dr. Devid how is the patient?' asked Salim rivaling Martin. Mr. Martin jumped ahead and catching the hand of the patient proved his entitlement. The poor lady still under the impact of anesthesia babbled something inaudibly. Mr. Salim as if not lagging behind leapt forward and almost tumbled over her. It was a scene that most harassed Shally.

Shally involuntarily caught hold of the back cloth of her husband's shirt tearing in the impact, 'Hold yourself Ji' admonished Shally. She was his savior from a real fall. Martin witnessed all in a sequence and finding himself not involved in the erratic act he thanked Shally aloud, 'Thanks Salama ji! Thanks for your timely holding otherwise this fellow would have thrown himself down on his face.' Martin remarked callously.

Suddenly Mr. Martin laughed. He laughed pointing to her hair. He had seen her hair cleared on the front head. Everybody including the doctor lowered his eyes, 'Sorry sir. We had not noticed the deep cut on her forehead. The blood had congealed there making mess. She needed stitching.' Sophie was upset at the shaving of her hair. Shally could see that the fair scalp on her head was matching with her skin. Salim Khan was angered at the doctor, 'But you had not sought our permission.' He was talking with authority. Mr. Martin resolved to refute Salim Khan. He appreciated the doctor acted as per the necessity. Sophie Juliet was disgusted at her balding head. She was weak so she could not react much.

The doctor departed instructing not to let her sit up, 'Operation requires precaution.' Salim Khan seemed to break the cordons and acting supreme he requested all not to let her sit up. His action proved spurious. Mr. Martin overlorded him instructing to restrict his excitement. Shally felt obliged to Martin. Rabbani was watching all and thinking that his master was playing an angry cock.

Sophie Juliet fell into a swoon. She had become weak and was exhausted. She in a state of delirium was babbling something scary, 'The spirit of the Buddha banyan, it has followed me. I fell on account of the avenging fury of Devi Kirpani. I had called the Bonga but they were too far off. I had called Martin but he was not available.' Sophie was inaudible but the suspense was not a suspense.

Shally slid aside fearing the slip of the spirit into her body. Shally had heard of the shifting of the demon. She feared the entrenchment,

'Kahan *sahib*,' she pulled his hand, '*Janab* stand away. The bad spirit seeks seminary in next body.' Shally was not acting sanely. She was sounding foolish.

The great man growled at her. The first time in life he roughened her, 'Stop your nonsense. Cannot you see Sophie is persecuted?'

Mr. Martin baffled at the changed scenario shouted at Rabbani without any apparent reason. Rabbani was shaken. He repulsed, 'Sir *saheb* your woman has been possessed by the evil spirits. Your wisdom and loud rationalism would succumb to naught on the wake of this transaction. You need our assistance. I alone can be of help to you.' Rabbani was agitated. Before him the fair lady was lying a victim of the evil spirits. He wanted to salvage and ravage her simultaneously. Rabbani's dirty intention remained buried in his heart.

'Stop your nonsense,' shouted Martin, 'Stop this your stupid talk.' Martin hit him on his face. A piggish grunt poured forth Rabbani's mouth, 'Hit me and injure but your woman has become the prey to the evil shadows. Your Andrew Morgan's sin on the tigress has turned active. It will harass the lady *sahiba* till atonement is performed. Devi Kirpani influence!' He was talking in a wild flow. He had folded his hand and was talking rashly. In him his mean self was activated as he had spotted her underarm peeping from below the petty coat. Rabbani desired to hold the lady and poke his too into her.

'Stop this your absurd talk. Where Devi Kirpani? While the poor lady cat could not save herself, how she could influence revenge?' shouted again the forester then sobering he touched on the forehead of the lady lying still, 'Dear me. Wake.' He shook her softly but the lady was lying still. It was a most tense moment. Salim Khan took guts to shake the lady. He applied his softest means to wake her. He was encroaching on the right of the forester. Shally not jealous became sure of the death of the lady.

The thought of her death made Shally moved. She cried uncontrollably and literally falling on the body of the patient made her wake with pain, 'What happened?' the poor lady whined.

Normalcy was restored. Rabbani stood devouring the fair lady with his un-fair eyes. Her nice figure had lured him. Rabbani had caught her in his eyes a captive of his lust. He evaded detection. He feared Martin. He feared Salim Bahadur too. Rabbani wished he would someday land hands on the fair skin of the lady. He would attack her like a vulture. His eyes became wine. His mouth drooled. His tongue became dog. Rabbani groped in imagination through her saree and blouse to scavenge her flesh.

Sophie opened her eyes weakly and surveying the room felt that the room was stinking of hospital odor. She noticed Rabbani and abhorring the way he was ogling she turned her face to her man. She looked at Khan Bahadur and wished he had supported her in her mission. She turned attention to Martin and thought vaguely if ever he would shift his point of view vis a vis the Indians.

Shally Jaan was no more than an extra in the story. Her mind was hung out to her *Rehmania*. Shally had been occupied by a fleeting desire to shift her residence to her dream clouds. She was confused and was no more than a scarecrow. She was popping through the ripples of imagination in her Mughal time past. The masquerading images of her royal lineage from the King to her father strolled past her eyes and she felt like a fool. She could not notice that Sophia was looking askance at her as if she was trying to access her. Sophia was not growing critical. She was curious to explore if Shally had English genes as her fair skin and nice figure resembled her to Alice Joseph, her mother.

'Do not you resemble in your facial features to my mom, Alice Joseph?' suddenly Sophie remarked and startled all. Shally was abashed. Her face flushed red at this remark. She became speechless. Rabbani and

Salim Khan and Martin looked at Sophie startled. Sophie then closed her eyes to hide embarrassment.

Shally, Martin, the lecherous Rabbani and the stupid Salim Bahadur together stood phantom like in the hospital ward waiting for something drastic to happen.

* * * * *

CHAPTER 4

STORM IN THE CUP

Sophie Juliet, back from the hospital was a sullen fellow not finding herself settled in her world of solitary ganging of importance and synthetic superiority. She had lost her baby fetus. She was weak in spirit and not ready to concentrate. She had strolled past the muddling phase and was trying to recoup. The surgical shock had been too much and she attributed her recovery to the grace of God. She came to realize that life was a trifle and shaping the destiny was subjected to its handling.

'I will give no importance to the importance we get as an English. I will try to live life out of the importance periphery. I have got a second birth. My life is now no more the usual life. I am bound to live it more meaningfully.' Sophie Juliet looked at the sky and discovered that in the daylight the half-moon was looking upside down and dull. But she said the same moon would illuminate the earth in the night.

'I was dislocated, torn asunder, a foolish guest

My new name 'Sophia' sounds not like a waste

Where am I adrift? Where broken off the shore?

But I will play Sophia, a Sophia with hesitant core

I shall chase the path of the heart without sore

This I would not take in instalment

I am Sophia, the half-Indian in the English frame

I will act Sophia to fulfill it without shame.'

In a state of poetic trance Sophia cried as she reached underneath the Buddha banyan tree. She tried to concentrate on her recollection of Gautam Buddha and his enlightenment under the holy Boddhi Tree. She stressed on her recollection of Buddha and failed. Her head was aching. In her mind the Bonga tigers and Andrew Morgan and the tigress Kirpani turned cruel ghosts to haunt her, 'I am not afraid but fear has caught me.' She had developed anonymous phobias in a cluster and was on the whole not in a right shape, 'I will run away. I will jump into whatever that will save me from the haunting. I am on a wrong direction. My life is adrift to the bleak shore.' She was not fighting the depression. She had gradually felt that the nervous bout in her was due to her disparaging dislocation from herself, 'I am not what I am and in me the depression is leaking from the system I have been locked up. I am an English and this has become my curse. The fell injustice of our breed, the racial arbitrariness of our men, the thumping dominance of the English anywhere in their colonies and here in this land of the Buddha and Mahavir I have begun to feel guilty.'

'Born from English genes, brought up on Indian soil

I am the alien body with my soul in turmoil

See I am desperate to balance between the two

But miserably I have no adjusting clue.'

'It seems my skin has caught infection of my racial superiority. It has become a disease. I shall get rid of it. We English are gone mad not to relieve the Indians. This is arbitrary. I will fight it.' Sophia became angry and openly alleged the English for doing wrong, 'These struggling Indians are not enemies; we have made them enemies. We are giving them sufferings. We have stolen their freedom. I simply know we have no right to steal their freedom.' She sobbed, sobbing underneath the gloomy banyan tree like Sophia.

She sighed and catching a hanging snake root of the banyan tree she kissed it, 'My baby again I lost him. Only if I had caught the amulets from the hoary Molvi. Reshma had been insisting on it.' She kissed the snake root with reverence and confessed to herself that she was a party with a breed of the White who was not white in executing justice, 'Shut up,' she cried, 'Shut up everybody arguing that we White people are rendering white justice to civilize the Brown race. We are no god-sent agent to teach any nation right and wrong.'

Sophie felt like running and being chased by Sophia. She was the Mermaid on earth: half English, half Indian.

'I am not divided, not at all destroyed

I have re-discovered myself definitely alloyed

My half-self, born from the English roots

My half-self, built in Indian shoots

I am to the latter side

I am to the Sophia side.'

* * * * *

She returned to her bed chamber and drew a sketch of a girl hanging from shackles. The python coil of the shackles having torn her flesh she was looking wounded. The sketch had nothing artistic but it embodied pain, pain in silent bulk of helplessness. She began to fill the sketch with the color: blue, yellow, red and purple randomly and finishing there it she let it hang from the nail in the wall. The sketch spoke the language of grief. The wind made the paper rattle. It seemed to grow in volume and fill her universe, 'Sorry the angel in chains. Sorry dear we are your tormentor. We shall someday, any day release you. The real Gandhi outside and the one developing in Indian wombs will together deliver you. You shall have your heaven of freedom.'

She lay beside the hanging and waited for Martin to come. Her Sophia-self was proud. Her Sophie-self was depressed.

Salim Khan was not her alternative choice. He was a hope to her to manage the freedom scene, 'I shall ask him to lend his tenants to make crowd in the street. I shall ask him to goad the crowd to create tension. I shall myself join this building tension and raise slogans against the rulers. I am on behalf of the freedom, freedom that is the right of each alive nation. Salim Khan, I hope will lend his hands. I will approach him.' Sophia talked within herself.

* * * * *

Martin came in the mid of night. He was looking weary, anxious, frustrated and angry. He had returned from a secret meeting of the English officers from all the strategic departments and had been loaded with pressure. He had taken wine and was quite tipsy, 'What this nuisance drawing is hanging from the wall?' he snapped at the drawing. The sketch looked like a hooting comment on him. His feet were unstable because of wine. Sophie Juliet had never before seen him in this state of collapse. He looked at Sophie and the sketch of the girl and hatefully uttered, 'What for this girl of the chain is looking miserable? What the hell the sketcher is trying to message?' Then he hiccupped like the street drunkard, 'Who drew this sketch?' Then he escaping the eyes of Juliet said, 'Chains are the control tools on the fellow persons to be held under check. Honor the chains as the leash of control. We English put the chains on Indians to control them.'

Sophie was pricked at the un-ethical definition of the chains, 'Shut up sir. Just shut up. Imagine the same chains fetter you. Imagine we are leashed to control.' She was not quarreling. She knew Martin was past the influence of her sober dialogue.

Martin reacted to her words inordinately. He had never been crude but at that moment he was. He hissed and fretted. She noticed his face getting hot red. She knew he was enraged but this did not scare her. She knew she was on the right. She let him sizzle with anger. His blood pressure had risen. She avoided to notice him, 'Ju you do not know what breed you are! You are the world's best breed, the ruler community. If you think you are supporting the rivals I fear you are losing me. Your sketch of the chained girl seems to hoot us.'

Marin tried to hold Sophie. He was staggering as he was not sober. Juliet did not abhor him. But she did not feel like supporting him. She slid aside, 'Martin we have no right to throw chains on anybody. It is against the moral scruples. Freedom, freedom of being un-enthralled and operating on will is the birth right. God grants it and we have no authority to curb it.'

'Julee, my Ju I am surrounded by pressure and threat. Our empire, our great empire it is sliding.' He cried like a child. His wine was making him cry. He was in pain and he longed to shed it by sharing it. Sophie was not callous but she was not available to him. She had been in the anguish of her own version vis a vis her understanding of the happenings. Sophie became stiff. She became stiff not to defeat him. Her stiffness was the outcome of her validation of her version of understanding vis a vis what he was not. She withdrew from him. She dug a distance. She got un-pinned to him. Her transformation had erected walls between him and her. It was not ruthless but she was looking ruthless. Her husband sobbed and sank to the floor, 'No body knows what torments I am passing through. I need support in this crisis.' He flung his arms wide to take Julee in but the girl got stiff. She had gone delinked.

'Sophie Mam come, let us celebrate the depressive news of our defeats on different fronts in war and let us celebrate our virtual surrender to the Gandhi of Hindustan.' He talked like a mad man and then he began to whine, 'We English are going to have counted days, maybe a few months here as the Crown is going to shed this Burden of Kingship to the Hindustanis.' He cried and became furious. His fury was the frustration of a beast caught in a trap.

Sophie forgot her grief and felt pity for her man, 'What happened sir?' she asked. But the man could not narrate the story fully. His wine had made him unstable. He was crying like a child in the lap of despair. He had lost dignity and pride and had become a picture of misery correctly embodying the pain that the girl in her sketch was suffering, 'She supported him to the bed and said with guts in her words that the English people were not just to others and that injustice was the most unjust of all the vices. If the English powers are dwindling it is because the others are getting aware of their right to self-dignity. Our colonies and our wars both were dependent on our manipulated support of the natives.' Sophie was talking not in hostile terms. She was just exposing the reality of English mushrooming of powers, 'Sir ji Martin *saheb*, mind that stolen powers hardly stay fixed. Someone like this Gandhi gets up and raises his community and then the picture begins to change.'

'Then do you want to celebrate the dwindling of our power?' cried Martin.

'No dear. I do not feel like delighting in the dwindling of English power. I just want to suggest that our power was stolen one. Our mean divide and rule policy was a morbid policy.' She was not taunting.

He heard and un-heard her and uttered a pale word, 'Silly.' She did not quarrel. She had never quarreled with him. She knew he was the kindest brute in terms of being never crude. Sophie Julee found herself slashed. It was not her victory, only a justice to her Sophia-self. She hugged herself and kissing her arms said, 'Sorry Sophie. Sorry dear. Your expiry was due. I am a Sophia of the Indian upbringing. She recalled episodes in the school when with Reka, Rakhi and Sulekha she spent the leisure time playing typical frog-jumping in the school premises. Then she would feel like wearing full-length shalwar instead of the body-hugging pantie.'

She sighed and the picture of college days invaded her mind, 'How I cherish to be in the company of Rakesh Sharma. This guy abandoned me. He left India for England. His departure on the train still hangs in the memory as his waving hand had vanished in the fog of distance. The train had carried my first love away.' She shed tears. She wiped them, 'India gave me the nascent feeling of love and snatched it.' She said it as a secret, 'This feeling was like freedom inviting me to the journey through the heaven of it. It was like my existence meeting more meaning. I was in the pang of joy and pain and Rakesh was to me not a betrayer. He had left me to gain wisdom and knowledge the English are proud of: rationalizing fulfilment!'

Martin slept on the bed whole night snorting and *nightmaring*. He would shudder and cry and would sit up then fall asleep. He looked like one sleeping on thorns. She was herself perturbed but she sidelined it. She looked at him with compassion, 'Poor guy he needs my support. Poor my fellow boy he has alienated himself, alienated from the natural compassion slot for others. He will suffer I tell it. He will find himself deserted.'

Sophie then visioned the English setbacks on war fronts and its different colonies. She sighed relief that the fall of English powers was going to build the house of freedom for those who sought it, 'I just want freedom reaching to the aspiring countries and communities. I am not against my England. I am in favor of the conditions which lead OTHERS get freed, freed from the paws of slavery. Every individual nation and community deserve being freed and allowed to get its own government.' She stopped debating the issue

She looked at Martin and discovered that he was in shock. She pitied him. She cried in love-throe and kissed Martin in absentia. She felt like at kicks. Rakesh replaced him and then she shifted to Salim Khan, 'What cruel constriction I am in!' She found she was lonely. She dreaded this condition. She leapt about feigning to writhe. She was on the phase of transition. She shook her man. It was a rash shaking of a sleeping guy.

The emotional upheaval being over the man next morning awoke weary and low and asked if he had vandalized and on hearing that he had been mean to her, he apologized and said that the excess wine and tension had distempered him and that he would not behave like that again, 'Sorry Ju. Very sorry really. I think I had never been as rude. I like you. You are my precious gem. I want you to be beside me. But I notice these days you are straying. Your conducts I doubt them.' He was talking sense and nonsense, 'Okey but you should not have taken excess wine.' He suddenly told that she had changed. She calmly admitted it. She said with clear mind that transformation of soul is a phenomenon that noble minds acknowledge, 'Transformation? Okey. Transformation and to the side of the foes. Really it is unfortunate. Preposterous! Dear, I am bound by my culture and reputation. This English reputation it is my prestige point.'

Mr. Matin rubbed his palm in a gesture of frustration. He said that the hold of the English root was fast loosening. Then he suddenly stopped. He took a glass of water and washed his face. He asked for some cold drink. The June month in India was a terrible month for the foreigners particularly Martin. He cursed the heat, its sultry attacks on his skin. He washing his face again and again said that he was fed up with the Gandhian *Jumboore* outcries, 'I wonder what creature this naked-fakir of Gandhi is! His loin cloth, his seemingly ugly face, his thin body, his brisk gaits, his energy and charm. This Gandhi seems to defy dignity and redefine decency. He does not look like any effigy among the suited-booted English discussing matters at Round-table! Where from this fellow human gathers pride that looks like divine glare! I wonder if he is BIOLOGICAL. I wonder if he is a human incarnation of some sort.'

Sophie did not feel excited at Martin's assessment of Mahatma Gandhi. She said calmly that such messengers of God come off and on and they come to give meaning and direction to what we call heaven of freedom, 'He deserves salutes sir. He is a UNIVERSAL man, a saint indeed! His non-violence and passive resistance are two tools in his seemingly weak hands but he is the bravest of the brave. He is the commander of an army of the armless truth-seeker. India and the world henceforth will remember Gandhi as a tiny GIANT.'

Sophie sighed. She had been looking at her husband and wondering that a man of his stature too was likely to get upset at Gandhi and talk in despise of him a truth that the whole world had praised about, 'Do not ask about this living saint, the naked-fakir is the warrior of all time, a king of patience, the monarch of simplicity; his weapon being not bloody bullet and baton; his tongue is not the spear of the metal; he is the only human in this dehumanized world. I have gone enamored of his power and I submit to him. Yes, every good soul will submit to him and say that he is not a beggar of freedom for freedom. He is the Messiah of the bereaved and powerless anywhere in the whole world. Let us fold hand to him and hear his soul's prayer. Let us learn humanity from him.' Sophie found herself tugged to a twig in the storm raging within. Her Indian-self had made her split.

Sophie brought two glasses of chilled Roohafza *sherbat*, red in texture but not bloody in taste and offering one to him she said, 'See the red texture of this drink. It is pure Indian, a preparation for the cooling of our guts and saving us from stroke.' Sophie drank it. Martin too drank it then Martin said softly, 'Really this pure Indian drink is our savior in severe heat.'

The heat of June had reached its peak and the fellow Martin was readying to go to his office. He gave a soft smooch to his wife, 'Dear in this land of the foes you alone are mine, a support and a relief.'

'Your idea of me is your sustainer. But my idea of myself is changing. Your idea of me is your authority on me, maybe to control me. I am not revolting but I feel I have my dignity and right to hold opinion about Indians. As for your feeling forlorn in my absence I can assure one thing that we English have made India and Indians forlorn. We could have peacefully assimilated with them, made them belonging and feel tied together. But no, we preferred an arrogant distance. We proved that we were superior and this was our despair. If you think that amid them, we would be at stake this is our making.' Sophia was not talking a total lie. She had discovered it.

'Brave lady. You are living in a paradise of the fools. I tell you point blank that we are foreigners to the Indians and their Gandhi and his doctrines would go shoo once the mass would capture freedom. I foresee a blast, an explosion of the volcano! I can predict mass scale violence will spread out and we would be targeted.' He then talked about the intensifying disturbances in Hindustan due to Gandhi pressure, 'These Civil Disobedience and recent Quit India Call and our setbacks on the global war conditions I feel we are surrounded by black days.'

Martin stopped suddenly, lit the pipe, smoked his chest, looked grave, sat stiff and waited for Sophie to open talk. She did not open the talk. In her mind the Buddha banyan tree, the tigress Devi Kirpani, the Bonga myth, her abortion, the face of Rabbani greedily glaring at her legs, the past with Rakesh and his departure on the train all together assaulted her. She enjoyed the assault. She did not suffer the assault. She had turned a patient Gandhi able to bounce the attacks. She said to herself that peace and patience went together if the person had managed the soul force to take care of eventualities, 'Gandhi could survive eventualities because he had developed soul's force to shield him from the eventualities.'

* * * * *

Their attention shifted to the movement outside as they felt the door curtain was disturbed. It was like some human shadow sliding to one side, 'Did you notice the movement?' said the man. He leapt to the door and found no suspect there, 'Strange! I am sure I caught the movement,' said he and returning to the bed he asked if she had noticed, 'Yes I also noticed it.' Sophie was not scared. She had begun to compromise with the ambiguous happenings, 'But who was spying on us?' she looked tense. He had no cause to ignore it, 'If things are going to disturb us deliberately, we shall not tolerate it.' He said with deep frown on his face, 'You know Ju if things are not checked immediately, we shall have troubles.' He took his gun. He found security in his gun.

Sophie Juliet teased him, 'Sir *ji saheb* you belong to gun-culture. You are a pure English believing in phantom security under bullet and blood.' Sophie was not taunting her man. She was summarizing the English mentality.

Mr. Martin admitted that gun, a handful of corrupt Indians as boot-lickers in English camps and the creative bogey of English supremacy made the Angrez the ruler of the world.

A horrendous sound of something thrown from the sky came from the courtyard. It was like a big thud of a falling foot on soft earth, 'Julee! Dear notice the sound. It seems something heavy was thrown,' shouted the man. He was infuriated. He had the right to turn mad. He took his gun, loaded it and rushed out to the courtyard to investigate. Juliet too rushed after him feeling sensation of fear mixed with nervousness, 'Take care sir. Make sure if it was some wild animal, a beast!'

'Damn your obsession with the beast. I fear it was some human thing, these rebels of the Gandhi men! We have been alerted of attacks.' Martin aimed his gun upon an imaginary moving body.

There was nothing real anywhere. The trees and the wind were as usual. He could see a couple of long-tailed monkeys chattering and mocking. He shooed them and they in return shooed him. The lady pulled his shirt from behind. He was frightened and in a nervous panic would have tumbled her but for her timely recession, 'Are you mad that you almost tumbled me?' she shouted.

Mr. Martin then looked to the banyan tree, its snaky prop-roots hanging and sighing he said he would get this ancient tree cut, 'I have a nervous dislike of the hanging snake roots. When I was a child, I used to imagine the Banyan roots would tentacle people like octopus.' He suddenly stopped talking as he thought he had seen a huge lizard-like creature leaping about on the tree. He concentrated his eyes and found the creature evaporate, 'Did you see the lizard?' he asked, 'No. Where you found it?' The lady looked around and imagined her version of the Bonga figure. She cancelled the vision, 'I do not think that the Bongas are real.' Then she desired strongly to experience the Bonga effect, 'What strange name! These Bongas are to the villagers their savior. I wonder how much the villagers have been saved, saved from their relentless miseries and poverty.' Her mind became a noisy platform.

'Anyway dear, we the English here are passing through a critical phase. We are not safe here. We are targeted.' Mr. Martin looked sad. His eyes flashed fear, 'Dear you are the only support to me here. We are alien in this hostile land of the muddles. Here survival is hard if we are not adaptable or at least not ready to face the odds.' He was sounding disappointed unlike his usual self.

In return she said, 'The Indians are not hostile. We are adversary to them. They deserve pity and attention and we as the rulers have been heavy on them.'

'No. Not us but these cowering Indians are adverse. I fear once they got the chance they would pounce on us like a fury.' Martin was not absolutely wrong. He had the inkling of the suppressed rage and vengeance of the Indians, 'Your villagers, have you noticed in their cringing is the wriggling ache, the ache of the serpent when battered.'

Sophia did not argue. She extended her hand to Martin Julius. He held her hand but she found herself un-connected. She discovered that he was also drifting from him. It hurt her. She felt scared. She thought of the Bongas and the villagers and Khan Bahadur even of Shally Jaan and inferred that she needed Martin more. She regretted her getting adrift from him. She caught his arm strongly and hung from it. Her sketch of the girl in chains flustered in the wind. There was a storm in the cup.

'Why did your friend Andrew Morgan kill the tigress Kirpani? What necessitated this destruction of a poor cat? Was it not a callous meanness of a fellow English who claim they are the superior race and rational too.' Sophia tried to check her anger, 'I am upset.'

'I can see that you are upset dear. I can answer only this that Morgan was not fair. I never could convince me that he killed the tigress to kill his fear of the cat. He confessed to me that he had been *nightmaring* of the tigress someday tearing him down. It was his phobia! Morgan should not have carried it.'

'I wonder this Morgan was in a foolish trauma about the cat tearing him down.' Sophia then asked her man to do his best to protect the remaining two tigers which the villagers called Bongas. Martin heard her and never revealing his mind said her to think of England and the nice Thames and the kind world of comfort there, 'What happened to your mom in England?'

Sophia did not answer this query. She knew that her mom in England had taken the other *man* and she had quit communicating with her, 'My mom is disconnected from me. I do not know of her and vice versa. After papa's departure I became a virtual waif, then you came in and now I am facing a different crisis.'

'Your crisis is your making Ju. You have chosen to invite it. You have virtually deserted me for a phantom love of the Indians. My silly love I would tell thousand time that racially they are alien and we are alien and that once they got the chance they would fall upon us like thunder.' Martin caressed Sophie and the latter this time gave herself in.

'I would tell you only one thing that however sacrificial you turn you will remain alien here. They are insiders and we are outsiders. They are different and we are different.' Martin repeated the same statement.

Martin's mind was occupied by the recent developments locally. The boulder episode and the daring of the villagers to march up to the Bungalow alarmed him of something untoward. He did not mention it to her. He was beginning to design moves to control the storm in the cup, 'I know if it is not checked today, the daring would turn someday lethal. The Indians' Gandhi will become diffused with his idealization of non-violence but I predict it will gush forth like pus and blood from a morbid wound.'

CHAPTER : 5

THE BONGA TIGERS

One morning when the inclement weather had left the entire Chandrapura dazed by the infernal heat, Mr. Martin left his bed drenched in sweats. His limbs were burning. On his balding head the heat had sat coiled. He was feeling damn. His lungs were dry. He was having troubles in breathing. He looked around and saw that his wife was lying crouched on the bed. She looked oppressed. He wanted to touch and check if she was okay. He left her un-touched, 'I do not doubt her for having had term with Rakesh of the paper clip. I do not have doubt about her leaning to this Khan Bahadur. But I doubt her intelligence when I find her believing in the Bonga farce. Is she correct in the mind? What has happened to her English sensibility?' Martin was getting swamped under these pressures.

He ran upstairs to the open terrace to escape the pressure, 'My God, my dear Lord please release me from here, this terrible country of the alien gangs of howlers! I would rather resign my job. I will take a long leave. I will go to my England, my pretty England!' He struggled for breaths. He did not know that he, too, was pining for a heaven of freedom, a freedom that he could not locate, 'Ah God where I am stuck up. This Andrew is heard to have been granted a long leave to visit his native country. Andrew killed the tigress because of his *nightmaring*. His poisoning the cat was a crime but he did not get punishment.'

Martin saw the crows settling upon the banyan tree. The snake roots hanging from the tree looked like spreading gallows. The forester was in a very uncertain mood. He admitted blatantly that the English policies were contrary to the natural codes of free-living, 'We have ruled here by arbitrary means.' He did not allow the mind to muse further. He changed the topic. He visioned the scene of the boulder rolling down, 'It was not an accident, an act of God. It was the human mischief. I tell the villagers are the culprits. I am sure a few of the daring hands had dislodged the boulder.' Martin passed gas. He passed gas thrice with loud boom. He felt a bit relaxed but inside him the fear and suspicion kept turning, 'We English are un-safe. We are in a version of impending risks on our lives.'

Martin fanned himself with a piece of cardboard. He was behaving like a prisoner in the open jail, 'We are here in an open jail built in the premises of our control.' His eyes caught the scene of the jungle far off looking dismal and antagonized, 'We English are ready targets,' he again returned to the same topic.

He had read in the newspapers that the Gandhi people had demanded the Swaraj, self-government and were going to enter provincial elections via Separate Electorate. Martin was against it. He was never regarded as a tool in the British system but he had the illusion of carrying the whole load of the British Raj. He was obsessed with every failure of the Raj politically and geographically and would behave rashly to keep the British prestige, 'Damn my life. Damn the conditions going to derail our power. Damn me and my fate that we as English monarch would soon stumble and become a history. Damn my faith in the invincibility of the Crown. I do not know why the histories make new histories and this breeding of history of the emergence of a new nation is becoming to me a snakebite?' Martin drew a big breath of frustration and filled his lungs with the hell-fire.

He heard a stray koel cooing. Its melody became mockery. He reproached his deteriorating taste. He loathed himself for his lady to turn lanes, 'Mad she has gone, mad and foul that she claims she is transforming. Damn her transforming! It is frustrating. My woman is getting crooked!

These Gandhi howlers I tell they deserve being deported to the Black Waters.' He searched his snickers pocket for his pipe. He did not carry it.

* * * * *

Martin recalled the rumor of the villagers going to do some ritual performance in honor of the poisoned tigress, 'Scoundrels! They are going to fabricate a drama. The Bonga tigress, I know its ritual burial will make news. The local papers will catch eyes and ears and then the Gandhi gang will pick it up. This will make them utter their hate figuratively on Andrew Morgan. I do not justify Morgan's act of killing the cat but I must think that this hallowing of the tigress would ignite fanaticism. Their heads fermenting the brew of religious wine! I know religion when distorted makes the heads mad. It will infect the whole of the community.' Martin reiterated that Gandhi was habituated to add rituals with politics and in his speeches, he had referred to them.

Martin paused and mused, 'Tigers! Yes, other cats! They are becoming the objects of their heightened adoration! I will send these cats to hell. I will arrange for their hunting. Hunting yes, hunting these cats and demolishing the stupid belief of the damned natives! I will see that their faith infection is killed. This will break their morale. I shall call the Khan and order him to arrange for the hunting.'

Martin came to his bed chamber. He saw Juliet lying crouched on the bed. Her legs were bare. His sex drive got ignited. He literally assaulted the lady. The lady evaded resistance. She surrendered to mean that he was mean.

He was panting from the exertion of the violence on her. He was sweating too. His smoking had made his lungs congested. He wiped his sweats and sat up beside her feeling guilty and ashamed, 'Okey. You did what your English blood does to the Hindustanis. You can do nothing else. Poor guy. You were a plunderer. I pity you.'

She did not cover her legs. She looked plundered and dazed, 'See this your definition of power over the powerless!' she pointed to the sketch of the girl still fluttering in the wind, 'Martin, you did not outrage me. You outraged my faith in you and in the decency, I thought you belonged. But you proved that you were capable of brutality only.'

Sophie Martin was angry. But her anger was under bridles. She had a respect for her man necessary to soberize her. She had the capacity to consider and re-consider matter, 'Okey for his excess. Okey for his seeming brutality. I can understand his state of mind. I now pity this guy. Poor Martin he is in panic. I will forgive him.' Her eyes were wet.

The fellow man was piping smoke again. He was looking genuinely penitent, 'Sorry,' he uttered this word in shame and she not hearing him turned her back to him like the East had turned the back on the West, 'Really sorry Ju!' he cried but her Sophie had recoiled his appeal. It all happened in a most dramatic moment. She was dislocated from him though she was not angry with him. She knew if she dropped him immediately, he would blast.

She felt pity and this pity made her speak softly, 'Dear Martin you and me, I tell are going to catch different paths. I appreciate freedom of choice; you seem to detest it. My understanding of freedom is vast; yours narrow. You look upon the chains as the control key. But I believe in universal shattering of chains. I believe in the shedding of the pressure tactic. My understanding of the value of freedom gives me bliss.'

She finished the dialogue and he looking upon her as a silly lady without full understanding of the gravity of situation said to her a hasty yes, 'Okay my lady of freedom. Okay. I agree with you and without insisting on your turning the right page of life, I predict that you are preparing your trap.' Martin patted on her back. He bowed his head and apologized.

* * * * *

Martin was smoking those days hugely. He had been also overeating maybe to kill tension. His tension was his creation and Sophie was not emotionally involved in it. She had her diversions mature enough to keep occupied. Her diversion was the freedom of India. She was sure that she cherished it to come. The Gandhi spell had made her enchanted.

She had the apprehension that she was an outsider, but it was not her heart-break, 'No problem, not at all! I am to India, to her freedom and Gandhi is my Bonga.' She found Martin not acting an obstruction. She found him tense and glad and looking mischievous. His smoking spree had doubled up.

'*Darling we shall go on a hunt*,' said Martin with mischief in his beady eyes.

'Hunting fellow humans?' she commented blankly.

'*Not them. Two Tigers! Two Bonga beasts. These tigers have grown fame in volume. These damned villagers treat them as their Bonga gods.' Martin did not wait for her to pull out of the shock.*

'You mean those deities of good luck, the beasts of good will, our Bongas?' she shouted.

'Yes, dear these worthless creatures! I want their haze of importance to shatter. This will trample their morale.' Martin sounded harsh. She heard him with shame in her. She hated people abrogating anybody's faith.

'What big you will hit by finishing those poor Bongas!' she was not arguing. She was talking wearily. She did not appeal him to refrain.

'Well Ju prepare yourself to go on a hunt. It has been planned and finalized. Please make sure you enjoy the expedition.' Martin had uttered this dialogue in an authoritative tone with ample supplies of smile.

She knew him and his rigidity and knew well that he was going on the tiger hunt as a punitive move, 'Then this expedition of killing, you think, you are going to prove yourself mighty?'

'Yes, dear Ju. Yes, these your Indians need shock treatment, a psychological blast. I am sorry but it is accommodative to my policy! We have to break their morale. They have dared defy the English morale.'

Sophie heard him patiently. She did not quarrel. She held calm and looking vaguely outside in the sky tried to see if God moved in the sky. She reverted and scratching the earth with her toe she made her toe bleed. In her eyes tears went dry and her heart became an angry prisoner, 'Yes, yes you have power and gun and support. You can go for any extreme.'

Martin picked his gun, checked its barrel, weighed it and kissing it on the butt said that he would use the gun to finish the Bonga nuisance.

Sophie looked away from him. She felt distant. She did not hate him but she felt like hating him.

'Dear my brave Indian-wife you are coming with me.' Martin's verdict sounded harsh. Sophie did not react. Her obsession with her love for India gained motion. She decided she would not go.

Sophie felt she was going to delete her honor for him. She did not delete it as she was a votary of justice and the justice prompted her to appreciate him as a morbid case. Inside her the Gandhi came alive invoking her to turn passively resilient, 'Gandhi does not fight fiercely with hate and nail. I will also not fight with hate and nail.' Sophie felt like hearing words of encouragement from the Buddha banyan. She felt like hearing the whispers of encouragements from Devi Kirpani. She heard the whispers of her conscience. All together came to heal her, 'I shall not participate in the crime of killing. *I shall ask the villagers to make a band of protestors.*'

She felt relaxed. An echo of confidence overwhelmed her, 'I am Sophia *begum,* yes Sophia of English blood but Indian make. I am no more Sophie Juliet. My choice of justice takes impetus from Gandhi, the saint warrior! My allegiance to Indian is my commitment.' She heard Martin again instructing her to wear the hunting suit and carry a gun, 'We will be only three, you, me and Andrew.'

'How you decide I will be in the killers' gang?' snapped the lady. Mr. Martin did not quarrel her. He had no moral trepidation. He was clean of it. He said again in severe tone that she would go. He patted on her back, 'My Ju dear this hunt will mean more than a hunt. This will be the hunt of Indian buoyance; their boiling point will be made to freeze. I know I have no grudge against the poor Bongas. But via them I will exercise my power over the Indians. I will show that the English-will is indefeasible. Okey, I will arrange the best for the expedition: good food, wine and your favorite mutton *kebab.*'

She slapped on his face aiming to hit a hovering fly. The hit was unexpected. He was angered but he did not react, 'Sorry. I wanted to hit the fly.' She apologized then continued, 'Do you think the Bonga killing will really kill the spirit of the Indians? I doubt *saheb.*'

Her words were arid but he was not embittered, 'Damn your warnings. I tell you we English are here to keep the Indians bridled. We cannot allow any move and madness that smacked of rebellion.' He dropped the pipe. The burning tobacco scattered on the floor, 'Well *saheb,* your thoughts are un-ethical, I would take license to term it '*criminal*'. Your hunting plan is a criminal plan. It is foul and un-fair. These Bongas maybe cats to us but to the villagers they are reverential.'

Sophie took up her knitting pin and accidentally poking the needle on her arm and she let the skin bleed. Martin saw it. Firstly, he remained unmoved but when he saw bleeding was continuing, he shouted, 'This is idiotic. What do you want to prove?' The lady hung her hand as he plucked the cut with his thumb, 'I am seeing you are turning crazy. Madam I tell you, your moves will someday make you repent. These guys here are not ours; they are different and this alone is a fact; all else is an illusion. You are chasing that phantom illusion. You will suffer and pay for that! You are an outsider and this only is remarkable.' Martin caressed her on the hand and kissing her said with grief that he would be left utterly lonely if she quit him.

* * * * *

Martin left her. She sat for hours hoping for his return. But he had turned cold. She felt helpless. She called Reshma and mentioned what transpired between her and Martin, 'Mam this will cause a havoc,' added the rustic girl, 'You know these villagers and others in the surroundings have begun to associate the Bongas to divine profile. I do not blame them. I have no cause but I would tell if anything untoward happened to their Bongas this would cause a mayhem.' Reshma threw herself unexpectedly to Sophie's legs, 'Please Madam,' she cried, 'Stop this unfortunate move. Tell your lord *saheb* to cancel the plan. It is a matter of the villagers' faith.'

Sophie Juliet became excited. She felt accountable to handle the case, 'Reshma if you can carry a message to Mr. Khan?'

Reshma was given a chit to deliver it to Mr. Khan, 'Mr. Khan this your Martin *saheb* is out to kill the cats, I mean the Bonga cats. You know

I have heard these villagers have associated the cats to some divine profile. I do not personally endorse it but I have a fear if the cats are harmed these villagers would go berserk. Matter is their silly faith. Matter is the safety of the Bongas. Please do something to stop Martin sir.' Her letter carried the weight of her conscience to safeguard the faith of the villagers.'

Reshma delivered the chit to Khan Bahadur, 'This is the letter from my Mam.'

'Which mam?' the Khan was bewildered.

'Your Martin's *bibi*, lady I mean,' replied Reshma.

The Khan snapped the letter with a thumping heart. He looked around to ensure that his wife was not spying. The Khan pocketing the chit pleaded Reshma not to reveal the secret anywhere. He wished to bribe her. But at that moment his pocket was empty, 'Reshma, I will reward you someday.' The maid was a born news breaker. She soon reached Shally with the news. Shally took it neutrally. She reverted to her prince of the fantasy. This was irrelevant but this gave her solace, 'My dream prince I do not know if I should really succumb to the chit-chat.' Then she became grave and said that she should not bother, 'Maybe the letter carries message of harmless contents.' Shally Jaan asked Reshma Sagar if she had any doubt.

The maid confirmed that the lady Sophie had been anxious about the Bonga hunting , 'Madam ji, Martin sir was angry about the Bonga tigers. The letter is about the hunting.'

'Why hunting? What wrong these poor cats have done?'

'No wrong sir ji madam but the forester presumes the butchering of the cats would trample the morale of the bloody Indians.' In the tongue of Reshma was hate for Martin. In the hate was violence. In the violence was the defeat of the Gandhi. Reshma was voicing not discontent. She was vindicating her hate.

'Whose morale?' shouted Shally. In her tongue was also anger but of different version. She had edited her hate of Martin. She wanted to ask a plain question as to why Martin was going to hunt the tigers and take proxy revenge.

* * * * *

'Dear Mam,' the Khan wrote the reply in Indian English filling each line with the humility that he could muster together, 'Good lady, my Highness, please let me gather guts to address the queen of the universe, the humble truth that this your servant, the hapless Khan has no courage to fold hand to the King of the size your husband is and plead with him. He has decided what he has decided and then the cats are sure to get gone.' Salim Khan folded the letter and hid it in his *sherwani* pocket.

'Well then,' said Shally sensing he had dispatched the reply, 'Now the Prince Khurram is out to hunt the new Queen.' The comment fell like a blunt spear on his heart, 'What are you up to?' he stammered.

The lady said with a sigh that she did not shit at what he was up to, 'Brave man get brave further and do not try to cheat yourself. I know you are carrying a love note in your pocket for the lovelorn lady.' The Khan was flabbergasted, 'Shit you are talking. This letter is about my helplessness not to be able to plead with the Martin.'

'Do not mystify. Tell what it is. I am curious to learn.'

'Okey,' said the man and produced the letter to her for scrutiny, 'Sorry,' said she, 'I thought you were *affairing* with the English monkey-face.'

Shally heard koel birds cooing in a panic. She ignored he panic. Before him was the culprit of a crime. She patted on her own back and adding drama to her words said that she was unlike the ladies on earth, 'I am open to market the truth that nothing like catastrophe befalls me if you turn disloyal. Loyalty and disloyalty to me is not a matter of shock. You are righted to take your flights. We cannot clutch a strolling heart and it would be too romantic a proposition. Choice and freedom should go together and freedom of choice should not showcase the downfall of it. Bravo! My great-hearted Lord you are there in your kingdom to rule and mar it as you want. I passively take it. I obsessively forget it. I despairingly welcome it. Salim *saheb,* you are permitted to select your flight zone. Yes, your dear route to be a passenger on your flight.' She used vague poetry and this made her light, 'Sir *saheb* go and enjoy.' She pushed him to the bunch of flowers on the flower pot and plucking ten flowers she offered them as a bouquet, 'This is the token of righting you *sir saheb*.' Her language was flavored with little ironies. Her person was not on the rollercoaster. She had lost nothing and gained nothing except that she had realized that her man was too flimsy a character in the book of her story. She was not sorry. She was not because she thought she herself was webbing deceitful dreams around her dream icon: the prince charming.

Shally Jaan was not crying. She was not sure herself as to why she had dialogued vaguely. She tried to sadden her. She tried to sink her in tears. She heard the cooing of the koel bird. She cursed the cooing bird and touching on her cheeks she assured she was alright, 'My folly. My silly suspicion. This Khan fellow is too spent for *affairing* with a lady. I am sorry. I harassed him and tormented myself. This half-liver fellow is too timid for arousal.'

* * * * *

Martin Julius was in his full form, fuming and raging, a picture of a bull in heat. He had decided the hunting contrary to the British policy. The Royal Bengal Tigers had been declared the endangered animals. But he was going to breach the law.

He had summoned Mr. Salim Khan and ordered him to arrange for men and matter for the hunting, 'Hunting of the tigers.' He pronounced the sentence stoutly to confirm his lordship, 'But sir this would cause a ruckus. These villagers as I know and you too know have a pagan belief attached to the tigers. The tigers to them are adorable. Then the Gandhi turbulence! Do not you think in this delicate time when things are going out of control, the Bonga killing will be an addition to the flames? These tigers are no ordinary beasts; they are Bongas, very special.' Salim Khan tried to highlight the fact. He did it because he had been goaded by the letter of the lady Sophie.

'Shut up Khan Bahadur. Mind only what has been told. The cats, yes, the cats I have a mind to book them.' Martin placed his gun on the table and told Salim Khan if he could not arrange this hunting he would manage it via Andrew Morgan, 'Morgan has had the experience of hunting the she-cat. He will come forward.' Martin was angry without reason. Salim Khan felt timid. It was strategic. His timidity gave him a shelter.

'Okey sir. But please reconsider it. This hunting would not remain localized. It would churn ripples on the national fronts.' Salim Khan wondered how he had gathered guts to talk so high, 'The Hindi dallies,' Salim Khan began in panic, 'Sir *saheb* the news added with fanatic overture would cause havoc. I do not think your government would appreciate this rash killing.'

'My foot the government! My foot your counseling! My foot the repercussions! I have decided to crush the spirit of the villagers. They have been displaying rebellious flares. Now they will see how they are humbled! Their tigers, I shall have them downed.' Martin aimed the gun towards Salim Khan. It was a feigned targeting. The Khan was nervous lest the trigger should get pulled. But the forester smiled mischievously, 'Not you man. But if you did not arrange the hunt, you will be made frontal in it. Your fake photo will appear in your favorite Hindi daily figuring the hunt. These villagers will find you the culprit behind it. Okey. You are supposed to arrange for the howlers, what we call in Hindustani : *jhalawa*! Your job done well I shall allow you to take the skin of the cat.'

Salim Khan stammered. He was cowering and raging simultaneously. But he was rebuked, 'Just shut up Bahadur Khan. Get the arrangement of howlers. If people of this village do not agree call people from adjoining village. Andrew Morgan can help you.' Martin shooed Salim Khan out of his presence.

* * * * *

Salim Khan returned home agitated. His face was dark with tension. He had never before been shooed by Martin, '*Badmash*, scoundrel. Passes orders! Tells I will become frontal, my fake photo as the hunter will appear in the Hindi dailies and my tenants would take me a culprit of the hunt.' He took a glass of water. He tried to cool himself.

Shally appeared from somewhere. She was absently present in his vicinity. He sought to share her feelings but she turned her face not in repulsion but in indifference. She was indifferent. Her waning touch with him having peaked she took a towel and began to dust the sofa. A storm of dust had been raised. The man was feeling choked. He coughed and gestured to stop dusting. But Shally ignored him. She had in the recent time gone out of his premises. It was not like her shifting lanes but it showed that she had got herself ejected, 'Stop this your dusting madness,' he roughly talked. The lady became a statue. She would not move and react. The man needed a live demonstration of even a feigned positivity. But she was frozen into a stone, 'Can not you behave in a normal way?' he shouted. It was a harsh shout. The lady endured it, '*Begum* you know this Martin thing has dictated me. He is going to kill the villagers' tiger. I have no sympathy with the cats but I know the tenants would find me frontal in it and would nurture grudge. I am in a moral dilemma.' He took another glass of water and sweated profusely.

The lady coldly said that he should let the tigers get killed and that he should carry no moral compunction, 'Not easy madam. Not easy at all. The time has changed and now that the Gandhi elements in the mass having ignited resilience, the villagers will react.' Salim was in a state of madding indecision.

The lady pulling the bed sheet asked him to vacate the bed, 'No issue at all. Just give up your pale resistance. The other option in Gandhi theory of passive resistance also implies a retreat till the opportune time comes.' She was indifferently wise but in terms of emotion she was blank, 'No. The tigers are the villagers' hallowed objects.'

'Then what can you do?' asked Shally. In her person detachment was demonstrative. Salim Khan looked at her woman with disappointment and retreated. Salim Bahadur was dangling between fear of being faked as the hunter and the desire to salvage the tigers. But he was nowhere. Martin's order was loud. He had no guts to disobey. In a state of torture of mind, he reached the lady Martin for healing.

* * * * *

Lady Martin was expecting him to contact her. The arrival of Salim Khan was announced by Reshma. Reshma was excited and confused and would not linger about as Khan Bahadur sat in the drawing room of the

Bangalow. Juliet Martin came in and instantly asked if he was ready to co-operate, 'Co-operate for what? asked Salim.

'Co-operate in gathering your contact persons, the tenants, anybody else to raise a revolutionary crowd' she said with anxiety in her words.

'But Mrs. Martin it is not practical, it is not possible.'

'Why not practical? Why you think you cannot push a crowd?' the words of Sophia resounded blankly.

Salim Khan was perturbed, 'Madam ji we are not in a position to offend the Master. We are bound by no principle but definitely by the apprehensions of retaliation from Martin sir. You know he is in power and ours is no condition to oppose it.' Salim Khan was sweating. He was taking deep breath. His mind was puzzled.

Mrs. Martin did not argue. She became disappointed. She asked him to take water. She said to him that Mr. Martin was out. She also said that she was ready to initiate the resistance, 'But for this she needed his support, support in raising crowd.'

Salim Khan was shaken. He hid his face in imagination from being sighted. He had no guts to enter upon this mis-venture, 'Sir ji mam,' he said in a visible scare, 'I do not think I am born heroic. Nothing like that is in me. Then I believe in no rash steps. My apprehension is that we would invite only troubles. My tenants are timid. Then my wife. I do not think she is the right support to me if I undertook to incite rebellion.' Mr. Khan revealed his mind.

Mrs. Martin felt discouraged, 'This timidity in your heart has been the cause why your country remained slave.' She rebuffed him. She thought it would prick him but he was stolid, 'We cannot jut rise and get involved madam. We have lots of obligations, many things to consider before we can take any step.' Salim Khan gave logic. Sophia waited for his turning of mind and was disappointed as she discovered that he was chicken-hearted, 'I did not expect you to cower. I expected you to show guts and frame resistance.'

Khan *saheb* remained as stable as he could make himself. He babbled, 'Sir ji mam your sir *saheb* is a rigid fellow and he has linked the hunting plan to his tampering of the villagers. This is like the battering of the spirit. The soul's battering I would say! He thinks it will break the spirit of the villagers. He believes and I fear his belief is only arrogant despotism that he would throw rein upon the Hindustanis, crush their morale. He admits that he would encourage the uprising if the spirit is not broken.'

* * * * *

Rabbani came with a letter of enquiry from Mr. Martin. The contents sounded harsh. Khan could hardly read through the lines. It carried the words of ultimatum. The Khan was duly shaken. He had no delusion of being a warrior to oppose Martin. His cowardly heart thumped like the caged rat, 'Okey. Okey. I am going not to stand against the winds. I shall comply. I will arrange the howlers.'

Salim Khan swallowed anger, 'But I do not think our tenants in Chandrapura would join in. These rustics are not going to join in the blasphemous act of Bonga destruction. To them their Bongas are hallowed ones.' Khan Bahadur was sweating. He babbled the holy verses from scripture to capture rest but inside him unrest had burrowed in. He asked Rabbani to carry a letter to Andrew Morgan, 'This Morgan will arrange for the howlers from his side.'

Rabbani tried to incite Salim Khan over the harsh language used by the forester, 'Sir *saheb* the ordering tone of Martin *saheb* was unbecoming of your status.' Rabbani failed to excite Salim Khan. Salim Khan had nothing of the Gandhian in him, Gandhian in terms of standing pressure on the wake of fighting for right and dignity. He digested the ordering tone of Martin. Gandhi's passive resistance in him flopped as the Khan was going to timidly succumb to Martin's orders.

He diverted the topic to the count of men to be engaged for howling, 'I think about twenty people with drums will suffice. The howler will have to make a wide circle and close it in circular order.' Rabbani said a blunt yes then trying to poke Salim Khan he said, 'Sir *saheb now* we are not hustled ones, the sacrificial goat. We have the backings of Gandhi. Sir ji we are not the former battered lumps of life. We can step forth and stir sir ji Khan *saheb*! The scene has begun to change. The Gandhi volume has widened! I hope we are going to shed off the English leech very soon. You can try to ignite the souls of the villagers. We are supposed to give ignition to Gandhian flame all over and our Chandrapura should not go un-noticed.' Rabbani exhausted himself and Khan Bahadur remained buried in timidity.

Rabbani fell flat. Khan Bahadur got leaked. In him the awe and power of the formidable English got impersonated as the Halloweens, 'You are talking the language of the Hindi Papers. Provocative and selling us for victims! The media is underestimating the power of the British. We can expect their quitting but still lots more are required.' Salim Khan's version of seeking the key to the heaven of freedom consisted of his withdrawal and timid retreat. He dreaded conditions leading to tussles and fights. To him facing the storm was a submissive burying the neck into the sands. He dreaded repercussions. He dreaded the English retaliation. In his mind the passivity of reaction was his rescue.

Salim's mind became busy designing the hunting. He had decided to get platforms raised on three places, 'I will ask Martin *saheb* to take me in the party.' He foolishly thought so and then eclipsing his mind he said in whispers that Gandhi's passive resistance implied the withdrawal from the hot-chase and wait for the right occasion. He then felt ashamed and said that he had no right to misinterpret Gandhi and that he was born weak so he would act weakly, 'I wish somebody brave enough should rise elsewhere! I am a hider, a non-performer! I seek the hiding in my withdrawal. I have no right at least to discredit the Gandhism. In Gandhi there is no scope for withdrawal. In him the hiding in fright is ugly and I am a hider, a poor fellow with timid heart.' Salim Bahadur Khan reproached himself and then succumbed to his withdrawal.

* * * * *

CHAPTER 6

THE BONGA TIGERS FINISHED

More than thirty drumbeaters had been hired from the adjoining district under Morgan's influence. These drumbeaters were aware of the Bongas and their sacred profile but they had been paid money and fed with wine and in their head greed for more had been stuffed, 'Bongas! Why for they are Bongas? Are they living deities or only the faking of mind? Okey. These Bongas will be doing us no wrong as we come from the distant villages,' the howlers argued. Then one weak of heart whispered, 'But if really the Bongas are the divine creatures, will not they do us scary things like haunting in the nights and strangulating our children?' These confusions of the howlers diluted as the Morgan's agents scolded the howlers to get engaged in the duty, 'I want you all just to go ahead with your duty. No useless waste of time. No more your ragging brain over Bonga folly. You have been paid and will be paid more.'

As the howlers opened their mouth and tried to beat the drum they felt like choked to the bottom with ladders of fright, 'We cannot move. Our limbs are getting numb. Bhagwan ji we are getting sucked dry of energy.' The jungle then howled, the jackals then the monkeys and bears and wolves and the birds and the butterflies all together became restless. The morning light got bedimmed and the sun as if looked like swallowed by the cloud. There was no motion in the limbs of the howlers. The agents of Morgan goaded the bodies and spiked on their bottoms.

The howling began like the slaughtering gurgle of the thousand beasts. A thick wall of the howling thunder began to move in a fury that wine ignited and Rabbani undertaking to relay commentary made Chandrapura drown in the fright of the happening, 'These howlers, the bloody ones are not from our village. They are hired from Morgan's village. Only if their legs got frozen! But no. Our Bongas are endangered and they would not release energy to stapple the steps. Dear Laxmi, Sarita, Nirja come together and cry. Cry like a child and wake the lethargy of the sky.' Rabbani could see that Laxmi, Sarta, Nirja and others were already praying and failing to get heard.

Rabbani ran about as if dismantled. He ran about crying and hoping his cries would puncture the walls of horrid mum. Then he heard a loud groan coming from across the mountain as if a monster was stabbed in the throat, 'Yes I can hear the Bogna getting activated, poked to realization that their freedom to live had been jeopardized.' He plugged his ears to the sound and to his dismay he located that it was the simple booming of the empty mountain, 'Then these Bongas are powerless!' said Rabbani to the villagers.

Laxmi, Sarita, Nirja and Ram Lal fought him, 'How possible that the Bongas we have trusted since long can be powerless? Our Bongas are our saviors. They must be devising means and calculating time to show powers. We shall only wait and see the miracle happen.'

No miracle happened. Nothing would happen in such a dismal time except that the madding drumming of the traitors mounted louder. The jungle had been arrested in the drum beat. Report was pouring in that the elephant Raja tusker was carrying the hunters. There was no trace of the Bonga Tigers showing any a-terrestrial gusto.

The poor Bongas were reportedly located loitering on the borders of the village mewing and cowering. The beating gong of the drum had filled their bellies with horror. They were hungry and harassed and they had nothing cognitive to guess the overhanging menace. Laxmi, Sarita, Nirja Thakur and Ram Lal together bound their heads and cried that their defenseless Bongas were faking their faith, 'Bongas! Bonga dear are you drowned in fright? Roar dear, jump across the mountain and land on the back of the elephant. Stop the march of the hunters and save us from the humiliation of faked faith.' The villagers gathered in a cluster and pitied the Bongas. They gathered together and cried too. Then somebody among the villagers shouted that they must not break heart and that their Bongas would sacrifice themselves to save the villagers.

'We have been cheated, cheated by Khan Bahadur and his wife Shally Rani and have been deserted likewise in the crisis of shame. Our Khan *saheb* could have challenged the Martin people and stopped them. But no. We are left with horror of the Bonga being eliminated, our divine Bonga!' Nobody was to hear the cry.

The jungle howling had gained volume and the sky was mocking at the inmates of the earth downward, '*Solution to the crisis lay only in the hand of Sophie mam*,' said Ram Lal. Ram Lal addressed the villagers like a hero in the films. He was not heard. The villagers were angry and sad and madding.

Nirja Thakur tried to fetch attention to the feeding of the Bongas. He repented that he had invested his hard-earned savings in bringing milk bottle, eggs and kheer to the corner of the jungle where Bongas were supposed to stroll to and devour the delicacies, 'My foolish wife had been goading me to bring these delicacies but today the energy of the Bongas got fiasco. Instead of roaring they are reported mewing,' he abominably turned his face towards the Banyan giant tree, 'Tell the banyan Bonga are we not cheated?' Nirja kept his thought to himself. He feared the stolid head would not hear him. The snake prop roots of the banyan tree wriggled and nothing ghostly happened.

The Bongas were in dangers and the drumbeating was gaining fury. In the grim situation the only hope was Sophie Juliet.

* * * * *

'The Bongas were no more than the phantom creatures, coming shyly and vanishing shyly. They were reported roaming like shadows in the moon light. They looked thinning out of vision when eyes chased them as if they despised being spied upon. This was the major clause in support of their divinity. We must admit that our Bongas are the rare cats for our succor.' This one day declared even the boozy Ram Lal. All the village praised Ram Lal. Gobardhan was assigned the duty of care-taking of the Bongas. Gobardhan was a bad chap given to adding and subtracting to the miracle fabrics related to the Bongas just to prank the gullible fellows. The freedom of imagination in him was at the most active when he was sure the villagers were listening to him, 'Sarita Maie,' once he opened his mouth, 'there I was dazzled to see our Bongas dancing on two legs and carrying something like a big pitcher on the head. The dance was weird but around the cats I saw light beams falling from the sky.' It was a blunt lie but Laxmi and Nirja Thakur were hearing it with great attention, 'Could you really see this weird dance as long as you desired?' This was the curious query, 'Shut up *chacha*. How any lad of my virtue could see the weird dance longer than it was ordained. Soon the Bongas became shy and they retreated.' Gobardhan was lying. The story of the weird dance ignited imagination on individual talents to conclude respectively. The Bongas became more reverential and more mystifying. Gobardhan became more available ever since with tastier stories. On the whole the poor cats began to lose their characteristic animality.

To this credit must go to Gobardhan and the villagers' vulnerability, '*Maie* these cats are like our Bonga grandpa, chewing morsels toothlessly and ogling around as Bonga grandpa did. Do you remember the drooling mouth of Bonga grandpa? The old fellow ogled around vaguely at the faces and not finding any clear face grandpa like a Bonga joker sat with his front limbs expecting somebody to support his bony body. I used to be frightened of the grandpa Bonga but as he was harmless, I became gradually aligned with him. These Bonga Tigers are like our phantom grandpa Bonga.' Gobardhan was shooed and chased by Sarita. But he completed his tale about the Bonga that the tigers looked harmless due to age so they were Bongas, 'You know *maie* when I touched the skin of the Bongas they purred like domestic cats and would not stop till their chins were caressed.' This was the plain lie that Gobardhan spread about the Bongas. He spread the lie and laughed to himself. Ram Lal heard it and rivaled him.

The drumbeaters were in frenzied action. The gong of the beating and the shouts of the twenty mouths had smothered the jungle silence. Only the desperate stampede of the jungle folks was felt through the gross trampling of the vegetation. The hirelings were worked up under the influence of threat and wine as they continued to coil the body of the jungle in python roll.

The poor Bongas frightened of death were struggling through the coiling space to the shifting hide outs. From their mouths no curse and cry were belching as they were too weak for such panic outburst. The poor cats did not know their crime. They also did not know the tagging of divinity. They knew only this that they were old and helpless and that they were targeted.

The villagers were in rage and panic behaving timidly as the howlers were closing the death coil upon the Bongas. The cats had hidden themselves behind harsh bushes and had been panting in exhaustion taken aback why they were being haunted. There was no answer, 'Sarita,' whispered Nirja Thakur undertone lest he should be detected, 'Sarita I bet the drumbeaters are not from our village. The traitors are from another village. Children of pigs they do not know what crime they are in.' His words hung in his throat. He was sounding like a phantom in agony.

Sarita who wanted to face the drumbeaters in person and scratch their faces was dampened with a shudder in her body that her folly would expose her to Martin. She dreaded exposure to the pink-face. She heard the gang of the howlers nearer. She cried in prayer and shed tears, 'Our Bongas! I leave you on yourselves. You are divine. If really you are divine, you will salvage yourselves.' She wished to utter this blasphemy. Nirja as if overheard her and chiding her told her that she should not doubt the Bonga power, 'Our Bongas are Bonga Bhagwa!'

Sarita repented secretly and telling nothing concrete heard the howlers howling like the slaughtered devils. Gobardhan had hidden his face in the lap of her mother and his mother had hidden her face within her trembling palm and Ram Lal was nowhere to be seen with his dirty dialogues, 'Come somebody, come my Krishna!' cried Sarita, 'Come somebody to save the village, our Bongas.' Sarita was kicked by his husband to choke the crying lest she should be detected, 'Our Village Bongas are going to be attacked. Our dear Bongas! Ah Bhagwan save our Bongas. They are ours! Our savior in the time of crisis. We sleep safe when the Bongas are awake in nights patrolling the jungle.' Each heart was in pain, each eye wet with tears but there was a disaster overhanging. Their great Bongas were in danger.

Then Sarita showed guts and she in a fury shouted, 'Jai Ho!' She was throwing her limbs about and letting her black hair unfurl like a fury calling to the sky to send help. No help was dropped from any sky and her words of prayer boomeranged. Sarita as if got choked and she threw up. But then she again went hysteric, 'I will fight the devils of the Andrew and the Marin, crack their heads, hold their feet, hang around their necks like a witch but shall stop them.' Nirja Thakur felt moved and ashamed and shaky in the legs. He felt like holding Sarita in his bosom and smooch her.

The tempest of the howling sound had by then filled the universe torturing the jungle and making the wild lives scatter in panic for life. Nobody was there to notice Laxmi, Sarita and Nirja. The sky had begun to crack with the boom of the gong, 'Ah, they have raided the jungle. Yes, our Bongas have been besieged. Yes, there is left no hope on the platter of life. The last of the route of hope to heaven of freedom has been seized. We will lose our Bongas to the brutes,' cried the villagers in a chorus. Their actual god was quite confused.

Then Reshma and Rabbani appeared like two good protagonists with wisdom in their heads and fire in words prompting the village to swarm in a bunch to Martin Bungalow and appeal to the great Sophie, 'Sophie mam is ours. Sophie the khadi-wearing lady-Gandhi we shall reach to. She is ours. Her red face wears sympathy for us. She will hear us and take our prayers.' The crowd thickened around Reshma and Rabbani. These fellows became the last glitters of hope.

The surging tornado of the howling having engulfed all, the ears could hear the screeching voice of Reshma, 'I know the lady sweet! I know her personally. She is kind and in her eyes compassion floats like angels float in the heaven. She has been heard fighting her man in our defense. She is a lady of justice. She will fetch us the key to what they say the heaven of freedom. Sophie mam is our Sophia! We want no possession of this heaven. We want no exclusive justice. We want enough of space to see our Bongas spared. We pray to our god to come down and secure the Bongas against the raid. Ah they are in danger! The red-face would kill our Bonga Raja.'

* * * * *

In a desperate bid to catch the last hope in Sophie Martin the legs began to pull bodies to the Martin Bungalow. The legs were dragging the weight of the phantom bodies as the villagers had nothing like the fire. They were the picture of defeat of guts; in them the Gandhi was hung up! Their legs were carrying the dummies of their bodies. Reshma and Rabbani and Laxmi and Sarita and Nirja and Ram Lal and Goberdhan and others in hundreds had reached the main gate of the Bungalow.

The gigantic Bangalow stood before them a formidable foe. Its magnitude seemed to devour their guts. The sheep-herd of the villagers felt their legs go numb. The Gandhi of the passive energy got frozen. They had worn the mask of Gandhi minus true Gandhi and were around the Bungalow, a cowering sheep-herd! Saita, Laxmi, Nirja, Ram Lal, the silly Gobardhan and Reshma -Rabbani duo were at Bungalow gate to hit it but they lacked the Gandhian guts.

The jungle cries of appeal and horror then seemed like turning into the cosmic sobs. The ears became numb with the resonating echoes of appeal to move for the appeal, 'Go ahead the surging despair! Go ahead to where the hope is tagged and hold the legs of the lady if you want justice descend. Lady-Gandhi, our Lady Bonga! She alone can save the jungle from the mar. Our Bongas would be finished if the Lady is not invoked.'

The words of the jungle carried on the wings of wind fell like hail storm upon the numb villagers. The hail storm became severe as Laxmi then Sarita then Nirja then Reshma followed by Rabbani caught motion, 'Sarita and Laxmi and Nirja,' called Reshma, 'Make a towering ladder of hope. Climb it. There the Lady-Gandhi, the Messiah, we shall hold her legs. We are built for holding legs. Our appeal we shell platter to her. Bonga we shall save; Bonga we could save by this only. Lady-Gandhi will use her acquired soul power, her resistance of the passive components!

Alas! We had reached her earlier! You hear the booming cries of the jungle folk.' The jungle echoed louder and louder.

Then suddenly dead silence fell. The howling ceased. The echo died. The legs and movements got paralyzed. The gate of the Bungalow flung open and the Raja elephant strode out carrying the killers on its ride: Andrew and Martin the two were mounting the Raja elephant to kill the Bongas. The riding crime vanished into the dark night as the human phantoms of the villagers froze down, 'Lost we all, lost the last shred of hope and now no use our being foolish and wise to reach the lady,' shouted Laxmi. Sarita seconded her. Nirja uttered the same. Reshma tore her hair. Rabbani caught her from behind and poked his tool upon her plump bottom. Reshma shouted defiance and slapped Rabbani. Rabbani was heated. He shouted abuse on her. Then the villagers turned in a mass into a ball of fire, 'We shall reach the lady,' the gang said in one volume.

'Lady madam we are going to be ruined if and when our Bongas are killed,' shouted the gang. 'Which Bonga? Where Bongas?' the lady was bewildered,

'Our Bongas, our great Bongas. They are the cats. The cats are at the gun point of your man. His Raja elephant rides to the jungle please stop him!'

The lady rubbed her hands in repentance, 'Foolish people you became too late. The hunters have departed.'

'But what! You are the only hope to us. We have nobody else to reach. You can control the disaster.' The villagers prostrated in front the lady. The lady Sophie was embarrassed. She had never been used to such awkward situation.

'You are our Devi Mata. You are invoked to save our Devata.' Sarita tried to catch Sophie's leg. The Lady shut her ears with her palms. She was never before caught in such damned situation, 'Okey I shall go. Come on,' she became a liquid lava. Her movement became a landslide, 'Come you all in a mass. We shall pluck the guns of crime.'

Sophie tightened the khadi-saree above her waist. She flipped the sandals. She went bare footed. In her mouth fire and words together mixed. In her eyes the ultimate hell made the hell alive on earth, 'I shall make them cease.' In her Gandhi-shadow took a sojourn. She looked like a white-lady-Gandhi, the replica of soul force and a brave creature built from bones and flesh. She had borrowed the words and the voice of the Gandhi, his gestures and gaits and was looking a prototype of the Saint of Hindustan.

The gang of the hooligans were stumbling, tumbling, turning and going. The jungle was whimpering. It was the eeriest wailing of the kind ever heard. Sophie was marching her army of the sheep-herd to fetch for them the key to justice. She had been mesmerized. She had been mesmerized of the Gandhi-magic and was going to see it perform.

But the sheep-herd of the vulnerable villagers she never thought if they should be trusted or not.

Laxmi and Sarita, Nirja and Ram Lal all suddenly got frightened mid-way, 'Laxmi,' whispered to Sarita, 'Is it not that we like a nightmare are marching from our hut to the jungle to stop the disaster?' Sarita was not loud to convey her sudden fright. 'Shut up,' snapped Laxmi, 'How that we can leave the gang midway?' Sarita whispered, 'I am having pressure.' Her bottom lost control. She sat squatting on the ground. Her bowels disgorged the poo. She felt relaxed, 'Yes now I am well.' The sheep-herd was on the move in the dark prompted by waning anger and madness.

Suddenly the jungle howled. The howling became loud. The gang trembled. Ram Lal took U-turn and vanished into the darkness. Nirja

Thakur felt foolish as to why he was *phantoming* behind the gang. He also took a U- turn and dissolved into the darkness. The count of the sheep-herd continued to fall one by one till only Laxmi, Sarita and Sophie were left in the gang. But these souls were not pinned up. Sophie sensed the thinning of the support. She kept goading her forth on the strength of the Gandhi-magic:

'Gandhi, Gandhi the beginning and the end of the good light

Give me strength, support and the right stride

I am not duplicating you, your lordship grand

But I hanker to cling the like of your plank

This sheep-herd I know would dissolve

But I shall continue on your strength resolve

Allot me guts and the understanding of your powers

I am yours, you are mine and the mission is ours.'

The jungle had churned the animals out of their hide outs as the howlers made the final efforts to upset the last lair. The poor Bongas then stuck to their den were poked to flee by the invading litters of the boars. The long-tusked boars were dangerous to the soft bellies of the Bongas. The Bongas were feeling timid. Their legs were trembling. They sought help and the boars were too crude to hear them, 'King of the Jungle,' taunted the male boar, 'The all-time plunderers of the animals why today the legs do not give support.' This was no occasion to give dialogue and hear dialogue. The poor Bongas were horrified of the invading drumming. They cried for help and their illusive majesty became a farce, 'Where to hide?' the Bongas cried. In their mouths their worn-out canine peeped and they pooed.

In the time of crisis when the fate staggers the chance to stand erect gets slender. The Bongas were passing through this slender phase. The poor cats were no Bongas. Gobardhan had made them Bongas. The irony of fate had endorsed Bonga-title to the poor cats. They had become famous as Bongas without ever having had any Bonga power. Their life had been staked due to this notorious Bonga-title. Then Alas! As the crisis had reached to the head these Bongas were fleeting for life and gun was chasing them. They were not safe as the gun had been loaded and the Bongas had been left to the care of chance.

The great soldiers of words, the villagers had thinned out. Any poking urge for freedom of heaven having blunted they were facing a nightmare, 'Laxmi we are mad if we are pinned to this spot. We are mad point blank.' Sarita pulled the hand of Laxmi. Laxmi felt his hand plucked from the body.

Sophie madam had never imagined that she would be left alone by the sheep-herd. She had marched forward with trust at the ganging support. She was betrayed and it was more unwarranted than strange, 'I believed these stuffs would continue en-masse.' Her head was buzzing, 'I am alone here. The jungle and the dark night and my bare hurting soles! I am still not foolish. Not feeling foolish. I am on a mission!'

Sophie babbled spasmodically. Before her the fate of her conviction of the freedom of heaven was tremored, 'The abstract Gandhi had wrapped her up. The Gandhi as a blank verse was making her move.' The sheep-herd had deserted Sophie, the khadi-lady and the Raja elephant was on the move.

'Where to find the hunters?' Sophie cried as her legs were hurt and bleeding, 'My folly that I got involved. My folly that I did not rationalize with me and plunged into it.' She repented. Sophie groped through the jungle undergrowth to find a passage maybe a human hand, 'All left. It was ethically a betrayal. But pragmatically the given. These guys never having had a taste for freedom, to them this betrayal is pardonable. I pity them. I will not blame them. I am not to blame them.'

The howling again gained intensity. The drumbeaters were at the last leg of their foul mission. Their boozy head was indifferently set to poke the Bongas to the forefront. The targeted Bongas were totally bewildered and would not know that they were the endangered creatures of the moments. Their faces cut furrows of unwritten horror. In their chests their hearts caught fright like the wicked child catching a desperate bird. The poor Bongas were running helter-skelter looking for any refuge in the bushes. But the search light had pierced the chests of the bushes to greedily spot the Bongas.

Sophie hurt in the soles was limping and crying. Her chivalry having drowned she became a picture of misery. In her the great courage bubbles had burst out as she had sensed the slip of the fugitives. She was left alone in the battle field exposed to herself, 'Shit! My men, they fled.' Sophie was dazzled by a flash of the light and it was most excruciating. She turned her face in shame and hid it in her khadi.

* * * * *

Martin not expecting the unexpectable had focused the light upon the crouching Bongas beneath the thin bushes. His gun ready, the finger pulled the trigger. The first and the next bullet hit the Bongas on their faces downing them like the stuffed-pigs. The light flash died and in the utter darkness Sophie could feel the sticky blood jet on her face. The warm blood dripping through her face made her look scary.

The jungle wailed. Jackals and hyenas and real cats wailed loudly killing the silence. Sophie sagged down on the ground trembling as her life became a shadow of doubt on her. She touched her limbs and skin and could hardly discover her back. She was a failed warrior in the field, 'Had I been potent enough to subdue the firing!' She felt sabotaged. In her, her guts were again transforming. She was again gathering her limbs and parts to restructure her and try to argue with her. The howling of the jungle suddenly drowned as the night got frozen over her. She fainted. She fainted by shame and the proceedings of the scary happenings. With her fainting her madding mission to catch freedom by forelock also got arrested but it was only a transitory phase.

Martin shouted hosana. He had downed the Bongas but soon he discovered that her woman was also down on the ground shaking with loss of pride, a fiasco in the picture.

* * * * *

CHAPTER 7

SOPHIE RESURRECTED

Three bodies were carried: two of the Bonga Tigers and one of Sophie Juliet. These bodies embodied shock and disgust embodying nothing grand. The Bongas had been downed to signify the victory of arbitrariness. Sophie beside the Bongas was the embodiment of the impact of tyranny not allowing justice to breed. But she was not the death of the will to fight for dignity and relief. Her body was carried with care as she belonged to Martin's family and was a plug in the circuit of future events.

Sophie Juliet recovered sense but was still dazed as she had been exposed. Her fire and temper having gone she was lying on the bed traumatized. On her pale face the tale of defeat was building infrastructure. Her body was aching. Her heart was paining. The broken skin on her body was telling a tale. She had been crudely bandaged on the soles. She was ashamed and angry and frustrated.

But she was not wiped out as a trash. She was not rubbished out of the story of the dignity and fight for dignity. She was built for freedom and freedom was her craze.

Martin Julius was hanging about looking at her in anger and pity wondering how the lady had thrown herself into the dramatics, 'Well done. Bravo! You are the hero of the history you made. A madrigal of praise and wailing elegy will be composed by the wandering minstrels on you. The epic of your good deeds will reach England to your country people to tickle them. Your Ammi Alice Joseph will hear it and laud it! I too will cooperate the narrative to spread like an infection.' Martin was reprimanding the lady who had no answer in her mouth.

'Then what madness made you lead the rowdy gangs? What folly that you came there bare-footed and met the result?' Martin shouted. It was contrary to his manners. Sophie sat up suffering the castigation. She had nothing in her defense. She was shamed.

Martin then sobered. He came to her. His breath touched her. She felt the warmth of his skin on her. He was trembling with passion. She could not discern it. She did not try to discern. She was ashamed and dazed. *She had committed a wrong for the right.*

'Dear my Lady Sophia,' he touched her cheek and brushing the dry blood clot on it said, 'You were supposed to show English blood. But you fouled it. Do you think your Madness did you any good? Did not you get deserted by the sheep-herd. I have been warning of it. I pity you for your folly. I have been warning that these sheep-herd are volatile lot. You are an outsider and you got the proof.' Martin was not un-kind. He caressed the lady on his cheeks, 'My compulsions, yes, my compulsions! I will not quit you, cannot as I belong and you would fool yourself if you trusted these sheep-herd.'

She was ashamed but not shaky. She confessed in whispers, 'Sir I would not have been out. I wished I had checked myself. But when I found you were on ride to the jungle with the bloody plan, I became desperate. I did not want the Bongas being destroyed. I had no other option but to enter the jungle. I entered there to counter you. But I failed. Your gun downed the cats. I could not save the poor animals.' She sobbed. She fell into a swoon. Martin became nervous. He sprang to the verandah and in a state of bewilderment he brought a pitcher full of water and poured the contents over her, 'Wake please my great warrior! I salute your spirit. I salute you for fighting a borrowed fight.'

Sophie was drenched to the skin. She was shivering. The dramatics had made her totally damned. She held his arms and wept. She wept and wept. She was behaving like a child in terror of a nightmare, 'Martin *saheb* you have power and position and you are still the supreme in this locality but you did a cowardly act. You killed the Bongas whom these rustics revered as their guardian deity.' She asked for a blanket to cover her. She covered herself in the blanket and holding his hand pulled him down on the bed with a force of an avenger, 'Sir *saheb* you did a grave wrong. You killed the innocent Bongas only to subvert the faith of the rustics. I tell you it was a timid act.' Her words fell flat on Martin. But as he valued her and had connection with her, he held calm. He heard her rave and rage, 'The sabotaging of somebody's faith is vicious. You committed a vicious act. I hate you and would hate the scene of the killing life time.' Sophie Juliet closed her eyes wearily. She was not planning to harness him. She knew that Martin was tough. She knew whatever he did was a part of his duty.

She looked blankly to the sky as if trying to catch the meaning of freedom. She contemplated. She discovered meanings of freedom, '*To Martin the pressure and control over the natives constitute of his picture of freedom. To me it is otherwise loose and expansive. I associate the term* to the *realization of its bliss in trying to diffuse the pressure and control.*'

She did not make any further efforts to move Martin to her point of view, 'His point of view is his asset. Mine is mine. I am not going to intervene. He is doing his labor to try to hold his version of heaven of freedom. Definitely it is unethical. Definitely it deserves castigation but from his point of view it is blissful to him. I shall not intervene.'

She asked for a glass of *sherbat,* 'Roohafza *sherbat,'* she whispered, 'Roohafza drink of the Indian hakim from Indian herbs I think will cool my anguishing soul. I am suffering from moral wounding.' She said more and Martin not trying to belittle her brought the *sherbat* and half drinking it from the glass offered the rest to her,'Take this your soul soothing *sherbat* dear. Your transformation is not salubrious in reference to the last night's folly. Why really you plunged into it? Were you forced by the rustics or was it your soul's compulsion?'

Martin sat down beside her and heard her, 'I am not on the side of any rustics. I am on the side of the poor conscience. I am a Christian and like a conscientious Christian I pine to see that nobody is robbed his freedom. These rustics maybe irrational but to them their Bongas were their imagination catchers. We as superior race must consider it. We cannot afford to shoo the rustics of their boo. It is against the principle of nobility. I am to this principle. You breached this principle. You are a wrong doer. You need suffer penalty.' Sophie completed her stormy dialogue.

'Delicious dialogue, darling. Your Gandhi rumble is only delusion. Meanwhile you are an un-blessed creature. You are fooled by your conviction. These rustics whom you lead did you mark they dropped out enroute? These creatures are not more than irritants. We English are here to rule. We have to be sure of ourselves and make sure that we do not get loose! Then dear so long as we are tough these rustics will remain under control. Otherwise they are infections!' Martin took his pipe to his lips. He did not light it. He was looking in tension.

He confessed, 'Dear madam,' he continued, 'You know we are meeting war setbacks. Our hold is loosening. This your Gandhi-type has noted and we are being subjected to blackmailing. Please dear do not build the same pressure from your side.'

He bent and took hold of her hand. He planted a kiss, 'You are precious to me. But I tell you that of late I am marking you are drifting. It horrifies me.' Martin embraced her but he felt that Julee was not his Julee. This was horrifying. He slackened the hold, 'Sorry Julee, sorry. I am holding as if trying to catch at the rippling tide. I am foolish to surround the emptiness. You seem to have skidded off!'

'It is sad,' said the man, 'sad and depressing that you are drifting from me at the time I need you most.' Martin looked away from her. He was sure that he had failed to convince her. She was not able to discern matters as per his vision. He also knew that Julee had been put on the spell, a Gandhi-delirium!

In his mind the scene of the Bonga hunting came alive. He could recall that Andrew Morgan in the crucial time when he was about to fire bullet had gone crazy behaving as if he were possessed. Morgan had attacked him and would have snatched the gun but for the physical scuffle in which he defeated him. The gun had fired three shots at random and these shots rightly plunged into the Bongas.

'Dear madam I would like to mention the scary moments when your Morgan had suddenly turned maudlin as if possessed. He had twisted his body, his eyes throwing out, on his face distortion of muscles visible, he had gone disoriented. He tried to snatch the gun. I fought him. He produced gurgling sound as if a devil was smothered to death. I could not know what was happening but my muscles supported me. My finger pulled the trigger. The shot was fired. The Bongas fell like two huge bodies. I could not at all understand the weird part of Morgan's behavior.' Martin paused to hear her explanation. She looked pale in the face. She bowed her head. She said wearily, 'Whenever excess is on way the soul of the nature gets activated. We would not apprehend the mystique of it. The nature acts in the eerie manners. Savior! Morgan embodied it. He acted the savior! Christ, you know comes as savior! Your gun fired depicting your failure to apprehend the sign of nature. The nature wanted you to stop. You were a villain there and the gun embodied the villainy.' Sophie rubbed her palms furiously. It was a state of frustration and penitence combined. She stood and walked to and fro on the verandah and looked pale by horror, 'You did an utter wrong. You killed the soul of the Nature.' She did not know what she was alluding to.

Martin did not argue with her. He simply digested the resonating horror. He offered to bring coffee. He then offered her to go on a picnic. He offered her to purchase her a pearl necklace. He was trying to divert her mind. He offered her to have sex. He was in a muddle looking strange and spent.

Sophie was recounting the last three minutes of the time when the Bongas were shot dead. She could vaguely recall that amid anguish of death the bodies of the cats had slid to her legs. The warm fir and the horror of a dead animal had made her traumatized. She had not cried but she wanted to cry.

Sarita and Laxmi had vanished leaving Sophie alone to suffer the desertion. In a panic bout she had thrown her limbs about and she had caught a snaky prop root of a giant banyan tree.

'There was something scary about the Bongas,' she said but Martin ignored her. He talked of the defeats of the English forces on different international borders. He talked of the Round Table Conference. He talked of history and the recent political developments and talked of the probability of Gandhian magic, 'I wonder how this Gandhi in his meanest face and humble cloth round the loin could massively capture world's imagination. I wonder how he without gun and violence could make his men shadow him.' He then whispered to himself that the old figure was a mystical devil, 'A fugitive from the heaven.' He could not explain his meaningless phrase and to soothe her he said that he too liked the old man.

'There is something infectious about Gandhi, something beyond comprehension, very catching, very divine and this is what makes him a saint. Gandhi is unbeatable, a fierce and cool influence on everybody who carries soul in him.'

Sophie stopped at the drawing of the chained girl. The sketch was crude and unfinished. It gave her some meaning to what she wanted to convey, 'This my sketch. Take it. See it. Nothing marvelous. Not artistically correct. But it is a solid depiction of pain and longing of the Indians seeking freedom.'

Martin tried to justify himself, 'We English are committed only to us, committed to our interest and mission and this is our compulsion. You do not know what dangerous situation would take shape if we English drop out of power. We cannot just turn and recede.' Martin was right and wrong and he was taking precaution to see that no further harm befell him.

* * * * *

Outside the Bungalow a crowd was building. It was a cowering crowd in the shape of the gathering storm. It was thick with bodies rubbing against each other and fearing to get identified. One would doubt if the crowd was charged with the passivity Gandhi prompted. But the structure of the crowd confirmed that it had the seeds of violence in fetal configuration. Sarita, Laxmi, Nirja, Ram Lal and others were wriggling and wriggling drawing picture of the building mob.

The Bungalow was indefeasible standing still proud. Martin scenting the building mob came to the balcony. He hissed and fumed. His gun ready to charge, 'Okey! The shape of the crowd predicts violence.' The term violence made him seethe with anger, 'Violence! Yes, violence against us! Damn the creatures of the Gandhi passion! I shall see.'

The crowd was carrying the load of the bodies of the Bongas. The Bonga bodies were covered by white sheet patched with the dripping blood of the cats. The Bongas seemed to question Martin as to the crime of the killing. Martin had no reasonable answer. It put pressure on him. Martin felt like loaded inside. It was not the load of conscience knocking him. It was anger mixed with frustration, 'They will attack? Their daring heart will it make them violent?' Martin babbled. In answer Sophie whispered, 'The mood of the mob is bad.'

Martin gave a call to the sentries at the gate. There was nobody to return answer. Martin shouted enraged and his voice reverberated through the empty jungle. The guard had gone. Sophie pointed to the blank space where the sentries used to stand watch.

Sophie could see that the thickening of the crowd had received dilution. She could see that the faces of the mobbers were growing vague as they were struggling to get deleted. It was a strange proposition. She wondered if the Gandhian passivity had overwhelmed them. She eagerly wished they had worn Gandhian passivity. She wished them to wear the passivity cloak as a shield, 'Poor my protesting fools,' her mind was a riot, 'Dear my poor protesting souls learn to be calm. This alone is admissible. The English gun would otherwise teach peace.'

Martin had turned un-expectedly calm. He was watching the movement of the mob. The mob had literally alighted the weight of the Bonga corpses on the ground. Martin was looking gravely at the white sheet smeared with blackening blood. He felt a little quirk of passion for the cats. He could not find out its sources. He cursed then Andrew for the strange behavior during the shooting time. Andrew had resisted madly the firing. Martin dismissed the scary thought. He asked Sophie to withdraw. He himself withdrew feeling a bit guilty for the cats.

Sophie stayed there in the balcony noting that the sky overhead and the distant Buddha banyan tree were looking grim. She appealed vacantly to the sky to shed the grim faces. She then suddenly saw that the Buddha banyan limbs were moving and growing in volume. She felt like getting infused with the weird energies, 'I shall join the crowd. I shall lead it.' Sophie was uncertain of the impulses but she was under mystic pressure. The sky overhead and the Buddha banyan together beckoned her, 'I am no warrior but I feel like getting pumped up, pushed to join the motion for justice,'

Then she refrained, she felt guilty and sad and she said to herself that she had been cheated, 'Yes in the motion to check the hunting the rustics had marched with me then had deserted me.' She thought and thought and was not made prejudiced. She smiled and admitted that the nation long clamped in slavery was likely to behave that way, 'It would struggle and falter enroute. These rustics would behave erratically. We cannot trust and distrust them. We can only pity them and feel for their feelings.'

* * * * *

The mob ceased to exist. It was like the spectacular lull before the storm. Suddenly the mob wriggled and its legs began to dance. In the distant Buddha banyan tree, the hanging roots began to wriggle. The jackals howled aloud followed by the wolves and the entire jungle became a damned domain of the weird. The legs got panicky but they caught a chaotic movement. Rabbani and Reshma joined the weird dance. They churned dust and fogged the atmosphere. The mob got swallowed in the chaos. There was no voice, only severe silence.

Sophie felt persecuted, the torture of the soul in the whirling tornado! 'Sir *saheb* this dance is the cosmic replica of the birth of a star.' Her allusion was redundant, 'Sir *saheb,'* said Sophie, 'We should fear. We should fear the untoward. These muddling rustics are lifted aloft to the scary consciousness,' Sophie was not able to convey meaning. She covered her head with the *khadi saree*. She felt like reversed to a strange self, 'Sir *saheb* give them their freedom. It is their right. We cannot decline it. It will be the cruelest thing on our part.' Sophie caught hold of Martin's hand and pleaded, 'Yes, they are not dangerous. They are desperate. Meanly longing for their due. We English have usurped their right. Their Bongas have been denied the right to a decent burial. They should have it.'

Martin heard her and swallowed her concerns. The immanent horror of the situation triggered his English hate of the Indians. He knew the mob would turn violent and this made him wary, mean and vengeful. In his eyes blood and vengeance boiled in a fury. He was afraid and desperate and this made him a dangerous person.

Without provocation from the mob he rushed into his bed chamber, took his gun, loaded it and would have fired it into the mob but for the struggle of Mrs. Martin, 'Are you mad? Will you kill them? You cannot at all.' She turned the barrels of the gun to herself, 'Justice you cannot do. Justice the noblest act of Christian ethics having died in you, now you are up to this meanness.'

Marin was flabbergasted. He was sweating profusely, 'Okey the queen of justice,' he shouted and pointing the barrel to the sky he fired the gun. The boom of the firing literally uprooted the demonstrating crowd. Legs fled like the ghosts fleeing the light. Sophie saw the fleeing crowd with pity.

'See these your gallant heroes,' laughed Marin, 'Good lady freedom!The right to independence is deserved only by those who can stand the threat of challenges. These plump souls deserve only slavery.'

'No. Not at all. We have choked the longing in them for it,' Sophie voiced her concern, 'They have been battered so long that their natural resilience has died. But they deserve justice. We have usurped it. We should sanction it.' Sophia argued, 'You may be right in your points but they are right in theirs. These villagers do not know actually how and why and when they should be allowed their due: freedom to act free and get their Bongas their respected burial.'

The Bonga Bodies were lying on the ground. The rustics dropped their limbs. In them agitation had sunken. Sophie was looking on blankly to the Buddha banyan and the pale sky hoping them to signal something. She resolved, 'Gandhi, his patience and control I salute him. I am not his copy but at this juncture I feel like his spirit permeating me. I would fight but not with hate and revenge. I should fight with the calm energy of the Gandhi. Gandhi does not fight the foe as a foe. He fights him in a cool way and here Martin is my opponent and I shall fight him cooly. Great is Gandhi. I am no duplicate of him but I take joy in duplicating him.'

Sophie repeated her new name 'Sophia' like some sacred incantation and felt like clinging to it like the baby monkey clings to its mother's breast.

Martin had left her and she was tangled in her Gandhi. The thought of the Bongas and her attempted rescue of Bongas then her disappointment together made a rolling ball over her memory slope. She did not rebuff Salim Bahadur. She wished he had supported her, 'But no. This fellow is a timid fugitive,' she commented and concluded that she would give the fight.

* * * * *

CHAPTER 8

SOPHIE TURNED INTO SOPHIA

Martin Julius returned. He was agitated. Anger and hate and irritation spilled from his eyes. His pink-monkey face was red with rage. He was turning an inverted volcano. His pride of supremacy had gone berserk but mingling with it was the streak of scare. He was hiding his nervousness in the shell of arrogance. The Bonga bodies were as if floating about him buzzing like swarm of flies.

He was pacing through the verandah of his Bangalow like the freshly captivated hyena in the cage. Sophia was nowhere. His confidence content as the supremo was getting hung. He had not guessed about the villagers going defiant, 'These rat souls, battered and bridled I wonder what made them agitated. Maybe my loose grip and Sophia's support to them turned them boisterous.'

Martin Julius called Rabbani. Rabbani appeared before him like a culprit, 'Then you too were amid the ganging fools,' thundered Martin, 'This lady maid, the stupid Reshma too was seen there.' Martin paced through the verandah, his smoking pipe giving smoke. On his monkey-pink face horror and hate was sitting aloud.

Rabbani was standing subdued, a picture of miserableness, 'Sir *saheb ji*,' he tried to open his tongue, 'Shut up you damned fool. You had been there *puppetting* the Gandhi. Reshma and all those rebels!' Martin broke the spirit of Rabbani by the thunder lightning. Rabbani was battered, 'Idiots you all thought your howling would scare the like of me. I would have sent you all to hell by shooting straight but for the check from my wife. This lady too you people maddened her.'

Martin stopped suddenly and sighing said to himself, 'It seems it is growing un-safe to live here. These ganging herds I think someday they would turn marauders. I can predict it as their Gandhi has volcanized them literally choking natural outing of inner rage. These creatures of cringing version I fear to predict will someday turn bloody. One day, someday these vandals would march upon us!' in the eyes of Martin disgust became vocal.

He thundered, 'Damned fellow go and fetch your Khan *saheb* Bahadur immediately. Drag him by collar and produce him before me.' The order fell like a hammer on the head of Rabbani Shadman.

'Yes sir!' Rabbani saluted Martin, 'Yes, my lord. I shall go.' Rabbani turned to go but Martin shouted the command, 'I want the names of the insurgents too.' Rabbani was tremored to the core. He had no guts to utter words of defense.

* * * * *

Rabbani was on the carriage rushing with scare and agitation to fetch Khan Bahadur, 'Sir *saheb* this the red-faced monkey Martin,' cried Rabbani. His eyes were hot with anger, 'Sir *saheb* this the red-faced monkey Martin has summoned you.' His eyes became moist. It was the outcome of his suppressed rage and revenge, 'Sir *ji saheb*,' Rabbani swallowed the imaginary demon of fright.

'What for?' demanded Salim Khan.

'He is going to shout at you, the scoundrel red-monkey! He is convinced that the villagers were abetted to rebellion.'

'Nonsense! Who incited the villagers?' Salim Khan sounded weak. He was getting overshadowed by some outreaching threat, 'I will not go. I do not want to face Martin. He is temperamental.' Salim Khan was afraid. He knew he was of no match before Martin.

Shally overheard the conversation. She without much reason to blame Salim Khan almost attacked him, 'This way intimidated, we cannot get the *sirkar,* our rule'

Salim Khan did not notice her. He did not seek and express defenses. He was upset about how he would face a headstrong ruler. He was upset about facing Martin, the fellow English whom Salim Khan took as a villain. The only option was to evade him. But it was impossible. Rabbani requested Shally to plead him to obey the order, 'Shally sir mam,' said Rabbani, 'You know *ji Bibi sahiba* this red-face is a crack fellow. Now that he has summoned Salim sir, he will have him in his Kothi. I am afraid Martin red-face is going to bring a crackdown upon the villagers.'

'Why for a crackdown?' Shally ejaculated, 'Has really your *saheb* Khan abetted the villagers?' Shally forgot her biases and sincerely asked.

'Yes, ji sir,' cried Rabbani, 'This red-face having killed the poor Bongas now he is going to plant the blame on the villagers.' Rabbani used swearwords to cover his dialogue.

Shally was abhorred at the swearwords and not chiding Rabbani she asked Reshma to confirm what Rabbani was telling. Reshma confirmed Rabbani, 'Madam ji sir I gathered from Laxmi and Sarita that the villagers were demonstrating outside the Martin Dera. Their demand was genuine. They wanted their Bongas to be buried there. This was like an insurgent act to Martin.'

Shally became anxious about consequences. She strongly felt for the poor villagers and their plight, 'The unfortunate guys would get implicated in police cases. Ah the arresting! Ah the jail and persecution. These *firangis* have been using detention to batter spirits. I recall my Ammi mentioning during the British takeover of kingship from the Mughals, the English used native forces against the locals. The *firangis* were handful in number but their strength lay in exploiting the forces by way of regional and racial disparity. These Master manipulators, the English created disparity then exploited it as tools against the natives. Shally Jaan tried to convey the thought but could not succeed.

Salim Bahadur Khan ran about in utter mis-mind asking Rabbani and Reshma for help and then entreated Shally to support him. He was puzzled, 'This Martin fellow he is a crack. I tell he is a ruthless crack. If he has told that he would put charges of the Bonga killing on the villagers he will do it. The poor Bonga worshipper will have no Bongas and nothing beside them to save them. He will bring the crackdown and arresting will happen.' Salim Khan looked upset, 'I can guess the higher authorities will summon me and institute investigation and this Martin will simply duck out pretending ignorance about the killing. Afterall the English people are the English supporting the English. I will be made the escape goat. I will be framed responsible. I dread being involved in nuisances.'

Salim Khan was babbling the apprehension and Shally not capable of hearing him was in the race against her imagination, 'I remember my Ammi mentioning the scene after Mutiny when every next active Hindustani had been made a suspect. This suspect-marking of the Hindustani had been the easiest tool to keep us intimidated by the Angrez. This the Martins have done for decades, intimidation and false charging! This time also the same clamp will be used. Matters of justice and punishment would mess up and the innocent villagers will get victimized.'

Reshma brought dry fruits on a tray. She stood like a phantom waiting for responses, 'Sir ji madam, take a pick of the fruit.'

Shally was irritated but soon she checked the irritation. She thought it unseemly to peeve at the maid and then asking Reshma to remove the fruits she ordered her to bring water. Reshma was too engrossed in the matter to obey the order, 'Sir ji mam if the arresting happened our Chandrapura will turn a detention camp. The forces will be stationed here.'

Salim Khan rebuffed, 'Reshma, stop this conjecturing. Idiot girl arresting in British format is the most unfortunate thing. Stuffing in the jail and no hearing and justice.'

Rabbani became agitated, 'Sir *saheb* this Martin red-face had ordered me to bring you at all cost.' Rabbani did not refer to the insulting phrase '*drag by collar*' but insisted Salim Khan on complying.'

'I do not think if the villagers' ho-ha had anything to do with the independence. I do not think these fellow beings in the villages have any understanding of the meaning and purpose of independence. These poor creatures were noisy in sheer frustration. Their dear Bongas were the question. They were wriggling in the crowd to get their Bongas a sacred burial,' the Khan held tears.

Shally Khan crossed him, 'I think the villagers were charged by the slant imagination of freedom. They have no plausible idea of it indeed but they are provoked by the inner rage of it. Silly villagers they are under Gandhi spell but wrongly.'

Shally Khan then reverted to her dream prince. Calling the prince she languished to slip into the voyage of imagination. She then supported the villagers and withdrawing her charges she said the nicest exit to freedom came from fantasying. She talked undertone, 'I would say this dream prince maybe my private whim but it embodies the exit to the relief side. I love this relief seeking. The villagers in their silly buzzing maybe given to seeking this relief. Their Gandhi permeating through their psyche might be invisible but it is there. I am sure the villagers are slantly desiring for freedom. I sound foolish but it I am not wrong.' Shally did not talk aloud and Salim Khan was too dip in bewilderment to guess what she was up to.

*****

Salim Khan again became panicky. He cried that he was being dragged wrongfully into the matter. He feared to face Martin. He shouted for exemption. He raved like a child in distress. But then he announced that he would go, 'Rabbani prepare the buggy. I shall go to Martin.'

Rabbani rushed out to prepare the buggy. Reshma removed the tray of the fruits and Shally Khan waited for his departure. But Salim Khan stuck to his chair, 'Dear Shall I am afraid to meet this English Martin. I know he will behave like a despot. His English blood and arrogance will make him behave despotically.'

Shally literally unheard him. She was engrossed into her escape fantasy. She intensely desired to evoke her dream prince to catch relief.

'Shally, I tell you our subjection in our own country will keep us nailed. We will not breathe sigh of relief unless this nail gets off.' Salim Khan talked in suppressed rage. Rabbani noticed that his master was timid and feeling impotent, 'I wish I had not been born! Only that I had dissolved into ether! I do not know when this Gandhi tempest would really uproot the *firangees.*' Salim Khan talked not loudly. His eyes were wet with tears. His lips were quavering in suppressed rage, 'Ah Gandhi will save us, yes Gandhi and his great movement will deluge these *firangees.*' But he was not still provoked for action. He looked helpless.

Shally became excited. She joined him in his helplessness. In her the channel route to dreaming got open, 'God give us passage to the relief. God hold our hand and take us to the door of heaven! Come my prince of dream, come my Remhania boy and take us ride on your steed to exit. I need the ride. I hanker for it. I am bleeding.' Shally Khan turned wild:

'Exit, an escape, a relief outlet

We are on the plundering horror inlet

Catch us by the hand dear prince of dream

Hurl us on the war-steed to plunge out of this thickened realm

I am suffocating

I am sinking

Freedom from the *firangees*, yes exit from their clutch

God pick us! Throw us somehow out from the wretch.'

Salim Khan was taken aback. He had never before heard her rave like that. He was face to face with a desperate Shall, 'How you think your prince of dream would pull you out of the wretch. What supernatural powers it wields!'

Salim Bahadur heard her explain, 'Sir Bahadur ji whenever I am upset, I turn to my dream boy. He does not descend from the clouds but he gets connected. He becomes my pain reliever. He serves me the key to my version of heaven of freedom. He becomes my Bonga, the silly savior! It is the same as your Rehana is your Bonga.' Shally became overwhelmed with her poetic falsity.

'Shut up lady. Get out of this false lock up. I cannot get to what you mean.' He gave a big jerk to her. The jerk was crude. It ached her bones. She came to senses. She was crying, crying profusely, 'Sorry,' said she and clinging to his arms she pined to get excused, 'Sorry my Lord. It was a nervous breakdown. It happens when somebody craves to pursue his heaven of freedom in his own grammar. I am feeling baffled. I do not think that the Gandhi elements in the villagers are really operational. I will tell the truth that you are not primary to me. I am also not primary to you. Your first love is Rehana. Rehana your first wife. She is your Bonga, the scary reliever! I am not ashamed to admit this. I am in the agony of loss.' Shally was vague.

'Dear my lady, do not club your private agony with the national one. You are not qualified for any judicial sentencing. The nation is taking turns and will be turning and turning without your help and cramped agony. Our Gandhi, the lone man is not lonely in his struggle. Behind him is the entire Hindustan. We shall have our freedom.'

Salim Khan was correct, 'I confess I am not out to contribute to Gandhi struggle. I admit I am wavering but my heart is with Gandhi.' Salim Khan vented his suppressed anger against the English and looked stupid to Rabbani.

Rabbani doubted his master. Rabbani Shadman wished his master really took guts to talk against the pink-face, 'Our Gandhi alone is truthful. All else, these villagers and Salim ji and his lady fantasy are jokers in the circus arena. I fail to portray them. I only hate them.'

* * * * *

Salim Khan reverted to his normal state. He remembered the words of summons from Martin. He was as if battered. In him his indwelling awe of the Angrez mounted high. He looked upon himself not as a victim of humiliation but as a supplicating serf, 'I have never dared to stand defiant before the red-face Martin. Yes, I dread to face him, this Martin whose blue eyes seem to swallow me.' He failed to give right expression to his disgust of Martin. He admitted that he was too weak for any dignified rebuttal, 'I know I cannot openly dispute Martin. I know I cannot stand before him and say that I hate him and his government.' Salim Khan wished that the Gandhi tempest should really mount and upturn the Crown. He bowed his head in shame. He did not curse him but felt outraged.

Shally Khan whispered, 'Sir *saheb* the only glitter of hope in this critical time, I guess is Sophie Juliet. You should approach her. She might be of some help. I have heard of her from Reshma. She values the Hindustanis. Every English by breed is not nefarious. Sophie mam may be of some help in the crisis.'

'Do you really hope this lady Juliet would be helpful?' cried Salim Khan

'Yes, it is likely. *After all she is an English and an English alone can be an antidote to an English.' Her words solaced Salim Khan.*

'Poison antidotes the poison

The English alone is hoped antidoting the English

We Indians have no more the outlet but via this hope

Even the Gandhi motion receives the outlet at the English slope.'

* * * * *

The ride to Martin Bungalow was hard as the horse was giving a bumpy ride. It was running against the will on the road to the Bungalow carrying Khan Bahadur to meet the hostile Martin face to face. Khan Bahadur was agitated. On his face the lines of agitation had cut extra furrows. He was cowering and reverting to defiance, 'I will show my anger. No body can dictate me. Freedom awaits us, freedom from this half -life. Our Gandhi will be our savior. I admit I had never been vocal but now onward I shall pounce upon him.' Salim Khan cleared his throat. He cleared it so harshly that his throat began to hurt. The hot sun was dancing overhead. The strong sun beam had baked his skin and he was sweating, 'Sir *saheb* do you want to use my towel?' it was an offer from Rabbani. The Khan wiped his sweats along with the tears, tears of frustration, 'Rabbani do you think we shall get freedom someday? Will our Gandhi turn the clouds of bliss and pour bliss? I am getting desperate. This Martin thing has stolen my peace.'

The coachman divulged his scholarship in terms of what facts and myths he had. He said that the struggles on different fronts would someday pave way, 'We can hope sir, hope and trust for the shedding of the shackles.'

The Khan adjusted his turban. He made a fist. He punched the air. He was building guts to meet Martin. 'Okey. Okey,' he said to himself, 'I will somehow meet the leady Sophie. I have heard of her soft corners for us. I have heard Reshma talking of her half-Indianness. I can understand that all English race is not the same. This lady Sophie is different. She has sympathy and space for justice.' Salim Khan flung his hands to an imaginary ghost of Martin. He caught the airy figure of the Martin by the neck. He felt like throttling the Martin's neck. He saw Gandhi overtaking him. He was grappling with that Gandhi, 'I know Gandhi sir that in your dictionary of struggles violence is prohibited. But I tell you that your method is inverting the inner violence inside. Your passive resistance someday, it will burst out violently. Someday it will blast.'

* * * * *

In some distance the Martin Dera appeared like a white devil. Its wings flanked wide it was standing like a giant solitary structure.

Martin had connivance of the superiors in handling the natives by foul means. He was the English of the time holding the forelock of time in his hand. He was given to battering the Indians as per his choice, 'Well Mr. Khan,' Martin addressed him rudely, 'Your estate Chandrapura has been reported to create nuisance. The village folks were instrumental in framing a rebel gang. They marched with hostile intention upon the Martin Bungalow. Worst still they instigated my Sophie to participate in the fray. I am reported that the Bonga Tigers have been killed. It is a serious legal matter.' Martin smiled ruthlessly, 'The killing of the Bonga things you know can be reported as poaching of the wild animal. It is against the law' Martin stopped and waited. He laughed mischievously.

'Killing of the Bongas, you know who was behind it? Killing of the poor cats, world knows was no poaching.' Mr. Khan answered toughly.

'Then what? I can transcript it as a poaching.' Martin laughed triumphantly. In him his devil was in full swing, 'Mr. so-so if you want to save your tenants, I shall have you reporting with a few names. This will save the entire village from a mass punitive action.' Mr. Martin had occupied his chair and was waiting for instant answer.

Mr. Khan who had been disgusted about injustice of Martin was completely bewildered. He became speechless. His mouth opened only after he had swallowed panic half, 'Sir Martin *saheb* but will it not be un-fair to bring the poaching charges upon the villagers?' this was a direct confrontation. Martin repulsed it saying something to the effect that he was no judge in the court of the laws, 'I am a plain fellow as plain as I should be and my way of administering justice hardly gets influenced by the court of law. Legal and not legal is not my concern. My concern is to make the frontliner baffled. Your village has committed the daring. They must taste justice.'

Martin signaled the Khan to take a seat beside him and with the gesture of his baton he said that the deal had to be finalized, either the whole village or a few rowdy ones!

Mr. Khan felt defeated. He knew that the order of Martin was the final one. He did not answer the opponent instantly.

* * * * *

A few sepoys came inside. They were carrying message of surprise on their faces. Martin turned to them. They were uncertain as to how to address their master. They were going to deliver a bad piece of news, 'Sir some of the detainees Ram Lal, Nirja and two ladies have been resisting and questioning.'

'Questioning what?' shouted Martin in a thunder. His words cracked upon the walls, 'Yes *hozoor,* my lord. There Ram Lal is the loudest. He talks of principle and legality. He has even resisted the had cuffs.'

Salim Khan was standing petrified. He knew the outcomes. He pitied for the foolish Ram Lal. He had no idea of his drunken state. He thought that he was under the spell of Gandhi, 'Poor guy he will meet severer treatment.' Salim Khan did not have guts to intervene.

Martin took his gun, loaded it and came out. The scene constructed a scene of hunting. Before Martin, Ram Lal, Nirja Thakur and Sarita were literally lying hand cuffed on the ground. Only Laxmi and a throng of the defiant villagers were standing aside waiting for the consequences.

The sky overhead was unkind, so was unkind the wind blowing strongly to upset dust. Martin had aimed his gun at the culprits. The culprits were as they were, ugly and cowardly and demeaned. They were lying hand-cuffed their ogling eyes staring blankly into the sky. Nirja

Thakur was looking miserable more due to the iron-cuff cutting his flesh than the pain of consequences.

The distant Buddha banyan seemed tormented. The hanging serpents of the pop-roots wriggled. A howling sound reverberated through the jungle. Martin was taken aback. Salim Bahadur took guts to wish the weird happen in bigger proportion.

Then a voice of defiance overtook Martin. It was the voice of his lady coming from behind. The voice carried thunder in it. Sophia Juliet was there. She was set afire, a mystery and a reality mixed in one, 'Stop this timid rumbling of order. Jut refrain Mr. Martin from your brave decrees.' She literally snatched his gun from his hand. In her hand the weapon was trembling in utter nervous rage. Sophie was the Sophia Begum, 'You have no cause to implicate the poor villagers.' She was panting with passion. On her face pity and rage coupled together, 'Martin, I demand you on what charges these fellows have been put under cuffs?'

Martin was baffled. His lady had overwhelmed him. Salim Khan was in the midst of the scene a cowering entity. He had expected something reasonable from her but never something so breath-taking. Sophie had captured the scene and was waiting for dialogues to zoom and boom. But Mr. Martin was absolutely speechless.

Sophie undertook the charge to get the detainees released. Ram Lal, Nirja Thakur, Sarita and others bowed their necks to her and turned to retreat. The Bonga bodies in the background were ready to be picked and dispatched.

Martin suddenly ordered the hands to cease to touch the Bongas, 'No Bongas to be taken away.' He ordered. His order fell like thunder bolt on the villagers. The Bongas were left un-touched, 'Decision about the killing of the Bongas is still pending.' Martin sounded unfair.

Salim Khan suddenly got electrified, 'What decisions on the Bongas? These have been downed by your gun.' Salim Khan shouted at Mr. Martin.

'Stop there. Yes, my gun downed the Bongas but the charge of it will shift. It will shift to the villagers. I have told they will be charged of poaching.' Mr. Martin declared his mind.

Sophie Juliet undertook to defend the innocent villagers. She jumped into the fray, 'No way injustice! *I will give my witness as to the killing of the cats. The cats were killed by Mr. Martin.*' Her words baffled the forester.

The Budha banyan tree looked relaxed. Its serpent pop-roots returned to the former state. The howling of the jungle subsided. There was a victory of the Bongas in a shaded term.

* * * * *

Mr. Martin withdrew. He heavily walked out of the scene. Mrs. Juliet Martin was left among the outsiders too stunned for her blatant support to cheer her. The villagers retreated with the Bongas. This was a retreat of a crowd that had won and lost nothing substantial but they were convinced that in their fight for right they were being supported by an English lady, 'We never thought that such an angel *devi* existed there. She is our living Bonga.' Ram Lal wanted to touch her feet. Sarita and Laxmi tried it. Nirja Thakur stopped them.

Sophia deserved the reverence, 'Freedom, freedom in any shape and size, intensity and gravity if and when it is obtained for somebody it becomes a signal achievement. I endorse it,' said she, 'I was there to pick it for them. These poor guys might have been thrown into jails but I could save them. It is justice on my part and it was injustice on Martin's part. The poor fellow Martin I know will live in pain that I did not support him despite myself being one of his ethnic kins.'

Julee Martin felt like being re-cast as Sophia Julee. She heard a commotion inside. She heard it celebrating at the gate of the freedom of heaven. She should have felt great but she did not. She should have puffed up her chest but she did not. In her was no pride. She was feeling humble and weak and was recalling scene in her Ranchi College days when the Indian students seemed to avoid her because of her ethnicity. She would then feel slashed. She would then slide to her friend Shilpa and Madhuri. She had since long forgotten their real names and faces and was feeling eager to repair the memory, 'I was alien to my Ranchi College friends. I am alien to these villagers. I am not tagged to my husband. I am an unbelonging persona, a thing without images. Am not I, a distributed burden on earth?' She mused sadly but did not feel disappointed.

She was becoming unsure of herself and vividly recalling the words of warning from Martin that she would not be able to leap across the walls of alienation, 'Am I an outsider? Can I break this slash? Will these Saritas and Laxmis and Nirjas ever, ever take me into their folds?' these questions surfaced and fell out. She smiled and said that she saved the lives of the innocent villagers, 'I did my duty as the ethics upholds. This is my reward. I should not expect any verbal gratitude.' Sohie touched her caressing on her arms and felt that she was fair more in complexion than in deeds.

* * * * *

CHAPTER 9

SCALES FALLING OFF

At Sophie's performance Martin had not quit Sophie. He did not turn her off his orbit because he needed her company. He needed to stay tagged to her because in India she alone belonged, 'Foolish lady, misguided and un-fated. She will have the returns in slaps,' he shouted. Then solaced, 'She will learn to open her eyes and see that she was misguided. Sarita and Laxmi and Nirja and Ram Lal all these stuffs would someday ditch her. She will have the bitter lessons for trusting the alien ones.'

Martin was drawn from her. Scale was falling off. His allegiances to her were thinning. She was being pushed to the reverse side. He as a man was still gentle but beneath the gentleness was the absent attachment. He was ever available around her like a doctor to the patient. His horizon had declined covering her. He was caring enough sans the cares. He would seek her at bed time and not ever touching her he would pass the night listlessly. At the dining table he served her extra slices of toast and poured into her cup tea that was too hot. He had become a divided man, compartmentalized to the precision. She was left this side of the space and left virtually alone, 'Martin do not you think you have shrunk away? Do you feel that a slash has been drawn? Is it not hyphenated life that I am living with you?' Sophie Martin asked once and no words of consolation came from him. He smiled meaningfully and offered her overspilling glass of *sherbat.*

She again one night catching him asked the same question, 'Do not you seem drifting away from me? Am I not falling off your circuit?'

Martin heard her complaints like the doctor hears the patient. He was a neighborly husband to her but not dangerous as he still had a will to keep watching her. He asked her grievously as to why she had supported the villagers. In answer she said, 'She did not mean to gain applaud. She did not want to come to limelight. She saved the villagers only as a true Christian saving the bereaved. Do not you know that the villagers were innocent of the tigers' killing? Had not you finished those Bongas? Did not you falsely charge the rustics with poaching?' She talked softly.

* * * * *

Ever since Martin hid his face from her. He was carrying the sting of compunction. But he was not corrigible. Whatever he did fitted his understanding of reaching the heaven of freedom, 'I did it to save me and to ensure that the villagers were intimidated. This was designed to make me feel secured. I could not permit the villagers to make their will overlap mine.' He sounded vague.

Sophie did not argue with him. She knew he was wrong. She also knew that as an English he was bound to commit only wrongs to prove himself right, 'The Christian sense of justice and goodness you lack my great sir.' She sighed as she served him a cup of hot coffee. Martin sipped the coffee and looked away from her seeming to confess figuratively that he was wrong. But he dreaded admitting it, 'My limitations Mrs. Martin! My limitations are too human. I belong to the ruling party. I have to execute justice and injustice in the same tone. I cannot be always fair for fairness's sake and get myself into troubles.' He lit the pipe and dragged a huge puff of smoke inside.

Julee was as she was. She had not been ejected by Martin. She did not give a thought to it. She knew he more than loving her actually honored her. The honor of her in his heart was built from his conviction that she belonged to him and that he was bound to protect her. She felt pity for Martin. She felt like dragging him into his bosom and kiss him. But she refrained from this passionate act, 'I will stand by him, stand by despite the difference of opinion. He is mine and I am happy that he honors me. I also honor him. My Martin is honorable because he is just to me. O that he had been equally just to the Indians!'

Julee had acclimatized herself to the new-fangled set up. She refrained from bothering him with questions and was growing more and more comfortable with her new climate assuring that she was on the right path and that he was unfit to relocate himself as per his convictions, 'He is what he is, rigid and principled enough simply supporting the Crown. *To him his approaches to the meaning of freedom lies in declining freedom to others. I am contrary to him. I am clearly a denizen of the god's wonder land where freedom is not restriction to others. I am mad at applauding conditions where every trifle element has the access to freedom in its own way. I* love freedom as the breath.'

One morning when the sun was on its pace shining and rising and the sky was high and lofty and nothing unusual was there to intervene their progress she said to herself, 'Like the nature enjoying freedom of mobility I too crave the same freedom for human beings.' Her line of thought was cut as she saw a few birds marking the flight in the open sky in different wave lengths, 'Birds can fly in their marked wave lengths. Even such a trifling worm and caterpillar would follow their own locomotive pattern. No restriction on the flow of wind, no check on the rippling passage of the streams, then why punches and pushes to human will?' Her debate reached no crescendo. She had an urge to pee. She ran into the bathroom. There in the unhindered quite of the wash room she imagined herself hand cuffed and dragged to the jail. This was a harrowing fantasy giving her full meaning of torments, 'I can experience the imagined horror of pain and humiliation. But what of those Indians who have been suffering it in daily routine?'

She became excited. She danced in the little space of the washroom. Her dance steps followed no dance codes. She freed herself from the determining codes. It was rebellious but comforting. She felt she had been ticketed for the journey to heaven, 'My heaven of freedom earmarks no demands and audacity. It craves for a straightforward outlet to naturalness. That is all.'

* * * * *

For several days Julee and Martin never came face to face with their respective clashes of principle and for more days to follow they remained as distant and neighborly as made them one day abashed, 'Are we on the travel in the same bogey like two strangers?' asked Martin then Julee sharing a slice of toast asked him to sit beside her. He obeyed. Then she took his hand in hers and pressing it with love she said if he was not going to review his approaches to the genre of freedom. He said with the same care that he was bound by principle to his duty and that he was not ready to breach his principle. She did not insist on his changing his mind and no wonder he too did not force her to change hers, '*We are typical. By blood and culture of the same ethnicity but by mind contrary. You are Un-English and my Englishness is not to allow alloying.*'

Martin laughed till his eyes became wet. He was not a very handsome fellow by English standard but on that occasion he looked handsome. She felt like caressing him on the cheek and ask again if it was not possible for him to review his approaches. She asked him, 'Dear Mart,' she began with hope to hear from him something positive, 'Are we too rigid to relent to the visibly ethical issue of sympathy, care, concession and a little compassion? The locals need our care and compassion.' She finished her line. Martin caressed her on the cheeks, 'But they are alien, the total outsiders. We are not their own. Whatever care and compassion we impart but they will answer like cobras only. Mark dear Ju that they will bite us when we get weak. The foreigners cannot accept the foreigners. Your illusion of half-Indianness will get you nowhere.' Juliet unheard him.

* * * * *

Reshma appeared with a tray of coffee and snacks. It was un-warranted. Reshma was looking morose, from her appeals poured like gentle rain. She was not wording the appeals but was appealing thoroughly. Reshma was appealing for the villagers to free from the charges of poaching. The maid placed the tray on the table and waited for orders, 'Okey your Nirja and Ram Lal and Sarita will be released,' said Sophia with authority. She had worn the face of the Bongas, the saviors. She had worn the face of Gandhi she had adored so long. She became a new definition of liberty seeking.

She was gyrating on the axis of air. Her legs had become dreams, dreams un-bound by words. She herself had become a fantasy, humble and wide but reassuring enough. Reshma had been sided aside to the fences of life. She had been shunted. Then Sophie struggled to demystify herself, give herself name and a local denomination. She failed to reconstruct her mental and emotional symmetry. It was a state of ennui that she fell into but this made her not lost, only happily reassured, 'Sophie,' she addressed to herself, 'Sophie dear you are now no more Sophie. You are Sophia, the second-half of my Indian self. I am blessed. I am glad. I have discovered myself in this medley circus of life and am going to realize meaning.' She did not say more as she saw the words were failing to mean, 'Yes words get constricting on imagination. I want to get freed of constrictions. I want to get going shoo, turn a vacuum, a void minus void and belong to the poetry of being.'

'Torn not at all, torn and wasted

I am not hustled to be hated

If not fully but definitely with some slant recline to the truth

I am the Sophia of the Sophie cute

And this too is my achievement

This is the reward, un-begging rewards true

I am happy, fulfilled and dew

My *Sophia self* is the savior of *the Sophie self*.'

The lady found herself released from her Sophie contents. It was like un-cocooning of the larva. It was like the clouds of the moon-lit nights had suddenly scattered. Sophie had no words to intervene to explain her rapture. She was lifted away. She spread her limbs and rotated on her heels. The gyring intensity reached a mad frenzy. She was looking like a menagerie outside the glass case. She was behaving not like any mechanical doll. She had widened her limbs seeking to catch the winds. The whirling of the lady reached the madding crescendo till her head began to reel and she was thrown out of the gyring circuit. She tumbled and lay scattered on the lawn. Reshma spotted her in the fall. But Reshma had been shunted. She would not miss-venture into action. Reshma stood silhouetted, looking bewildered. Sophia had won the powers to constrict her beyond circumference. She was out of her hyphenated life to the one that linked her to freedom.

Reshma wanted to rescue Sophie mam. She rushed to help her madam free from the ethereal frenzy. Reshma brought a glass of water. She tumbled in a hurry. She hurt her toes. But she never feeling pain and though bleeding she wanted to salvage her mam from the frenzy, 'Mam please take water.' Reshma tumbled again this time right over Sophie wetting her through, 'Mam, take it. Water!' The glass was empty.

Sophia took the glass, tumbled it aside and with tears in her eyes she cried, 'Reshma, I have got it, got the clue to freedom. I can see the path to freedom leading via the channel called Khan Salim, your Bahadur Khan. He has a slew of his Chandrapura people behind, Sarita and Laxmi and Nirja and Ral Lal and others. They are timid but they carry a fire. I have seen the fire in them to get freed. I have had them behind me in the Bonga hunting. They are the weak winds! They would get the direction when gathered together. This Bahadur Khan would gather them.'

Reshma could not elicit the full meaning of Sophie's wordings. The maid clung to the flimsiest side of the reference, 'But there on way is sitting his wedded wife, Shally mam.'

'I know,' shouted Sophia, 'I know for sure that Shally Mam is the legitimate holding. I am not going to dispossess her, steal her man. I am no home breaker.' Reshma held peace. She heard Sophia, 'Reshma, I am not going to infringe upon her right. I will just borrow your Khan's support and influence.'

Sophie became excited. Inside her odd tides began to ramble. She whispered to herself that she would raise spirits in Mr. Khan. She did not explain it to Reshma. Reshma was looking concerned about the sweating profusion of the lady. She offered her to shift to her room, 'I will massage your body. You look tired.' Her feelings had no match with the unrestful emotions of Sophie. Sophie sought for a glass of water. Reshma brought it this time carefully lest it should sprinkle, 'Reshma how do you feel in your heart about your independence?' Sophie made this question to get seconded on the need for freedom. But Reshma was too illiterate for satisfactory answer, 'Independence! I have been hearing it being flung in slogans. Our great Gandhi has been flinging this term like dreams. But I do not know well what creature it is. I have never tried to know it.' Reshma became exhausted in the mind. Sophie pitied Reshma that she was unlettered about independence.

'Then do not you feel like you carry a load of chains, something that weighs your soul?' Sophie was talking in wild frenzy, 'Do not you feel like un-shedding the weight, breaking the chains and coming out of the grills?'

Sophie was talking idealistically. Reshma was not born to evaluate things in idealistic measures. Reshma then took up this issue with some care, 'Madam ji independence of what we hear Gandhi ji talking. I have also heard Ram Lal talking it when he is boozy. I have not understood its relevance. I do not have any taste of what new it will bring.' Reshma sounded dull. Sophie wanted to hear something alive from Reshma. But Reshma was rustic enough not to inculcate the right spirit into it. She was disappointed then she turned to herself whispering, 'The years of bondage in Reshma has erased in her the will to be the winged one.' Sophie was poetic and foolish, 'I can understand that I cannot infuse the feel of freedom in a subject long enthralled.'

She then asked Reshma to leave her alone. Sophie wanted to be alone and write a letter to Bahadur Khan who had fascinated her, 'This Khan has a slew of the rustic horde of people behind him. He may become useful in my mission.' She shuddered at the quickness of her plannings. Before her eyes came a full view of her army of rebels surging about against the Crown, '*Enough of the Crown throttling the spirits and bodies of the Indians. Now I think these bondages should snap.*'

She made a clear story in the mind. Sophie Juliet was then sighing and imagining and the more she entered the core of her will the more she felt she was thrilled, 'I will raise a parallel army of the rustics. I will take

Khan Bahadur to operate the mission. I will see that my Martin does not get too much hostile. I will not fight the battle of principle on the code of a battle. I will try to influence the existing battle. This Gandhi initiative I would subsidize. I would not create nuisance in ugly shapes. My mission will be symbolic not aggressive!' Sophie Juliet felt safe within and yet happy that she would contribute to the general motion of the Indian independence. She drafted a letter for Salim Khan.

'Dear Khan! I am going to address you as a friend and if you really find me worth friendship, I would like to initiate the letter with the admission that I am half-Indian and half-English. My half-ness is a cruel dilemma. I feel obliged to obey it. Born from English seeds I was brought up in Indian soil. My father was an Indian doctor serving in rural India. He had no loathing for wherever he used to be posted in the remote areas. He was typically tolerant of heat, squalor, noise and poverty of India and would love to eliminate his Englishness. I was his favorite and copied his ways. In my childhood days I used to live free of the sense of discrimination. I never had thought that I was an outsider. I experienced it only in my Ranchi College, a grand college in academics but a vaguely bad one in terms of assimilation of the foreigners. I was the only English girl whom my friends treated with care, extra care lest I should be offended. I remember my friends Malti and Sulekha and those whose names I have forgotten. These guys looked disturbed signally each other to silence when they happened to cluster together and discussed politics. I was ousted in this chit-chat. I knew why. But I would not bother them to include as I thought it was contrary to norms. I am confessing the situation to bring home to you that I was half-Indian but not treated as an Indian. Was it not unjust? Was not I paid undue of what I meant to get paid?'

'Well coming to the point, I would here mention that my half-Indianness is prompting me to address you. I have the awareness that the colonial power is waning and that your side of people are getting desperate to enter their heaven of freedom. I do not think I would be much help but I believe if you come forward you can influence the freedom struggle'.

'I have the understanding that you sufficiently control a huge tenancy. You can manage to activate a combined force of your peasantry in your feudal domain to influence the freedom struggle. I plainly want to offer my support to you. I can come forth with a positive vibe to steer the necessary local pressure. I think you are able to comprehend it.'

'In lump sum I want to organize a revolutionary body to influence freedom movement on local level'.

'This letter I am writing to make you convinced of my innocent desires and make you feel that I am not an adversary.'

'Khan Sahib, I want to run a parallel independence squad. I want in a plain word your co-operation. You are in command of a huge slew of your people in Chandrapura. You can activate and organize these heads. We can together create lots of pressures.' She signed the letter and left it on the table suffering pressures of confusion and apprehensions and this continued till she suddenly crumpled the letter and would have torn it but for an inner voice that asked her to check herself, 'No I should not act like a cowardly one. I have been a part of India. My duty unto India calls me.' She was enthused to get forth and declare a revolt. But then she vividly recalled the warning of her Martin that she was a foreigner and that she would be ditched sometimes, 'Yes, I have experienced this in the Bonga time. These Sarita and Nirja and Laxmi and others had gradually thinned away and I was left exposed to Martin. This is strange but true that my Martin is not a crude fellow. He did not treat with me roughly. He only warned me and shared his apprehensions and shared the feelings that he would be made lonely if ever he missed me.'

* * * * *

The letter from Julee Sophia was delivered to Khan Bahadur via Rabbani, the un-trustable fellow who by way of curiosity replete with hostility leaked the secret to Reshma and the latter a gossiper soon had told of it to Shally Madam, 'Then the letter really it was written by Sophia lady?' shouted Shally controlling her anger. Then she sighed hugely and feeling strangely relaxed and weak and strangely sad without resentments she said to Reshma, 'We human beings are strange creatures not ever stable. We languish to hover about and reach other's court. I too am this wanderer. I too am adrift to my silly prince charming of the cloud world. I am betraying in the same term as my Khan is doing.'

Shally was not upset. She was typically a lady without jealousy. Reshma felt like drawing her mam's attention to the possible hob-nobbing of Sophie and Salim khan, 'It is a matter of concern definitely,' said Shally, 'It would not affect me. I am a lady of different mental makeup. I do not want to draw cordons. If really my man gets shifting to Sophia then it is my luck! I am not an ordinary lady of foolish doubts and possessive overture. I do not like my Khan. He is a wavering character. I pity him. He is known to have been pining for his Ruksana Begum, his first wife. I have forgotten her name and have never bothered to relocate her and get me tormented.'

Reshma sat beside her hearing her madam talking calmly of the possible drift of the Khan, 'But mam you should somehow steal the letter and read through its contents.' Reshma had expected the letter to be sounding like Juliet's sob, 'Okay. I will not steal the letter,' said Shally Khan, 'I will directly demand it from him. I know, he is not a dubious fellow. He will comply.'

The matter was soon held up as Reshma spotted the Khan in the vicinity, 'Your Khan sir,' said Reshma, 'He looks excited. He is carrying the pink of the romance on his face. You can check if this pink on his face is the outcome of the Juliet effects from the letter. It is high time you took moves to intercept him.'

Reshma was abetting Shally. But Shally Jaan ignored Reshma. She did not get biased of her man. She suddenly felt a lot of relief. She got the relief of the version nobody on earth had been sanctioned. In her mind no antagonism was activated. Shally smiled and patting on the back of Reshma asked the latter to move out to the famous peepal tree, 'Sit under this Buddha tree. Sit here with me and suck the sober air and get refreshed. Think that you are watching on the screen of life a rare drama of dream and fulfilment. Do not divert and get prejudiced.'

Shally was talking in a trance. The trance was hardly in matching with the trance she had had earlier in realizing the importance of dream and fulfilment. Reshma tried to pull her out of the waking trance, 'Madam ji you are typical of a creature woman unlike your species that instead of getting upset you are casting a shell of relief around you. I want to tell that our Khan Bahadur would slip out of your premises. I want to predict this mishap. But you are ignoring the destined.'

Shally Khan laughed and seeking the sky overhead to turn exclusive she said that she was celebrating the transference of wish fulfilment, 'My man when he gets overtaken by his chosen Sophia it would be like myself being overtaken by my quixotic prince charming. I do not know how to elucidate the matter. I do not at all feel equipped to address to my relief and congestion. I only know that theoretically he is gone and he deserves being appreciated.'

* * * * *

In the branches of the peepal tree, she saw a swarm of black birds chirping. The congregation of the birds had no relevance in her story but it was giving her strength of belonging to herself, 'I will allow him to take a slip. I will not object. I will check to see that I am not depressed. I want to be no hurdles to him.' Shally spread herself on the ground under the peepal tree and strongly wished the adjoining surroundings to co-operate her in maintaining her sacrificial gestures. She felt like a martyr. She began to hum her favorite *gazal* from her memory. She missed the actual lines but she could add much of melancholic strains. She confirmed to herself that she was not betrayed and sinned against.

She confirmed herself that she belonged devoting to a version of freedom of choice, 'My heaven of freedom to anybody does not imply restraints, jealousy and choking of the spirit. If really my Khan wants to take a departure from me, I will not feel bereaved. My dream prince will salvage me.'

* * * * *

The letter in the pocket of Salim was growing weighty as per its contents as the Khan was absolutely misfit for the proposed turbulence Sophie cherished. He had read through the lines repeatedly and the more he had exerted his mind to catch meaning and ignite the mind the more he became horrified as regard the consequences. Salim Khan said to himself that he was a man of practical vision, 'I am not a stupid revolutionary. My problem is that I do not want to take risk. I am afraid, plainly afraid of entering the wrong lane. I am comfortable with my status quo. I am no more a man daring to invite troubles. I know nothing very particular is to be achieved if I jumped into any valid battles to accelerate the freedom. Already the agencies are working and things are happening in a positive tune. My thrust would not do any additional wonder. I am afraid, afraid of consequences and I do not feel that I am fit to take risk.'

Salim Khan visioned the torture of those fighters in jails who had been instrumental in keeping the freedom struggle ignited in their respective way, 'I tell myself every individual is not likely to gain a profitable and prominent position due to his action. I also admit that life's system does not remain bereft of the supports and pushes in the lack of one not being really useful. I am not that version of a useful element. I am a subsidiary character never capable of playing the main protagonist. I am an extra in the story of freedom struggle.' Salim Khan did not appreciate the line of rebellion Sophia was trying to place him on.

The letter in his pocket was getting weighty. He felt like his existence was under the load of the letter. He recalled the slip of the boulder from the mountain that had to take a tug at the base to evade damage. He recalled the scene of the Bonga hunting in which Sophie was involved and she was reported to have returned injured. He recalled his position as the zamindar of Chandrapura and recalled he had had no troubles in holding his dominion. Salim Khan said to himself that he was a practical man and to him the advent of independence was not a subject demanding his intervention. He said, 'I have been okey with the English and have had no hostility from their side and the most overwhelming truth is that freedom would come without my intervention as well. There are others taking care of it. I am not awaited to add to its momentum.'

Salim Khan smashed the letter, rolled it into a ball and would have flung it out of his life but for the honor he felt for Sophie, 'This Sophie thing, I wonder she is really martyring her passion for the realization of our independence,' He repeated the phrase '*our independence*' several times, 'Yes this will be '*our independence*', our heaven of freedom. She is a foreigner and will remain a foreigner.' Salim Khan then felt guilty. He felt guilty of uttering the most ungrateful line, 'Sorry Sophie Juliet, sorry Sophia mam I am not ungrateful. I am a practical man to think practically and conclude practically. To me getting idealistic is an idiocy in summary.'

He imagined his position as the zamindar and his influences on his tenants and discovered to his horror that he had never been remarkable to them. He also reviewed his tendencies vis a vis his affairs in his zamindari and came to realize that he had been an uninvolving creature, 'Even when these rustics were out to salvage their Bongas I had been nowhere in the scene. Of course, I had tried to dissuade Mr. Martin from the hunting but when he proceeded ahead with his plan, I did not create any nuisance. I am a man of peace, a good for nothing fellow to be most critical.'

Salim Khan took out the letter and read it twice, 'Sorry Sophie madam, very sorry that I am not going to spur my men and get them into trouble.' He became clear. His position vis a vis the story that Sophie was on way to start was humbly grilled to the naught.' He sighed a breath of relief and not feeling unheroic he said that he was not made for creating fire and making combustion.

* * * * *

Shally Khan appeared from somewhere. Her appearance was not of any momentous nuances. She came straight to her man, as straight as was due and not behaving like a detective she asked him to put off his overcoat, 'Your overcoat. I think it is getting too hot. You are sweating. Your overcoat you can put it off.'

The man hesitated. His hesitation was referential to his guilty sense. He did not dissuade but he felt like resisting. She said that he would not un-wear the coat. He knew the letter was in the coat pocket, 'No problem, madam. I am comfortable with it.' He literally clung to his coat. But the lady determined not to expose him with the sinful letter said calmly that she wanted the coat, 'I want it to brush it. It has gone dirty.' She knew that it was not dirty and he knew that it was not dirty but she was insisting on his un-wearing it, 'No problem, madam. I am comfortable with it.' repeated the fellow man. She un-heard him and thrusting her hand into the left-side pocket she seized the chit of paper. She threw it like a waste on the ground. She then picked it apologizing that it might be some important paper, 'Sorry sir. I un-intentionally threw your chit.' She picked it and opening it she handed it over to him. By this time, he became bold, bold enough to talk of the letter and its contents and the lady stood transfixed to hear the narrative, 'You know this Sophia mam is boiling. She seeks me to join her hot-pot! She has proposed to gather my foolish tenants and form a gang of the howlers. It is dangerous and risky. I know what consequences it would bring.'

Salim Bahadur handed over the chit to Shally and asking her to guide him he requested her to keep the matter to her, 'You know in this sensitive time it would be dangerous to get exposed. We are not supposed to enter into the hostile camps with our masters.' His apprehensions had substances. She had never thought of the other side of the story. She was face to face with a man who was going to revert from a natural line of action to support the advent of independence, 'You mean,' she ejaculated, 'you are not going to support Sophia in this adventure. Will you decline your supports?' Her tongue slipped. She wanted to chide him, may be reprimand but she talked contrary, 'Then do not you think it is your ethical duty to support the lady on the cause that directly refers to independence.'

Shally jaan was talking excitedly. She had suddenly been overwhelmed with the past of her mother's time when after the fall of the Mughals her family had been exposed to the *firangee* tyrannies, 'The Britishers after the Sepoy Mutiny had become haunting dogs. They had cracked upon anybody and everybody suspected of mutiny. Bodies after bodies were being hanged and left hanging for days. Such a horror had blanketed the sky! I was only a little child hearing my mother narrate the tales of woes.' Shally hankered to see the British punished, 'Bahadur Khan ji this is the time to take revenge.' She recalled in sheer imagination the death of her father by the British agent. Shally recalled in vague imagination the humiliation her family was reported to suffer after the Mutiny was crashed. She wanted Salim Khan to take revenge on the British but he was too timid for any such folly.

Her man knew the possible outcome. He retorted, 'Madam you fail to evaluate the gravity of situation. We are not in a position to take revenge. We have no cause to disturb the hornet nest. You only fly in the dream clouds. This is not like trysting with a romance, a flight to your fantastic prince. The consequences may be grave. I am bound to the Crown in principle. Forming a gang of howlers against the English would be like inviting Draconian troubles. I do not have any capacity to handle them.' Salim Khan was right.

He plucked a twig from the rose plant and in sheer ignorance of the thorns he cracked it. The thorns clung to his skin. Shally noticed the bleeding but strangely cold as she became to him, she reported of staining his kurta sleeve, 'Mark your kurta sleeve will get bloody.' Her man wiping the blood from his hand did not mention the pain, 'We are caught in the situation like this.' He did not explain it.

Shally read through the letter and looking slantly at her man she said, 'You think, you should escape, run away from the duty as you have been used to. Does it not look ugly? You have been so nobly harmless all life and you will be proving it at this too.' She was not taunting but her words carried barbs. Salim Khan bowed his head in shame. He recalled stages in his life when he had been a failure to her and she had suffered it with patience. He also realized that he was a fugitive in many versions. But he preferred to remain calm hearing her like a guilty person, 'I would suggest you to un-clench your guts. I would not press you but would like you to feel pressure on your conscience to consider the words of Sophie madam. This Sophie is doing whatever in our favor.' Shally then wiped the blood stain from his skin, 'Sir *saheb* whether we escape or hide the struggle is overhead. Let us follow the Gandhi formula: non- violence. You can instruct your people to stay calm but demonstrative of rebellion.' In her mind the flurry of riot was storming her in terms of revenge upon the British for their utter wrong her family had suffered after the Mutiny was over.

She picked the twig with the thorns and examining it she said that the twig represents the Gandhian credo, 'The thorns embody the urge to get violent. But the rose reminds of passive resistance. You can at least try the latter. You should not outright withdraw. Sophia Begum should be consulted. This poor English lady is going to help for conscience's sake.'

Shally Jaan then became agitated calling her dream prince to come down. She yelled wildly wailing in ancestral throe. The pitch of her wailing gained bass by the negation of anybody hearing and caring it. The faded image of her father emerged from the womb of history calling her to wake up. Her mother Dildar Agha came in the fantasy like a tortured dream. Her entire slew of ancestors breaking out of their tombs stood before her asking her to review the Mutiny and its aftermath. Shally Jaan became a bout of question from her history in Mughal lineage. She did not know why but she was enraged and was urging her Khan Bahadur to join the proposed Sophea gang. Even the Buddha banyan hissed and roared and pestered her to act. She heard the Bongas whining and *sloganing.* She was caught in the nightmare of sort in the waking morning. But all succumbed to silence, 'I know we unknow what most torments us. This boil in my heart will sink to silence.'

The Bahadur Khan sunk down throwing his limbs and looking like a tattered scarecrow he stood before her surrendered, 'I have no guts to face the Martin fury. A whole battalion of army is behind him and I am no match to him. My redemption lies in withdrawal. My succor lies hereat in being un-involved. I cannot miss-venture. Sophea mam should not expect chivalry from me.'

* * * * *

CHAPTER 10

WILD WINDS BLOWING

The whole of Chanderpura those days had turned a land of the buzzing unrest. Sarita, Laxmi, Nirja, Ram Lal and others were angry with Martin. They had heard from one another that Gandhi had negotiated with the English administrators and the latter were quitting India. This had caused a domino effect, bringing chain reactions. Sarita had brought the news that he British were evacuating Delhi and Laxmi had brought news that the Delhi government was to come to Gandhi men and to this Nirja Thakur had endorsed on the strength of Ram Lal's information that some Nehru thing was going to sit on Delhi throne. Gobardhan had confirmed that the Nehru thing would set up his cabinet and take control of entire Hindustan, 'We are freed sir and mam and we are going to have our own Rule, the self-rule and so we will have the bridle of Hindustan in our control and we will do as we like. These pink-face enemies will return to England and our Brown people will ensure that the pink-face never return back.'

'Laxmi dear,' shouted Sarita, 'Good lady, prepare your heart to thump and bounce at will. We have had lots of orders now we shall order. We shall order these monkey-face to do this and that. We shall see the English crawl before us.' Ram Lal shouted hosana. He shouted defiance to the phantom image of any English, 'Our Gandhi, the great has liberated us and the liberty now will bring trayful of tasty food and beverage bottles and we shall sip whatever wine we fancy.' He was confused so he looked around and for support he nudged Gobardhan but the brat was looking pensive contemplating things from a different angle.

The villagers were growing rowdy, foolishly quite decontrolled as the day and the heat began to grow in volume, 'Bonga Memorial,' shouted Laxmi, 'Our great Bonga shall have the shrine on the spot of our selection. This will be the first victory and final conquest.' Laxmi waited for supporting howling of the jackals and got it in ample quantity, 'Yes, yes, we shall have our Bonga Shrine there before the Bangalow gate. We shall snatch the land from the scoundrel Martin. Our Gandhi and the freedom together grant us the right.'

Gobardhan came out of his pensive clutch, 'But Laxmi *maie* do you think this Martin will allow the shrine to stand before the Gate?'

Gobardhan left a question rolling and rumbling, 'Shut up Gobardhan, just stop your ugly mouth,' shouted Nirja, 'We are now free and are in the control of our fate.'

'Fate? Which fate?' shouted Gobardhan.

'The same fate that had been slave to the pink-face but now we have our control. We shall build the Bonga shrine there.'

Sarita, Laxmi, Nirja, Ram Lal and Gobardhan together bound themselves in a pack. The pack became a rolling ball imitating the mysterious boulder. They began to roll over the slope and this was the reconstruction of the scene of the falling boulder, 'The boulder had slipped from the mountain at the push of the Bonga. There was no human mischief. But this pack is deliberate and destructive. We have the grace of the Buddha banyan. The wriggling roots of the banyan prompt us to capture the Martin-forester and strangulate him. We shall throttle him if he hindered us. We shall have our Bonga shrine there. This will be the testimony to our emancipation. Our Gandhi's passive suffering gets deleted at all. We shall go to any extent of violence and force to get the Bonga the due.' The voice of the villagers became the voice of violence.

Nirja Thakur regretted, 'Sir ji madam,' he folded his hands, 'I seek forgiveness on behalf of the Gandhi of non-violence. I seek an urgent forgiveness here telling that the Shrine will be erected and for this any violence would be materialize. We are not the thin-bodied, spectacled Gandhis with long folded hands and voice of a patient petitioner. We are the freed denizen of the new India. This India does not fear consequences. This India does not appeal for justice. We shall have our way and the Pink-face shall not obstruct.'

The rustics had got the tongue of courage. Now to them the Bonga Jungle and the Bonga mountains and the Bonga sky were no stealth entities. They had in one collective symmetry ignited the imagination of the villagers giving them the tongues of courage. They felt they were not orphans. Behind them was the Bonga mam, their ideal lady Gandhi, 'The real Gandhi may be so and so but our Lady Gandhi is our strength. Sophia mam is our Bonga savior. She will help us in crisis.' Sarita picked a thin stick and waved it like the baton which she had seen an English surgent wielding. She felt strong and authoritative. Then Laxmi chided him. Nirja too chided him. Gobardhan leapt upon her and snatched the stick, 'Chachi, you are *ghosting* the English *saheb!* '

'Yes, I am *ghosting* the English *saheb*. Fear me. Fear Sarita and Nirja and every Indian as we have got *azadi* and will have our way. I can wield this stick even on Martin-forester. I can revert the poaching charges on him and throw him in jail.' Sarita would not throw the stick.

Nobody cared her. Nirja laughed at her. Ram Lal looked on her and imagined that she had gone unhinged, 'Has really our *azadi* made us crazy?' He asked a genuine question and pondered over it for a long time. He inferred that the sudden advent of *azadi* had really crazed him and others and that the Gandhi principles of patient suffering and the so-called passivity had diluted, 'No doubt we needed passivity as a tool then but now that we have fetched *azadi* we do not need bother about them. We have returned to our natural self: irritation, anger, reaction, intolerance and abortingof the silly baby called forgiveness.'

* * * * *

Wild winds were blowing, wild because the winds carried dust and dry leaves and would not stop. The nature had gone erratic. The sky over Chandrapura had turned dusty pink at the sun set. The Buddha banyan was swinging in a fury un-marked of fury and beyond in the horizon the recline of the sky had been obscured. It was a state of total chaos and unrest as the rustics were not ready going to their fields. They had been arrested in the apprehensions of Martin brewing any new plot. They were thankful to Sophia mam for her intervention to save them from poaching charges. But soon they were ungrateful as they thought that after *azadi* they were sure to be released even garlanded with yellow and pink flower-garlands, 'These freedom fighters anywhere in any jail will be released from the jails and honored. This I have heard from Ram Lal,' said Nirja Thakur and felt authoritative.

'Laws and rules in the new India will be revised and the British rules will be abrogated. The old rules of the British time will become old and in the new India every individual Hindustani will have his fill of *azadi* to act and perform as per his will. We shall have our wild days!' These thought in Nirja's mind germinated like weeds. He became arrogant. He became as haughty as he knew Martin was and in arrogance his blood boiled. The boiling blood made him shout slogans, '*Jai Ho! Zindabad*! Angrez quit us!' He was attacked by wild passion. He felt un-hinged. He strutted about. He strutted and fumed.

Then he felt like a cold shower of fear mounting him. He suffered cold sweats, 'Sorry I was madding!' said Nirja Thakur and to hide himself from the eyes he ran madly to the Buddha banyan, 'You are my savior Buddha. Your species somewhere had saved the real Buddha. You will save me from English rage.'

A dog barked at him. He was alarmed. The dog barked at him and receded. The dog was not a bad animal. It had recognized him and was wagging tail and its hind part, '*Sala badmash*,' Nirja swore and ignoring the supplication of the dog he said like a secret to himself that we were like the dog the supplicating creatures to the English. He soon forgot the remark and puffing his chest he walked on earth like a live martyr, 'At the advent of *azadi e*very Indian in Chandrapura and elsewhere in Delhi, Calcutta, Bombay and Madras is a live martyr, live because he has lived through the ordeals of the English tyranny. I am a live martyr despite my decades of cowardice and shame.'

* * * * *

The Martin Bangalow had become an obsession to the villagers. They could not open and close any chit-chat without reference to Martin, Sophie Juliet and their Bangalow. To them their little universe orbited round the Bangalow, an existing enigma where lived the hostile Martin along the kind Bonga lady, Sophia mam. They hated Martin. They hated the red-faced Angrez Martin because he had killed their Bongas.

Sarita, Laxmi, Nirja, Ram Lal and the whole slew of people in the village though adoring Gandhi they were ignorant of the true spirit of his principles, 'This anti-Bonga red-face, the Martin Angrez we wish the god should devour him. He is our enemy. We would rather behead him than bow our head to him.' But then Sarita laughed mischievously, 'But we have cowered all these days and do not you remember we withdrew from the protest recently? Such a demon image this Martin thing is!'

The villagers then agreed that they loved Sophie mam who despite her Angrez body was not Angrez like and had the soul of the Indian, 'Our Sophie is ours,' said Sarita to Laxmi passionately, 'She is pink-white on the face and rose like soft in the heart. Her Angrez face is hers but her heart is ours.' Laxmi said nothing particular to endorse Sarita. Sarita was not disappointed. She looked to Gobardhan to support her, 'Gobardhan do not you feel that this lady is like us?' Gobardhan mindlessly said a meaningful truth, 'But she is a foreigner, a stark *videshi*, an outsider and we do not accept anything that is not totally indigenous. She is called our Bonga but she is not. We have a strange dislike of the foreign race. Does not she look absolutely an alien in the poorly saree-clad body, pink in complexion and *gitmitting* English. I doubt if we will ever acknowledge her. We are not wont to accepting things alien.' He said further, 'In us the hesitation of inclusion is it not our mental rot? We cannot endorse her existence minus the hostility we nurture against the Angrez.' Gobardhan was talking sense via nonsense. Sarita and Laxmi heard his sense via nonsense and did not react.

The Bonga obsession of Laxmi incubated into a full-body phantom, 'Our Sophie if she were left un-polluted, she will come forth with the might of Goddess Durga, destroying whatever demons come forth,' said Laxmi. She folded her hand in reverence. She closed her eyes visioning Sophie as a holy deity. She whispered in low tone something equivalent to what she uttered in un-refined prayers. Sarita followed the gesture of Laxmi so did Nirja Thakur. All the three folded hands and closed eyes to imagine a live Bonga in the form of Sophia mam.

Gobardhan doubted the fidelity of the three. He did not say anything hard lest he should be rebuked but he repeated, 'We are not wont to accepting anything alien.' He did not say it aloud. He heard with disinterest the following overflow of the seeming lie from Nirja Thakur, 'Laxmi and Sarita have you noticed that our Sophia mam has changed not only her skirt for Gandhi khadi but she has begun to talk our Hindi. Her alien Hindi punctuated by her English makes her sound odd but she loves to utter it. She tries to look like us, talk like us, pose to be de-alienated but the poor lady she looks so very dazzling in her pink-white skin against our dusty color. Her saree is only her outer cover not her skin. She is as foreigner as she is but she is trying to stand to our side. She is reported to have been fighting like a cat with her man over issues related to us. Recently when our revered Bongas had been killed and Martin had designed a trap on us by declaring us as poachers this great Sophie had saved us from jail and persecution.'

All except Gobardhan felt further reverential to the lady and chanted, 'She is no Sophie Juliet rather Sophia Devi, a lady of the Bonga spirits maybe more relevant to us than the Gandhi Bonga. She is a goddess of pity, compassion and salvation. Our existence revolves around her, she being our planet and we only her satellites! Our real Bonga Tigers get pale in comparison.' The entire villagers began to chant the name of Sophie Juliet like some verse from the holy scripture. The chanting deepened into a crescendo of noise rising into the clouds and booming like the rumbling thunder, 'Our next and next Bonga is our Lady Sophie, the mighty savior to us whenever we would fall into troubles.' Gobardhan too joined this spree fearing being nudged but in his vague mind his words swelled and fell like the garbage bag on the sea shore.

* * * * *

Wild winds were blowing. The villagers together sat in small clusters and as the night became cold the cluster merged into each other forming a mass of the human throng singing and chanting and wishing the visit of the Bonga to them. It was impossible. It was impossible to get the

Tiger Bonga come alive. But the villagers were in a trance believing that the Bonga would return, 'We are under the Bonga effect of our Sophie Mam,' said Nirja Thakur. Sarita and Laxmi endorsed it and all together again went wild like the winds bashing and blasting about and expecting a weird beginning of guts to spur them to action.

'We shall raise the Bonga memorial, a tiny but prominent memorial to mark his death and life together.' The whole village yelled affirmatively and became ready to contribute to the raising of the memorial whatever matter and material they could gather, 'We shall all take whatever risk and danger and will construct a house of honor for our Bonga *devta*. He is our savior.'

The site selection for Bonga memorial soon became a matter of contention. Sarta, Laxmi, Nirja and every mouth in the village was open and quarreling as regard the selection of the site, size of the shrine, funding and design. They had no material resources to raise the Bonga shrine but they hoped and dreamed that they would complete the task, 'Shut up Sarita,' shouted Nirja Thakur, 'Shut up and first decide which of the three: Gandhi, Sophie or the real Bonga tigers are our Bonga?' Everybody was taken aback at this juncture. Then Ram Lal took charge to review Sophie madam as the living Bonga in the same context as she had been visioned, 'Our lady pretty, the angel of innocence and compassion, our Sophia mam is the real Bonga,' he said shaking hands with Laxmi and wishing to squeeze her body. Laxmi was bewildered at this daring but she tolerating it heard him, 'She has been fighting for us. Our savior in the time of crisis.' Ram Lal had been pushed aside with a loathing, 'We should reach her, touch her feet and seek *ashirvad,* blessings,' these were the words of Dwarika long out to Ranchi and had recently visited Chandrapura.

Laxmi glaring at Ram Lal literally out-sounded him, 'This our Sophia Bonga is the only hope to us, hope to fight her man for us and save us from hazards.' Sarita then felt like overtaking Laxmi. Sarita pushed Laxmi and hitting Ram Lal on his face without any reason then shouting hosana she voiced her in-felt regret, 'But remember we had been meanly to her. We had abandoned her in the midst of crisis during Bonga hunting. I believe this time we shall solidly stand by her.' Gobardhan jumped in uttering little swearwords and repeating his doubts, 'Only if we did not waver. I wish we remained stuck to fidelity and not cheated her. She is a foreigner and I wish we really acknowledged her as ours and not used and thrown her.'

Sarita and Laxmi and Nirja together folded hand to Gobardhan and bowed their heads to him as if he were a Bonga. Before they could have promised not to cheat her, Ram Lal diverted minds by shouting, '*Pagal,* mad are you that you are behaving like Bonga worshippers to this tiny creature? This urchin Gobardhan is talking nonsense.' All villagers endorsed Ram Lal and hands pushing Gobardhan in horror shouted at Gobardhan. The boy was baffled.

He was literally destroyed, 'Our heaven of freedom,' said Ram Lal scratching his head, 'Yes, seeking our heaven of freedom is the main matter. Gobardhan's doubts and Laxmi's slogans nothing matters more than our securing a site for the Bonga Memorial. But alas! This site seizure is a Herculean task. This Martin do you think he will agree to dispense with the plot near the gate of the Martin Dera? He is the python of that plot and we need it.' Everybody bowed his head down. It was a sign of resignation. Sarita, Laxmi and Nirja had no tongue in their mouths, 'Yes, the shrine site will have to be shifted,' Gobardhan put in. Gobardhan was angry with Ram Lal, 'Okey then we shall capture the land plot of Ram Lal for the shrine.' He taunted. Sarita and Laxmi even Nirja laughed at the joke.

Somebody said, 'We shall seek Sophie mam's help for the site selection. We have no guts to do physical fight. We have had no such culture. We are brought up submissively. Our heaven of freedom, the gate to it tugs upon Sophia Bonga. We shall reach her to cut path to it.' Ram Lal finished the dialogue.

The scene suddenly changed. Gobardhan in a dramatic way catching the loose end of Ram Lal's *dhoti* and pulling it dangerously shouted, 'Here take this Ram Ji Lal. Take our hero Ram Ji Babu. He will lead us, lead like our new Bonga to Sophie mam and place our petition.' Gobardhan laughed mischievously.

Ram Lal was shunned. He had not hoped for such a rash appointment as an emissary. He shouted defiance, 'No way myself. I am suffering from anemia.' His excuse made all laugh, 'Then no problem. We shall make you drink a bottle of fresh blood from Gobardhan,' said Nirja Thakur as he poked his hand into the pants of Gobardhan catching his little tool. Gobardhan shouted in anger. Sarita, Laxmi and others together patted on the back of Nirja ignoring the wrong he did to Gobardhan. Gobardhan pounced aside holding his thin arm, 'Why my blood? Why not from Laxmi?'

A complete chaos ensued. The matter of forwarding the petition to Sophia became a challenge, nobody getting ready to undertake it. The villagers started throwing word volleys of abuses on each other till their ears caught a thunder voice coming from the jungle side. The sound was eerie. It was like something cracking wearily. The eyes then could see a weird tremor in the body of the jungle, wind shrieking, the morning seeming to go berserk and a sudden havoc to launch. Sarita clung with Laxmi and Nirja not finding anybody clung with the tree trunk. A dread of the dark engulfed everybody except Gobardhan who as if stood invincible smiling with pride. Gobardhan had detected the source of the tremor. He shouted that the thunder was a dynamite blast in the mountain, 'Mining blast.' He said and then he waited for the next blasts.

The panic reaction of the rustics confirmed that they were too timid for any message delivery. Sarita, Laxmi, Nirja and Ram Lal felt like melting away. Inside them their inheritance of awe of the Britishers compounded with their servility made them liquified. They sneaked away from the front line leaving the rest stampede.

The matter to get the message to Sophia got hung up. Nobody undertook to carry the petition but then the gang of the fools became one body moving like a phantom mass without motion to Martin Dera. Their thick steps carried the dead mass in a surge of the winds onward. It was a sliding of the human walls prompted by panic on a mission. The jungle in the background was gagged up. The sky overhead was throttled. The earth underneath had gone numb. The dead mass was slouching like a mystery to the notorious Martin Bungalow. Soon words began to drop as if upon the molten lava of desire and sizzling the whispers gained hissing loudness. It filled the air and loaded on the hunches of air began to boom and boom till the world around began to echo one consolidated crescendo of noise that hit the ear of the Martins.

The march to the Martin Dera to seek help of Sophia Bonga began with shaking steps and continued with the same till the mass of the village-bodies reached in front of Martin Bangalow and froze in panic and doubt.

* * * * *

Sophie Juliet, the lady of wild opinions not ever having had any real conflicts with her man heard from Reshma about the villagers' boiling and cooling. She heard from Reshma that Sarita, Laxmi, Nirja Thakur and others in the village had been fermenting the idea of raising a Bonga shrine, 'Madam ji,' said Reshma with excitement and scare, 'You know Ji these villagers are desperate to raise a shrine for their Bongas. They have been desperate for site selection rather site allotment. They want the memorial to set up at the empty land plot belonging to forest department in front of the Dera.'

'In front of Martin Dera? In front of the Bangalow that Martin holds as his pride and prestige?' Sophia shouted not to scare Reshma. The lady soon sobered and without thinking gravely about the consequences she said to herself that she was to the side of the villagers, 'These creatures: Sarita, Laxmi, Nirja, Ram Lal and that tiny fool Gobardhan are hapless fellows in need of being supported.' Sophia felt infected with sympathy. She became wild. She did not then fear the consequences, 'Let what happen, happen.'

Sophie caressed the folds of her Gandhi-saree. She kissed its fabrics. She felt like de-cocooning English-frame. She felt like submitting to Gandhi, the old hero of the shrill voice. She closed her eyes in prayer and folding hand to the absent image of her Gandhi she felt that she was in the ashram of Gandhi. She visioned her transference. She became the Gandhi-phantom exiting from her English-frame!

'Gandhi, Gandhi my Man in loin cloth

You are the lion in the old, thin frame

Come on, let me steal your guts, the voice of the brave

I do not want any more to stay imprisoned in the English-frame

Pull me out, pick and thrust me into the fray

My Sophia-self seeks to churn the day.'

Sophia whirled about and chanting the name of Gandhi as if drunk she reeled in wild motion. She lost her mind and lost her control strings and losing her in the given wildness she cried, 'It is high time that I should pay the debt. I am half-Indian. My existence is indebted to it. I am not alien to them.' She whispered confessions, 'I belong here, belong to India, belong to the nation that is bleeding to seek freedom. Ah that I had not been born! Would that I had dropped my breaths before things had trampled the hope for freedom. The heaven of it I tell madly lies in being released unconditionally, released from the yoke of slavery.' Reshma became nervous. Reshma shrank back to a corner in fright. Reshma pleaded her mam to hold control, 'Sir ji mam please do not excite yourself. I fear your words would fling forth to Martin sir.' Sophia retorted, 'Shut up Reshma. I am not raving. I am talking of justice and right.' Sophia got overhauled. She got herself transferred into the Gandhi-phantom.

Then as if woken from her wild dreams she asked if the village gang demanded a land plot in front of Martin Dera, 'Sarita, Laxmi, Nirja, Ram Lal these stupid mobbing horde of the villagers they are madding to seek a wrong plot in front of the wrong site. The Martin Dera is the pride and prestige of Martin *saheb*.' She shook Reshma by her shoulder, 'Dear Reshma cannot you argue with the fools to seek a land plot elsewhere?'

Reshma folded her hands, 'Sir ji mam,' cried Reshma, 'we pray for your help.'

'Help? What help, Reshma? How help dear? This demand is crazy. You know our Martin would rather die than submit to allot it.' Sophia became angry.

Reshma whispered stealthily, 'Sir Ji Mam this gang of the fools is desperately clung to this crazy demand. Their Gandhi in them has hibernated, gone dumb and deaf from its principles of passivity. They are going to go berserk, get de-controlled.'

'Go berserk? De-controlled? You mean they would go for violence. Why for? How can they afford to get aggressive? Will not then they be exposed to penal reactions?' Sophia shouted and sighing she said that the Gandhi magic was only the jugglery of its kind, not a complete spell to tranquilize the morbid passion, 'The advent of freedom I fear would render the so-called peaceful mass into a violent avenger. This would happen as the mass has been over-cabled and short-circuiting is natural.' Sophie finished the line, 'I do not know if I am going crazy but I fear to say that the way Gandhi has over-cabled hearts with supplies of moral and emotional check-mates the threat of short circuiting has increased. We suspect this would cause havoc when the release gate of freedom is opened. Then the mass would go berserk punching vengeance upon whatever they found vulnerable.'

Reshma began to press the legs of Sophia. She asked her if she would like to take coffee. She was declined coffee. Reshma then asked if she would like toffee. Sophia was tickled, 'Am I a baby to go for toffee?'

'Ji madam,' said Reshma, 'You are his wife. You can use your wife's authority. These stupid villagers are too weak for defenses. They need protection, mercy I mean.' Reshma suddenly came to the point.

The lady closed her eyes. In her mind the ghost battle was going on. She was reviewing the boulder incidence. She was reviewing the scene of the Bonga hunting. The Bonga blood had drenched her as the tigers had fell at her feet. She had an eerie feeling of cold sweating. Her heart was revolting as if it would crack the ribs, 'I have never forced my hubby, never quarreled with him. He has been considerate to me, good and a kind and a right husband material.'

Reshma had left her. Sophie was alone facing herself in the blank room. She knew the villagers would receive harsh reaction, '*Martin, I know will crack upon them. He is an English, a nervous foreigner bogged down in the insecurity abyss. He is arrogant but in-secured, nervous to the core because of the ganging villagers. His cruelty carries the pock-marks of the phobia of attack. He would secure the security by bullet. I hate bullets. I hate bloodshed. But to Martin this is the security fence.'*

She shut her mind and held the breath, holding her breath she heard the big thud-thud of her heart. There was no option left to her but to invoke Gandhi.

'Gandhi, Gandhi lion man in humble loin cloth

Come to Martin's succor, stop him from the plot

I am weak against him, weak in powers to hold his legs

The villagers demanding the Memorial they be given pegs.'

* * * * *

Sophie Juliet told Reshma that she was waiting for the reply from Salim Khan, 'This fellow zamindar I had written a letter and I have not received any response. I do not know if the letter was delivered.' Sophie asked about the letter and added that the letter must have reached the fellow Khan, 'Yes madam I had delivered it.' said Reshma and expecting Sophie to write reminder she brought pen and paper, 'No, this time I am not going to write a letter. I will call your Khan to my place.'

'Reshma, go to your Khan *saheb* and give him my message that I want to hold a meeting with him.' Reshma was quickly ready to go. She almost ran down through the street to Hawa Mahal. This building, the same magnificent building was nowhere changed in the course of time. It was standing there waiting for aging, reluctant to the outstanding changes in political scenario. Reshma ignored the status of Hawa Mahal as she was anxious to reach Salim Khan. She was feeling safe as she had only the words of mouth and Rabbani would not steal it.

Rabbani intercepted her, 'Hey you my fleeting butterfly! Your haste tells that you have some crispy message for Khan sir.' Rabbani guessed rightly. But Reshma dodged him, 'No such message.' She slipped from his grip. She was anxious to get him heard. She had chalked out many delivery modes and lastly, she dittoed the one she thought was the finest.

She literally tumbled over Mr. Khan sitting on the chair and without any loss of time she delivered the message in the telegraphic codes, 'Sir *saheb.* This our Sophie mam sends you a message summoning you immediately.' Reshma looked then exhausted and foolish. She realized her excesses and apologizing she shrank away without receiving any reply.

As she was running back Rabbani intercepted her and pulling her hand he caught her lustfully, 'Devil thing.' He planted his smelly mouth on hers and sucking her dry demanded what message she had delivered. The girl was overcome by hot sensation and desire and she surrendering to the man admitted all.

'My poor Khan s*aheb!* This brave effigy of Gandhi he is too cold for any use. To him staying stranded in cowardice is his safety-pin. I predict he will cower and cry and crumble back not giving any support to Sophia *sahiba*. He is a showpiece only, a wooden-owl.'

The Hawa Mahal looked at him abominably, 'I will not meet her. I will not answer her. I know my limitations. I am not going to invite troubles,' Salim Khan was running from room to room as if he were being chased by ghost, 'She expects me to turn a martyr. But no, I am not of that mettle.' Salim Khan fought himself. He feared the consequences, 'These bloated dead souls, my tenants I know they would foam and fume but when the real test will come, they will slink.' He recalled the ganging march of these villagers lead by Sophie mam, 'But what ultimately, they succumbed to? They evaporated from the scene. I know these chick-hearted fools.'

In agitation he was toing and froing as if he would measure the circumference of the earth in one go. But he was not going to get himself ready for the mis-venture, 'I can understand the wrong side of this folly. These Angrez fellows they know how to batter the foes.' He shuddered at this thought and for the first time in life he sincerely wished to join the company of Shally Khan and seek solace from her, 'I wonder if the lady would push me. I need her support. I doubt if she will support.'

Salim Khan soon checked himself. He decided instantly not to discuss matter with Shally, 'Shally is the progeny of the escapists. She holds the roots of fantasy to hitch out of troubles. Her poor cloud prince of dreams, she has no more than that! She will not help me find exit from my indecisions. I am alone, left evacuated!' Salim Khan Bahadur looked at him in the reflection of the smoked mirror and found him graying in the hair. He saw that his face skin was wrinkled. He lifted his arms and discovered that he was aging before time, 'I am growing old. My advancing age pleads me not to go berserk at such inciting pressures. *I am not worth any heroic folly*. I must contain myself and hide somewhere. This is the only way to pluck the key to my heaven of freedom, freedom from exuberant heroism.' Salim Khan became a shame to himself but it was not a shame at all. It was his survival kits.

Salim khan did not feel moral compunction, 'Every man is not likely to get excited and get carried away on the wings of rebellion. *I am comfortable with my withdrawal.* This is remarkable as my survival kits. Angrez people are dangerous. I cannot face them straight. They have become more dangerous like the cornered cats because they are nervous. This Martin is the living specimen of the nervous clan. He would take defense in bullet-shed!' Salim Khan was frozen down.

* * * * *

He instantly decided not to go to Sophie mam, 'This hybrid of an Angrez is unnecessarily over boiling. Okey. Alright she can overboil and whatever but I am not a privileged one like her. She is an Angrez and would not meet harsh trials but myself if I am caught, I would be battered. I do not have guts to meet battering.' He admitted that he was a man good for nothing. He did not feel humiliated. He touched his arm, pressed it to check its muscles and discovered that he was a sagging effigy, 'I agree I am a pulpy thing. *Of course, a good for nothing stuff. But it is no shame to me. I am what I am, no windy revolutionary. I do not blame myself,*' he stopped in the middle of the agitation, scratched his head and said that survival mattered more than stupid heroism, 'I am not one from the rash chargers. They maybe grand but my grandeur lies in my sneaking, avoiding to get caught in troubles. To me my life is precious, if not precious at least worth much to live somehow. I do not belong to the rebel school. *My simple credo in life is to run away, withdraw wisely and this has been my life's key to my heaven of freedom.*'

Shally Khan Khan, a lady with in-concrete base of mind was a votary of escapism. To her every solution lay in the flight. She was a harmless lady, harmless in the sense that she had developed dreamy outlets to escape. She dreaded meeting life straight and seeking viable solutions. She had a back-door escape route for everything that stood defiant. Her dream prince embodied it. She had long reached to and withdrawn from him in the time when she was most tortured in the mind. This realization of her escape had revealed itself recently when Reshma had casually referred to her fantasying as a ripple in the tides, 'Mam you are not solid with your chase of the dream prince. This is a lie of your vision, a condition that simply lifts you up from the troubled grounds. You are an escapist.' Reshma had then taken some wine. She was feeling light and reeling in the mind. It was a condition of the mind when she was talking above her mental worth.

Shally had gravely evaluated what transpired between her and Reshma and not openly appreciating her maid she told her that she was talking under the influence of alcohol, 'Yes mam I took a little of it just to experience its influence. It moved me to daring. I am feeling like invading any adversary. Even your great Martin would be beaten down if he appeared before me. This is the power of alcohol.' Reshma laughed and foolishly asked if she would take some. Shally Khan upbraided her and told that her meeting with her fantasy king too raised her morale. Reshma point -blank refuted her, 'Sir ji mam,' she said with the authority of a drunken man, 'Your fantasying and my wine has no match. My wine has given me powers to face life with guts and your fantasying is a shooing thing, a pretty escape route.'

Shally answered, 'Yes, it is my command center, my support for reaching my version of heaven of freedom. I seek it via escape that does not give me exertion and disappointment. I feel quite secured. It gives me the feeling of achievement. My dream prince has taught me with this.' Shally cleared her throat. She felt something smelly in the mouth and avoiding to explain it she looked away from Reshma.

Then the maid stretched her arms and seeming to catch the void told with bold whispers that she might climb to the podium where our Gandhi stood to address the mass and from there she would hugely deliver a big speech, 'Give me the mike, the *loud-voicer* and I tell I can yell slogans and raise slogan and defy the English, the whole slew of the tyrants and tell them that they are cowardly clencher of freedom not the monarch of the crowned head.'

Reshma was looking hot. She was looking like a volcano suddenly erupting. In her eyes life and death had caught the legs of hope and despair and pulling them, 'Sir ji madam, give me the platform to talk and I shall prove that I am more a volcano of passion than anything just a flimsy bloody rustic.' Reshma was needed to be stopped otherwise she would topple all thrones, 'Okey. Okey. You the great volcano of words please stop bragging. Your wine inside you, talks! It is time for the morning meal to prepare.' Shally Khan patted on her cheeks. Her cheek was hot and soft and sensational. Shally had an ugly desire to catch hold of her body and squeeze it.

'Reshma,' said the lady softly, 'My dear maid I have been thinking inside why after all, these English people do not un-leech us?' Reshma heard and unheard it and then after sometimes she told that the lust for power to keep other cowering and slaving was the lust of a beast of the jungle to dominate the herd.

Shally Jaan could understand the meaning and then yawning she said to herself that far easier was escape than organizing struggles and that her escape to fantasy was her right swing, 'I am okey with what I am. Everybody is okey with what he holds and he is. We are all free to design our defenses and mine is the coolest one, my escape to the safety of flight.'

* * * * *

The demented crowd of the villagers, without arms and guts to carry arms and seeming at a glance the boisterous disciples of Gandhi mustered at the gate of Martin Dera, buzzing and fusing and looking like a storm in panic. Sarita, Laxmi, Nirja Thakur and Gobardhan chased by desire to meet Sophie mam were standing dwarfed against the giant metal gate. They were standing on the spot they had fancied to capture for the Bonga shrine and not daring to inspect it they were each of them poking others to initiate by a howling. But words had as locked up in their throats as they would have desired it lest they should be identified. They were like the storm in panic. They looked dazed.

Mr. Martin, the only truly angry creature in the story was informed of the daring villagers at the gate. The information had come from Rabbani and had been confirmed by Reshma, 'Yes sir *saheb*,'rushed in Reshma with her mouth open like the devils in the dream, 'The ganging villagers, Sarita and Laxmi and Nirja along with all those fools have captured the site.' She heaved for breath and panted. Mr. Martin not used to such a ganging of the villagers, was perplexed. He then regaining his sense he leapt to pick his gun for safety and almost tumbled, 'Sir *saheb*,' Reshma literally caught him and throwing him as if he were a python she shouted, 'Not the gun sir ji. Gun will kill. They need dialogue.' She finished the line in horror. Mr. Martin till then back to himself jerked the maid and gnashing his teeth upon her ordered her to stay away.

Rabbani was then repenting for the treason. He stood aside praying to the god to intervene. He had no guts to stop Mr. Martin with the gun, 'Hunting this time I will do of the human pigs. I will kill the whole lot of these vermin.' The fellow English made a noise that awoke Sophie from her nap on the arm chair.

Sophie rushed to the spot and found her man in the middle of the gang. It was dangerous. She saw that her man was carrying the gun but his gun was limping in his hand. He looked nervous. He looked for the first time also anxious. The gang was desperate but dim in guts to harm him point blank. Sarita, Laxmi, Nirja and others were closing the coil of hate and enmity and would have choked Martin. But nothing hazardous had turned harrowing.

Only the Gandhi failure as a collective tool of resistance was apparently visible. The Gandhi in their blood had turned berserk giving them devil's shape. The ganging crowd looked volcanized, dangerous because of the festering rage. They were behaving like the tense wound with pus tending to burst forth. The ganging bodies were whirling round and round Martin then trapped in the hostile tempest. He needed immediate rescue, rescue from the python coil of the mob.

Sophie plunged into the coil, 'Shut up you, fools,' she fought with the might of a savior. She was struggling with the bodies mounting threat upon her and was looking like one slammed into nothing. She was struggling against the mob, struggling not to diffuse its frenzy. She struggled to absorb its frenzy. But the mob was getting *mobbier*, dangerous in proposition. Martin was thoroughly sucked in gasping for breath. The bodies had choked upon him layers by layers. He had turned a prey in the python grip. In his hand the limping weapon hung like a dead weight. Martin was horrified, 'Sophie, get me out! Rescue me.' He prayed. The ganging bodies flexed aside giving passage of escape to Martin, 'Stop you all. You cannot harm my man.' Sophia acted the savior. The yelling order of Sophia was heard amid the buzzing rage of the rioters. The mob loosened. It loosened not in fright of her but in reference to her divine grace. Sarita, Laxmi, Nirja and the rest of the mobbers felt like experiencing a shock and jolt. It was in answer to their awe of her. She was to them a Bonga thing. But she was caught in the trunk of the tornado looking helpless.

Mr. Martin rescued from the passive rage of the ganging crowd was standing on the verandah looking foolish and traumatized, 'Thank you Sophia mam, thank you that you rescued me.' He said with gratitude and seeking his gun again tried to foam and fire but the riotous mood of the crowd dampened his spirit, 'Okey, I will tackle it later,' he said slipping from the site of incidence. It was dangerous,'Sir *saheb* you are alone. Anything untoward might happen. Good that nothing unbecoming happened.'

Sophia was caressing the arms of Mr. Martin. Martin was looking pale in the face. An uncertain havoc had set upon him. He was looking dismissed and weak, 'You know Ju these vandals would have attacked.

They have come to this extent.' He was fuming and raging. In his eyes fury was lurking like a shadow. He was nervous and angry and was looking at the crowd still wriggling over the land plot, 'Will they dare seize this land plot?'

'No, they are not out to capture it. They have gathered in collective prayer to seek it allotted to them. They want the land plot to raise their Bonga shrine. They want you to allot the land piece.' Martin reacted as if stung on the bottom, 'Damned their prayer, these bloody rustics they will make it habit to fetch attention and permission in so many other avenues. I shall not allow it. Nibbing in the bud is the correct measure!' He suddenly got infuriated. He again picked the gun and rushed onward but this time Sophie did not check him. She stood frozen upon her feet waiting for the consequences of the rashness. Martin suddenly ceased and flinging his arms of defiance fired two shots of the gun. The panic soon captured the crowd. Sarita, Laxmi, Nirja and others stampeded. Their stampede caused dust to whirl up. The legs were running helter-skelter and Sophie was behind them shouting order to stop, 'Stop you running goons. Stop, wait, fight!' Her voice captured their legs. She was acting the Gandhi in its new version. In her call was no rage but it was effective enough.

Sarita, Laxmi, Nirja and others seized their legs. The fleeting gang as if got frozen. They tumbled into a block. The Buddha banyan tree laughed in approval. Its arms hurled up cheering the mob. Ears could hear for the first time the groaning of the Bongas. The Bongas of the mind came alive to vision.

The scary outlines of the mountains became vibrant with life contents. The birds and the insects and whatever relevant as creeping lives took their necks up watching to see something tremendous to occur, 'Do not run from the duty. You cannot just run away and turn a rat. Stay with the time. Hold the strings of it.' Sophia thundered so hard that blood came in her mouth. She coughed and vomited blood. She sank down on the ground looking miserable but not feeling devastated.

The mob ceased there. Sarita, Laxmi, Nirja and others surrounded Sophia and hands lifted her like a trophy of war. Mouths were howling slogans and articulating joy that filled their universe and made Martin feel subdued. Martin had picked Sophie and was pulling her from the clutch of the gang. She was caught in a tug of war meaning to start and end a struggle, 'Shut up you, fools,' shouted Martin order trying to secure her Sophie, 'Stop pulling her.' His order fell flat on the daring mob. The mob was pulling her to its side, 'She is ours! Sophie mam is ours. She belongs us. We shall take her home and set her in the shrine of hope and honor. She is our live Bonga!'

Martin relaxed the grip. He did it to check if she was to his side. He realized that he was bound to be disappointed. The lady was adrift to the foe side. He noted with grief that she was across his borders, 'Martin please,' she pleaded, 'Martin do not drag me to your side, your path of autonomy. Leave me relaxing in the space of my own. I do not belong to you. I am to their side, the side of justice, compassion and freedom. *My heaven of freedom lies in belonging to them.*' Gobardhan at this juncture simply backed out from his previous statements, 'Yes, I was wrong. She is to our side, she is ours. We must accomodate her. She is our real Bonga, our savior.' She is half-foreigner. We can trust her.'

Martin did not force her. He relaxed the hold. He looked to the sky overhead and read from the face of the sky the lesson he had never cared to notice, 'Sophie,' he said with grief in his words, 'Sophie you were dear to me, will remain so but with grief I tell you are to the wrong side. I have warned always and again I warn that we are foreigners and will remain so to them. You will not find you belonging to the side you turn.'

Martin did not apply physical force to snatch her. He let her slip to the side she thought she belonged, 'I am still hers thoroughly but she has changed the lane, this is her path to the heaven of freedom but to me my path to the heaven of freedom is to hold me up. I will not compel her to return. I will allow her to operate on her whims. I will warn still that she would suffer, suffer shock and humiliation. We are foreigners and will remain so to them.' He was sad for her, sad and sored that she was trying for the heaven of freedom for those who would never belong to her.

* * * * *

The mob lifted her precariously overhead swinging her like a trophy of war. Sophia Martin had been taken by the mob and she was exposed to its vagaries. The hundred hands had been callously groping her female parts. She was being molested. She squirmed in pain when fingers groped through her clothes to her unprotected pussy. She shouted for succor. She cried too but her cries got swallowed in the wild spree of shouts. Sophia was being hurled from hands to hands, a play thing being bowled wrongly. Her mind became numb as the outrage reached the ravishing peak. The frenzied waves of bouncing having swallowed her shouts she pined to fall into Martin's fold. She had become an aerial lust center to the molesting hands poking her here and there. She had become virtually naked, a lust morsel to the revelers. Her baring legs had become the butts for fingers and nails to tear her. Martin discovered her getting ravished. He pumped in guts and jumped into the reveling mob. She was rescued from the outrageous mob.

'You got what you deserved Ju,' shouted Martin and Sophie feeling ashamed clung to him like a deserted pet, 'Sorry, sorry,' she whimpered but strangely not feeling vindicative she pleaded for their forgiveness, 'Sir *saheb* mean they are but needing forgiveness. I can understand that they are naked vultures but they need pity.' Sophie was trembling with fright but was not vengeful, 'We cannot punish the mass for the wrong of a few.' She wrapped herself fully from the saree and trembling she held him by his hand.

Martin looked at her with pity, pity for the appeals she made and pity that he was not indignant at her. He did not feel estranged from her as well. He knew she belonged to him and knew that he was consistent in loving her, 'In this land of the aliens, herein I have nobody else her to return to. She was mine, she is and I cannot quit her at all.' He was in the quest of his heaven of freedom in remaining him bound to her, 'I admit she too is after her version of heaven of freedom in getting herself flung to the wrong side. Poor creature she will suffer, she will suffer and repent but I will not force her to break free from the illusive love of the bloody locals.'

He was caressing her on the back and without asking where on her limbs she had been outraged he felt the wound of outrage on his soul, 'My foolish Ju, my silly lady she got virtually ravished before my eyes and I could not do anything.' He felt like picking his gun and shoot the culprits. He did not pick the gun. He sobered and asked softly if she would need ointment for the bruises. She smiled distantly, smiled like the deity of forgiveness, 'No ointment sir. I am okey.' She was not okey as her body parts were paining, '*This outrage on my body is an atonement for the outrage the English did to the Indians.*' She foolishly began but her dialogue fell flat. She bowed her head in shame admitting that she had been wronged.

Sarita, Laxmi, Nirja and others were gone leaving behind dust wind and questions as to why Sophie was madding to favor them. Martin asked her solemnly this time without rue, 'Dear Ju admitting that you are not going to change. Admitting that in you your half-Indianness having fogged your mind you are not left with reason to argue with yourself but I think I have the right to ask after all what prompts you to turn to their side. I would tell and tell it for sure that they will not belong to you yet what mesmerizes you to think in their favor?'

Martin was not unreasonable to ask this. She in return clung to him like she used to cling decades before and bowing her head in shame requested that she wanted to see justice wear the face of justice and hear the voice of conscience, 'I am not mad but it maddens me to think that we humans are turning bestial by enslaving people without compunction. This is against the law of life. Have you seen these oceans tending to enthrall the powers of tides? They roar and hit the shores at will. Are not we safe under the sky inhaling and availing the God's bounty undeterred? We live without the nature resolving to confiscate our natural freedom? I understand that I am foolish from your point of view but I am happy that I am not bluffing myself in the belief that every living human kind has the right to freedom, see freedom whole and enjoy its natural flux. We have no right to clutch others' neck and halter the heaven of freedom that matters in terms of upholding dignity to life and living via choice. But we humans by way of the inherent envy and arrogance are given to stealing others' freedom. Our tension, greed, the negative thoughts to overlord others and intention to supersede others have dehumanized us.'

She paused for a little while and watched Martin. She found Martin was incorrigible, 'Okey sir,' she continued further, 'If not for pity on others, pity yourself and pause for a while and check your pride and greed to control others. I tell it will open venues of peace. You will feel most remarkably free when you leave others free. I'II tell you dear Mart that the horrid truth about the usurpers of freedom is that they never feel free and happy despite whatever control plugs they create to hold others.'

Sophie was exhausted. Martin heard and un-heard her and dismissed to mean what she meant but he felt compelled to utter the previous warnings, 'Whatever your wish Ju but let me reiterate the same lines of warnings that we are here only foreigners. Our status is fixed. We cannot shake it up. Well, your whim dear, your whim. Okey, keep giving time to them, give your best of love and attention but you will find them in the last the same ungrateful goons. I was yours, I will remain yours and if we strayed, we will be the losers.' Martin's voice became hard. He was fighting the tears. He did not seek her shoulder for support. He wiped the tears and said, 'My dear love we would be most lonely in the aftermath of this departure from each other. I can tell you I will be most hurt one but most wronged either!'

He paused and looking gravely outside continued, 'Dear my dismal friend you keep talking of heaven of freedom, I agree that it is worth considering. I undertake to explain it. As a votary of power keeper, a virtual upholder of British power I would make you concede to the fact that our colonial mechanism works only on the conditions how we control others. We do not treat it as usurpation. We treat it as the act of management. After all we the colonial fellows have sacrificed the comfort of our home-land. We are staying here virtually homeless. Whether you agree or not this our *statelessness* makes us feel unsecured. I personally feel most unsecured so my excessive reaction.'

He tried to gather her opinion but she kept mum. He continued with a sigh, 'Madam Sophea you must know we are not cruel to *your countrymen*. We do not extort them. We simply take fees, fees for our care-taking. We are just taking returns for our contributions in some degrees. We deserve it madam. We deserve to be admired.'

Martin was talking in a flow what was his understanding of the truth. Sophia was not going to agree with him. She was not a common quarreling wife. She laughed at his stands and taking a dusting stick she began to dust the crockery items. The dusting caused him cough. He signaled her to stop dusting, 'Ju you know I have dust allergy.' He protested. Juliet stopped the dusting and calmly said, 'The choking you suffered is symbolically the same the Indians suffer under you, the choking comes from the denial of the freedom of living. Sir *ji saheb* it is unnatural to curb other's freedom. Imagine what you would feel like if you are taken under control?'

'Dear Ju we English are not robbers of freedom,' he said with the pride of a ruler, 'We are here as benefactors. We take nothing from them. We only give, give new meaning to life and of course light and a new taste of living. Our hold on the Indians is not unjust. It is no extortion but only a mild reward-taking.' Martin did not expect appreciation but he rigidly stuck to his point, 'We cannot just give away this country, give away because we have nothing to do with it now. Sorry! Very Sorry we gave it away to the Indians. I regret that the Country which we civilized it would now fall in the hand of the novices. The poor successors, poor in intelligence, resources and maturity I wonder if they would keep it intact.'

Martin finished and Sophiea not countering him heard him attentively. Martin was in a loud flow, '*Sahiba*,' he said with a deep sigh, 'What astounds me is that the successors are determined to make India a democratic country, a country where election and parliament and elected leaders will lead this country. My foot what hell they do! But I laugh that a draft committee for constitution has been initiated and the scholars are going to draft laws and provisions in the secular face!' After a little pause he then again fired up, 'Madam Liberty this India is going to begin as a secular nation while its daughter nation Pakistan will follow Islamic tenets.' Martin drank two glasses of water and bloated his belly. Sophia wondered that her man was bloated with misgivings and bad thoughts.

'Sir *saheb* do not please torture you with envies. I tell you if this nation is going to earn freedom it definitely knows how to learn freedom.' Sophiea was vague but true.

'Okey Lady Liberty I will see and you will see how this your Hindustan leads its freedom.' Martin then became serious. He said something irrelevant predicting bad things about this country then said, 'We are here and anywhere in our colonies at stake passing life of risk amid the hostile natives. *What you call our arrogance is actually our summary defense mechanism. We are most unsafe amid the natives. Whether you admit it or not you are far more exposed to risks than me. I fear dear Ju someday you will realize it. You will repent but by then it would have been too late.'* Martin sucked in a lot of air to check if his lungs were correct

Sophie argued. She argued like a progressive thinker. She was determined not to allow his bad logic to overwhelm her, '*Our staking to risk is our making. Sir we never tried to assimilate with the locals. We maintained a cold distance. We gave them surgical treatment.'*

'Surgical treatment! Yes, this surgical treatment to the natives gave them a lot. We taught them scientific way of thinking, gave them a progressive push, made them HUMAN in terms of humanity. We gave them acts and tact and gave them more than we can give a count. We civilized them, initiated them into the world of science and on leaving them we will give them a tease to Remember us whenever they will feel perturbed and nostalgic.'

* * * * *

Her ears were trying to catch the strange gurgling sound coming from the jungle. It was the sound of animals and devils creating pandemonium. She had heard such sounds earlier but that day, it was eerie, 'Mark the howling of the jungle. Maybe it is in resonance with the spirit of time. Their Bonga thing, I fear it has been activated.' She was ignored as a silly buzz-hearer.

Martin was trying to relate the existing factors related to the fall of English army on different fronts. Sophie was not interested in the narrative. She continued with a concession, 'We both are correct on our stands,' she said. Then she lent her attention to the sudden silence of the jungle, 'Can you read the mood of the jungle?' She asked foolishly. Martin patted on her back. 'Dear Ju you are turning superstitious. I do not see anything unusual. Your ear drums are sounding. Then it is a sign of your turning lunatic. Okey your half- Indianness! I fear soon you will be hearing the voices of your Bonga things like some scary whispers.' Martin laughed.

He was anxious about Sophie getting off-beat. He loved her as the outcome of his possessiveness in some degrees. He wanted to pull her out of her lunacy. But she was growing crazier. In her a tempest was inside, 'I have begun to suspect something untoward. I have read in the books that the mystical powers exist. I have no logical proof but I can perceive it. I fear the Bongas would gain the oscillatory cabling in this matter. Afterall these Bongas have been assassinated, their ghosts I fear are loitering about. We should have been just to them. We manipulated their killing by deceit and brutality.'

Martin was preparing the strange coffee over sweetened and over embittered and as he was stirring harshly the content in the cup was spilling out. He was stirring it in a passionate display of anger and helplessness, anger at himself for failing to handle his wife and helplessness as he was beginning to lose his confidence. The coffee in the cup seemed to mock him, the whirl pool in the coffee was turning giant and he was feeling sucked in, 'Freedom in any gesture to me and them and to Julee is beginning to harass me. I am feeling obsessed with it and failing to justify what Julee upholds and what I get to feel about it.'

He brought the strange coffee cups to Sophie who sipped it and finding it detestable she felt like throwing up. But she soberly sipped further and further the strange brew with no strange expression of reluctance and horror, 'Did you like it?' asked Martin. Martin expected bad remarks from her but she smiled soberly giving a touch of compromise and acknowledgment and said with a gravity of a philosopher, 'Sir *saheb* life is like this over-sweetened and overbitter mixture of compromise and acknowledgement and freedom of heaven really initiates at this portal.' Martin heard her and not arguing with her said something that sounded compatible.

Martin finished the strange coffee and not battling inside he recapped the past events in a quick flash. He allowed the shooting scene of the tigers to come to his review and oddly said to himself that it was irrelevant. He also confessed that the tigers were wrongly killed and the aftermath of it was unpleasant. He tried to evaluate the consequences and found that he had been a bad master and the way he had been hostile to the villagers he would invite troubles, 'I will not disagree that I have made foes and these villagers are the open enemies now. They will harm us.' Martin drew a deep sigh and tried to escape from the apprehensions of attack. *He took his gun and looking at it with grief in his eyes he said that the loss of the English rule in its colonies was due to the bullet and gun culture.* He did not elucidate his point as he heard a noisy clamor outside the Bungalow.

'What after all I got from my service here, service to the crown and what the lady was going to get from her silly drift to the Indian side. I agree that she is prompted by a romantic impulse. I admit regretfully that my gun wielding policy and her ultra-love for doing something positive to the people are going to go in waste. We are on the loss side. The loss, real loss would be mine and hers.'

* * * * *

Sophie came with a storm in her bosom and like a poetry of passion she caught hold of his hands and without voicing her grief and pain she looked at him like a statue in the stone body crying like a child, 'You will become my memory and likewise I will become yours but the truth that we sought the key to the heaven of freedom in our capacities will make an un-recorded history. You did whatever you thought was just as per your vision and I did whatever I thought was fair as per my understanding and what is brilliant in the ultimate conclusion is that we never became abusive. We maintained a decent distance and appreciated our dissention in totality: you stuck to your ways and I to mine!' Sophia felt like hyphenated but not fractured. In her honor for him was also not the outcome of a passionate love. She liked him because he liked her.

Martin looking away from her said that in the life they passed together they gained nothing classic and lost nothing epic but they realized that life is not a drama of total conflicts, 'Your key to the heaven of freedom,' he said, 'would not match with what this Salim Khan would seek and understand and likewise these villagers would seek or understand. Every individual has his own version of the capacity to understand the heaven of freedom. This is remarkable and nothing else is whether they really obtain the key and enter the freedom domain.' Martin drew a deep sigh then he said with grief that *his gun-wielding credo and her khadi-honoring emotion* was not going to do anything remarkable, '*You will remain a target for violence when the passive Gandhi in the rustics will turn vindicative.*' He paused and heard her attentively, '*Then your gun-wielding credo too will fail sir ji. You will also realize that your gun-control was a fiasco.*' Sophiea was talking the other side of the truth. Both patted on each other and said that both were going to suffer. Then Sophiea said, 'The only signal gain in the whole story is the gain of freedom to the Indians and that is their due.'

'Madam make ready your luggage. Make ready for a flight from here. I can guess the Gandhi-fomented non-violence will soon be cracking shell. It will belch forth the ghosts of violence, erratic and cold violence that will befall each other in the name of religion and division of the land. I can predict a savage riot, riot all over India that will break the backbone of passivity and make India a den of crime against each other.' Martin chewed his lips. He looked emotional. He looked like one feeling unfortunate. It was not his love of the country he ruled. It was a certain penitence in him that his colonies world over were crumbling. He said that our gun-wielding culture did not uphold our supremacy, 'We as the English monarch of the world are gradually crumbling. The history will remember us with divided opinion. We will be remembered as the tyrants and we will be defended as the path-makers alike!'

Sophie ignored his words. She did not deliberately ignore him to hurt her. She ignored him as she had secretly admitted that the English colonial system had been the tentacles around the neck of freedom. She touched him on his cheeks and feeling the warmth of the flesh, she let her soul get warm and enlightened.

'Freedom! The opening of its wings and its flight in the sky

It is the wonder

It is the miracle

We can imagine its elation, the bond and tie

Freedom anywhere, in any rhythm and fancy

It is great

It is high

I love it beyond words to catch and try

It alone is the achievement of superb supply.'

She became tearful in the eyes. In her passion tides were mounting and Martin who could see the advent of a disaster patted on her back feeling very sad, 'Ju dear you are in absolute dream. I pity you. I will not blame you. Only I wish I am proved wrong but I can see a formidable black storm hidden in the womb of future.'

'Silly talk. Sir we will leave this land handing over its affairs to the able hands and their Hindustan will become theirs, duly theirs and we will be remembered in the history as the Givers.' Sophia was telling what she thought was due but Martin knew things otherwise. He smiled at her and sighed, 'Okey. Okey Sophia *sahiba*! Let us not get drunk in dream. Let us see how we are treated as Givers. Let us wait and watch.' Martin sighed and then continued, 'Dear my Lady Liberty we are in a country where morality and justice is not valued properly.' He sounded depressive. He said that he was not anxious about losing the rule, 'My anxiety is about the treatment when we are not in power. *This Gandhi thing will go volatile. The anarchy will overtake. Everywhere the marks of violence will be seen in the names of divisions.* What I am concerned is how you happen to be received and how I happen to cope with the future vagaries.' He was looking at the sky spreading wings from south to north and east to west, 'Someday afterwards this our sky will become bloody stranger to us dear. We will then find us captive. I do not know how we shall cope with the eventualities.' His words sounded like a panic on the lips of a visionary.

Sophia remained stuck to her status quo. She was not innocent of the possible upheavals but she was bemused in the hope for things to happen in right proportion. She was not to blame. He too was not to blame for his apprehensions. What was remarkable was that in between the husband and wife no conflict brewed up.

* * * * *

CHAPTER 11

WINDS TURNED WILD

Time till then had changed massively. Time of scare and withdrawal, doubt and nervousness on the part of the villagers had changed. Time of the freedom seeking had changed for freedom harvesting. The harvesting of freedom had made the villagers defiant. What had been an issue of panic had become to them a spur. Villagers had turned rowdy. To them the actual Gandhi had become a virtual Gandhi. This had happened because the freedom had got interpretations as per the choice of the beneficiaries.

From Delhi the news had been pouring about the shift of power from crown to the countrymen. Sarita, Laxmi, Nirja, Ram Lal and others in the local pockets were crazed out of control. They had gone berserk. The story of the nation shy of aggression had taken aggression as the benchmark.

Gobardhan known for bringing sensational news had come with the news of the independence at midnight, 'Our *desh,* the dear country it has broken the chains,' he shouted hosana, 'We are out from the fencing control. We are in the open sky of our own, the sky that is not subject to questioning. We shall have our ways, give jolting pushes to whoever we want. We are the monarch of our will, the king of Gandhi's Hindustan, every one of us.' He had skipped over the real Gandhi. The virtual Gandhi was in head head turning like a devil.

Ram Lal undertook to bind the hoosh Gobardhan, 'But the laws and the need for laws are still the same, it should be.' Sarita snapped at him shouting, 'Shut up. We are free that is all as free as our bulls are made in the morning.' Laxmi tried to add her version of idea of freedom and said that she was free like her hens and cocks. Her version of freedom made Nirja hoot her, 'Idiot you are that you resemble your fowl. I tell our freedom is like the moon behind the clouds.' He did not explain it. He said that freedom was like the stubborn pony. He heard the roaring of winds and heard thereafter the thunder of the clouds and said in whisper that the freedom to him was the tasty food and bottled drink.

Gobardhan was running amuck as if the wasps had stung him on his bottom. Sarita had turned the utensil boiling the rice and made the flame wet with the hot water. Laxmi had thrown her saree off her body and gone bare to the legs. Ram Lal had caught his *dhoti* off his body hurling it like a flag. Nirja Thakur copying others had begun to leap and bound like a monkey yelling wild words of glee, 'Get away from what had been holding you tight and dance in the open air,' shouted Ram Lal. His words quivered in the air not timidly as he had knotted the quivering tremor of words, 'Take your bottoms up and piss with your tools as you like.' His voice rose higher than necessary as Nirja Thakur slapped him on his face demanding, 'Why bottom up and pissing?'

He was interrupted by Laxmi who had reached the scene in the middle of the field and was demanding explanation about the revelry. She had fastened her saree round her waist and was looking like a warrior, 'I am here the second and third Laxmi Baie. I will ride my wind-horse and crack upon the enemies. I am no more the former Laxmi.' Sarita kicked Laxmi on her bottom, '*Harami* Laxmi Baie,' she scorned, 'Stop this your drama and tell what has made the village set wild?'

Gobardhan came forth with the explanation, '*Chachi* we are freed. We have got Gandhi as the new king of our *desh*. Hip! Hip! Hurrah!

The Angrez people are dropped off. We got the *azadi* for which our Gandhi had been struggling and we had been struggling behind him.' Ears heard Gobardhan with attention and Ram Lal who was jealous of the lad, pushing the urchin aside took the lead, 'Ladies and gentlemen,' he began with the flourish of a big talker, 'We lastly defeated the Angrez and thrown them out of this our holy land. We are today free and are going to tryst with destiny. We shall have our Bonga shrine. We shall have our own heaven of freedom, the freedom that will give us our own Raja, king. Come forward and take the fresh breath from the fresh air that is ours and write the writ of the fate in our own language.'

He was trying to capture attention of the villagers but the rouges were too rowdy for disciplining. The eyes and ears and bodies and legs and hearts and every organ in the crowd were operating in the fulness of the illusion called freedom, 'We are at the command of our free will and the control clutch that wore on our spirit has downed. We can act and do whatever without questions. We are sanctioned power to open and close our own path of understanding and action.'

Ram Lal got exhausted of expression. His head became dull. On his face the expression went zero. He felt suddenly jammed of words. He backed out and catching an obscure corner in the dingy lane of the village he tried to revive energy to talk. But he was not recharged and his position had been stolen by Nirja Thakur, 'Ladies and gentlemen,' he began like Ram Lal but soon he wore his own coat of tongue and uttered, 'Our life now will be different from what it had been. My way of thought and action will also be different. I will follow my lanes and will not tread on the rut. Too much of the bridling of emotions inside has made emotions rot. We have got Gandhi our King and we are all kings respectively. *Sala*, bastard we are all the independent Bongas! We are free. Freedom is ours. We shall act as per our whims.' The summary dialogue in his mouth had the same message as others had.

Nirja Thakur then demanded for a glass of water and when no hands brought it, he cursed and swore and became violent. He became a vandal full of passionate intensity and mean overbearing, 'Our freedom has broken chains, broken the chains of mandatory obedience. Now nobody will watch us and question. We are free like the wild winds.' He was running amuck like he had been stung by a swarm of wasps, 'Now that we are free, we must talk and hear and force others to talk and hear. This is our right and we are above laws of control.' Nirja Thakur strutted about and rolling his eyes in the sockets he behaved like an un-biological being. He felt like a Deveta, god had entered his body and wished he should be treated so. But he was dismayed when he saw every next person carrying the same delusion of the highs.

Sarita was standing with the pose of a queen of windy powers so was Laxmi and in between them the competition was making them look weird. Nirja took guts to address Sarita and Sarita ignored him as if he were a trifle. This was the arrogance that made Laxmi all the more insolent when she shouted orders to the crowd to come in a queue and hear her. But she was not heard as others were as much drunk in the wine of freedom as she was.

Sarita became angry, very angry and herself not knowing how she should counter Nirja she threw her arms wide and as if catching air, she voiced poetically, 'Sir come on. Ride the air. Sit upon the wind. Build a rainbow of colors. Wipe clean the sky of the patches of clouds. Lit up the moons of own liking. Dig new paths to the heaven of our choices. We are free. Free from rules and regulations.' Sarita pulled the hair of Laxmi and the latter pulled the hair of Gobardhan then Sarita yelled, 'Forget the clutch of control over the body. Shake off the fright of being spied upon. We are free. Our Gandhi Bonga is sitting now in each heart. We are the Bongas to us. Yes, big Bongas of our own! This is the achievement of the freedom.' Her dialogue sounded windy.

Others were too busy to give her importance. Her erratic words became silly buzz in the ensuing revelry when the entire village began to whirl and whirl in wild spree hearing nothing said and following nothing said, 'We are the monarch of our will. The Gandhi of Delhi, his passive magic, his insistence on control over passion, his cry for non-violent resistance all these nuisances are now outdated. We are updated ones, important and in control of the situation.' This was perhaps Nirja or Ram Lal talking but the mob was not hearing as it was out of the bonds.

But then Ram Lal attacked Gobardhan on his chest and literally taking control of him by subduing him by hair, Ram Lal poured words into the mouth of Gobardhan to utter, 'Tell Gobardhan to all that Ram Lal has decided to capture the land plot before Martin Dera and there we shall raise the shrine to our Bongas.' Gobardhan would not be released till he by utter physical force of subduing uttered the words of Ram Lal cast into his mouth.

'Bonga friends,' Gobardhan uttered hardily the words. The clutch on his hair was tightened and the mob seeing the violence on Gobardhan felt eerie creeps of pang and heard Gobardhan, '*Chacha and Chachee* get ready to march in a procession to Martin Dera. We shall capture the Bonga site. We shall take the site by force from the Martins.' Gobardhan was released from the clutch and he scuttling out to freedom vomiting volley of swearwords he cried hysterically what was not expected, '*Harami*, bastard Ram Lal, the son of pig, I wish he shall have the poking spear into the arse of his bottom from Martin *saheb*. Talks of freedom and the violence! Of course, the Angrez has sided aside but they are still powerful. May god Ram Lal of the pig's son get punishment for the torture he did to me.' Gobardhan was soon not being heard as the mob had gained a different lethal mood and Sarita, Laxmi, Nirja and others were boiling with uncertain hate biz.

The crowd squeezed into a punch of hate and not at all under any control and moving like the devil in the nights was now surging menacingly to Martin Bangalow. It had turned into an un-accountable lethal storm. Sarita, Laxmi, Nirja, Ram Lal even the agitated Gobardhan now cool and sobbing and cursing had lost the frame of human contours. Their identity having drowned they had become a psychopathic energy of hate and decontrol and were storming to Martin Dera. They had no Bongas in their mind.

Even Sophia Bonga and Gandhi Bonga having slipped off their minds they were the living fury in concrete mob-structure. They had turned wild winds.

Gandhi's passive coolness and his teachings of non-violence having gone deleted the mob was as dangerous as it becomes, 'We shall attack the Martin Dera,' thought of violence spurred Ram Lal as he stumbled over the same boulder once it had rolled down from the mountain, 'I shall kick aside the hated boulder,' he shouted as he felt his toes were bleeding. He touched the wound and pouring dust on it he walked with fierce energy at the head of the mob. He felt he was leading the mob. He felt important and felt like dismissing whatever Gandhi he knew, 'Gandhi my foot!' he kicked this time on a thorny bush and hurt his wound. He cried like a pig and seeking hand of support from Nirja he received again a kick from the hot Nirja. Ram Lal was limping and marching not a warrior in the gang. He was party with the gang of the vandals going to vandalize Martin Dera.

'Down with Martin Dera! Down, down with Martin *saheb,'* mouths roared into the air, 'Up with our Gandhi!' the mob hurled slogans like weapons of hate.

The mountain and the jungle and the silence of the surroundings responded with echoes returning in triple booms. Gobardhan got fascinated of this phenomenon. He diverted his mind to the repeating echoes and smiling with curiosity and awe wished to filter his voice and get it echoed. He howled like a jackal and this was a fascinating experiment as the jackal's sound out-beat the rest. The echo captured the air. Sarita, Laxmi, Nirja and Ram Lal forgot the slogans and concentrated on the jackal echo. It was sounding sweet and sleek and was making the mob bewitched.

The slouching of mob in batches had no rhythm. Ram Lal pretending to lead the mob growled directions to the mob. But mob was a mob. It knew no discipline. It was a ball of fire in the wild, 'Up with Ram Lal, the hero of Bonga march!' a mouth in the mob hooted him. In return the mob lifted Ram Lal into the air and poking fingers into his hole in the bottom shouted hosana, 'Up with Ram Lal sir!' chanted the crowd like incantation shaming Ram Lal and giving Gobardhan a chance to avenge himself. Gobardhan thrusting his hand into Ram Lal's *dhoti* caught his tool hard and shook it, 'Harami, bastard scoundrel.' Gobardhan got detected and would have been caught but then he slipped into the thickest core of the crowd.

Martin Bangalow was there standing in its full awe and its serene whiteness had a lot of glory and shine to dazzle the eyes. The Dera was looking innocent and scary alike and had nothing to do with the changed mood of the mob. The background silence from the mountain overhanging the Dera was the witness to one of the crudest mis-haps of the year. The jungle trees were silent so was silent the Buddha banyan, the tree that had appeared in the story signifying peace and appeal for enlightenment. But then the Buddha banyan had been ignored like Gandhi had been dismissed. Even the Bongas had been underscored as the mass was typically listed for the blast.

Jackals, real jackals suddenly howled signals of warning maybe in support of the Martins or may be against them and the mob sizzling with energy and inner fire scattered in patches all over the plot of land spotted for Bonga shrine, 'Here at this spot we shall have our Bonga relics buried,' said Sarita feeling charged as if she had got the Bonga soul resurrected into her, 'We shall dig foundation immediately,' she ordered the mob and herself she began to scratch the earth with bare hands. She got frenzied and pulling Laxmi by hand she forced her to follow her. Laxmi resented and she kicking Sarita growled, 'Shut up fool. You cannot dig hole with finger nails. We shall do it with iron spade.' Gobardhan unnecessarily got charged and without any compunction he started digging earth with his finger nails and soon a lot of the hands copied him leaving finger nails hurt and bleeding, 'Gobardhan,' commanded Ram Lal, 'Idiot boy, do not you know that our nails are no Bonga claws! Our dear Bongas you remember they had given up violence and adopted the path of peace. Oh! How I remember our Bongas who had become sober vegetarians and had abstained from hunting animals!'

Ram Lal was not talking to awake sense of peace. He was recollecting the virtues of the Bongas, 'Stop this Bonga preaching,' shouted Laxmi and herself beginning to scratch the earth with nails she called upon others to follow her. The mob captured the plot of land and sat stiff on the bare ground defiant of impending threats. The mob was stiff because their head had hanged reason. In their silly head the Gandhi and the freedom had mixed up making them brave and timid alike, 'We shall not quit the plot of land. It we shall capture to raise Bonga memorial.' This was the stark violence in the making. Such violence comes forth like the lava bursting from the volcano long subdued.

* * * * *

Inside the Martin Dera, Reshma was agitated. She had the news of the mobbing villagers. She had been the link as informer to the Martins and on that fateful day too she carried a tremendous piece of news. She ran amuck and dashed into the chamber of Martin. Her mouth was ajar smelling stale and she was excited to vomit the news, 'Sir ji mam they, the wild windy mobbers have attacked the Dera. Sarita, Laxmi, Nirja, Ram Lal and all others along with the tiny Gobardhan have raided the Bangalow. They are camping outside; these headless fools I would tell are threatening the grace and glory of the Dera.'

Reshma had more to narrate but Martin suspecting something lethal took his gun and shot out shouting war- cries. But his legs caught his steps. He would not dash wildly into the thick of the crowd, 'Okey. Okey. These bastards, I know their boiling is the result of their freed. They have turned mobbers, dangerous and mean I should evade them.' Martin fettered his legs. He tangled himself safe behind the door curtain. He wore the folds of the curtain round and round himself and peeped outside.

In a flash the radio broadcast of the independence in the midnight came alive to him. He was hearing the famous speech of Nehru's 'Tryst with Destiny.' "*Long years ago, we made a tryst with destiny. Now the time has come when we shall redeem our pledge---not wholly or in full measure—but very substantially.*"

Martin could recall the next vibrant line of Nehru, "*At the stroke of the midnight hour, when the world sleeps, India will awake to life and freedom.*" He closed the door of his mind. He found himself thrown into a blank tunnel. Martin felt the trysting with destiny was creeping to him like a monster. He felt lonely, absolutely lonely within his Dera. He suddenly felt like getting emptied of his pride. He saw around and discovered that even Sophie Juliet was nowhere around, 'I am left alone, alone and un-supported. My Julee she is their side.' Martin still did not hate Sophie. He knew she belonged to him by race.

A surge of pain and panic overwhelmed him. In his hand his gun seemed like a dead log. He clutched at the butt of the gun and felt cold in the hands, 'I am no more the Martin of the past. I am deserted and alone.' He was in panic, panic caused by the mobbing villagers. Martin was hearing the babbling fury of the mob outside in front of him and he was helpless despite the weapon.

Sarita, Laxmi, Nirja, Ram Lal and the mob behind them were looking formidable, sizzling with rage ready to attack. Martin craved to have Sophie Juliet by him but the lady was not there. He wished to drag her by her hair and hold her by. He had never before imagined to have had any cruel feelings but then in sheer panic he wished to drag her by hair to make her stand by and give him a sense of security, 'At this crisis time she should have been beside me but no. The lady, bitch!' he clamped his mouth with his hands.

He violently held it tight, 'But no, she stays distant may be giving impression of neutrality, but when the mob cracks down it will not leave her.' His eyes became red with rage. He clutched the gun tightly, 'At least this my gun and my guts will stand by me,'he said something that should not be recorded as it sounded outrageous. He was cursing himself, cursing his failing guts. He was taken by panic of the version he had never taken. He edited his panic and with trembling legs he froze down on the spot, 'Shall I call the police?' he asked himself and felt helpless that he had no means to call the forces.

Martin Juliet had guessed earlier that on the advent of the independence the long-diked passion would flush out and the people would turn turbulent. She knew that then the mobbing of the so-called subdued people would become a common sight here there and everywhere. She did not get panicky. She sighed deeply and not cursing said that it was the given. She was no sage at it that she had such premonitions. Even Martin had these premonitions but he had failed to acknowledge them.

Naturally she was not nervous. She had been quarreling with her man to curb him but he had always beaten her by arguments. She was hearing the angry buzz of the mob still not daring to attack point blank but she was sure any frenzy outburst would happen any moment.

She recalled that she had rashly joined the mob during Bonga hunting. She recalled that she had taken risk for them and recalled that she had been deserted midway. She smiled without grievances and sighed, 'These mobbers. Yes, these un-diked people I tell they are dangerous. Their freedom slot to them has un-leashed them. They are simply unpredictable.' Sophie knew that panic was no answer to the immanent dangers.

She yawned and putting her hand on the mouth sounded bore. She stretched her arms and legs and slouching out of the bed she felt listless and weary, 'What can I do?' It was a vital question that she asked her. She waited for Martin to rush back and hide somewhere but she was foolish to guess so. She sluggishly recalled the words of warning from Martin that she was a foreigner and this was her disadvantage. She agreed without hesitation, 'Yes we are the foreigners and to us this is the worst we are.'

She knew the mob anywhere in any frame is the collective havoc, 'This mob too is the collective havoc. We are going to face it. We would rather inflame its fury if we showed resistance.' She felt numb in the body. Her head became dizzy, 'We are exposed to its mood, the mood of the mob depends on its mood!' She waited for Martin to retreat in due course but finding that he was delaying she became curious to discover.

Sophia saw Martin standing in the pose of a defender, his gun ready and he looking like a novice hunter. She pitied him, pitied him because she saw that his guts had failed. He was a picture of misery in the booby trap, 'Poor hero of all time,' she taunted him without reason, 'His English guts having fused he is a pitiable victim of the situation.' Sophie yawned again and looking blankly to the sky said meaninglessly, '*The heaven of freedom, poor meaning of this phrase it has changed versions through the story. To me it prompted to reach it via quarrel, to Martin it meant otherwise a wild desire to hold control over the natives to maintain his Raj, to the locals it was a cause for the morbid- retention of violence now taking the outburst. My dear Salim Khan he took the route to reach the freedom territory via withdrawal and visible timidity. The good lady Salma Agha she remained clung* to her *fantasy of the cloud prince*.'

Sophia sounded inappropriate in the crisis time. She was sure that the mob across the walls of Martin Dera was in bad mood. She could guess that anytime the mob would go berserk and attack but she was feeling lethargic. She had no excitement. She had no energy. She had no desire to undertake to control the situation. She was behaving like the fate given to trysting with the destiny. It was unfortunate but it was happening.

* * * * *

'Sophie ji sir,' Reshma dashed into the room and catching hold of Sophie she shouted, 'Sir ji mam your man is in danger. These mobbing gangs are anytime going to get berserk and do anything untoward. Come see for yourself. You have been favorite to them. Plead with them to stop.' Reshma literally pulled Sophia out to the balcony from where she could have a full view of the sizzling mob outside.

'There see, Sarita, Laxmi, Nirja, Ram Lal and that tiny Gobardhan and others sizzling with rage. They are getting dangerous, would anytime go berserk and raid The Dera.' Reshma had no response from Sophia. Reshma was perplexed why her mam had gone reactionless. Reshma was in panic and this had made her feel her bowels upset. Reshma had an urge for pooping and she ran into the bathroom to ease herself. The nervous panic made her bowels drain out all that was inside except the panic. It was strange that she who had had no real favor for the Martins was feeling concerned for the life of the Martins, 'Sir Ji mam,' she shouted last time, 'If you do not move forward to save Martin *saheb,* anything untoward can happen.' Reshma found Sophie Juliet was stiff on her position as if ready to meet the wreck, 'Do you want get wrecked by the mob?' Reshma pulled Sophie and found that Sophie was heavier than usual.

In nervous panic Reshma ran to the other corner of the Bangalow in search of Rabbani. She wanted to get Rabbani for the rescue of The Martins. But she found Rabbani in a different mood. He was fell and tight and reluctant. From his eyes hate was spilling. Rabbani was there sitting on a chair he had never dared to look at. On the chair his pose was regal drunk in the liquor of pride. Reshma could not catch the meaning of this illegitimate regality and snapping him she shouted, 'Man mark! This chair, it is not meant to sit on illegally like that. You are the servant of this Bangalow not master.' She could not disturb the monarch of the pride out of the throne, 'Now this chair, this Bangalow, all its wings and flesh are mine. I have seized them.' He mused and it enthused him, 'Wow! Liberty can be so tasty I never had this idea. See the chair supporting my bottom, it seems it has jacked me up. Now I am the Babu, the monarch of my whim.' The chair was munching as the heavy load of his bottom shifted angles. Reshma saw him and scolded him, 'Idiot, Badshah ji,' she pulled Rabbani, 'You lunatic! What do you consider yourself. This chair is the honor of the master. This is a part of The Martin Dera not your bloody bottom-holder!'

Reshma was behaving like a savior. She had no practical reason to act a savior but she was doing it. She had shaken Rabbani, scratched at his face, pleaded and entreated but the Rabbani fellow had diffused her. He had captured the chair as a booty.

She heard the mob raving and howling. She paid ears to the uproar. Rabbani too gave ears to the uproars, 'Seems the rioting has started.' Rabbani Shadman lifted from the chair expecting the mob to attack the Bangalow. He rushed to the balcony to have a view of the rioting. But he could not catch full view of it. Sarita, Laxmi, Nirja and Ram Lal were wriggling like the lava, 'Are they mad making only howling sounds?' cried Rabbani, 'Why do not they attack the Bangalow?'

He in the hate blast caught Reshma by her breasts and squeezed them savagely. Reshma was squirming with pain fighting the brute. Rabbani was heard shouting war cries spurring the mob by words of vengeance, 'Come on Sarita, Laxmi, dear mobbers fall with the fury of avengers and plunder the Dera.' His voice got overtaken in the rising crescendo. Rabbani turned a blasting volcano, the lava of hate and revenge overflowing from his mouth he attacking the wings and the flesh of the Bangalow with teeth and nails, 'I shall pillage all, pillage its shape and size and loot it.' He gathered the house-hold articles in his arms and caught whatever from his teeth looking monstrous, 'Rabbani is the possessor of whatever he possesses.' He caught hold of the leg of the chair and tumbled over cutting his chin. In his mouth the leg of the chair looked like a bone of a prey in the hyena jaw.

Reshma locked her ears against the avengers' howling. She was horrified and was to the side of the Martins. She felt like protecting the Martins, 'My good Martins,' she cried, 'My pretty- pretty Sophie mam and then this pink-faced Martin *saheb* I am worried for the couple. This mob will ravage the poor Dera. I am Bonga thing! The real Bonga comes alive in me. I shall act Bonga, voice Bonga, be Bonga.' Reshma became violent with care. Her violence was no fury. It was like the Bonga activated inside to protect the Martins.

She looked at Rabbani prayerfully for support but finding him cold she cursed him. She was helpless and had nothing except prayer. Her prayer got stuck to her throat as she heard a fresh bout of howling, 'These avengers are going to invade the Dera. God save the Martins, my pretty-pretty Sophie mam and this pink-face monkey! Admitting the pink-face had been cruel but the cruelty of the mobbers I hate.' Reshma howled in horror. She herself did not know her compassion plug had been triggered. It might be the horror of bloodshed!

Rabbani was callous, entirely a ruthless devil given to avenging. He swept upon whatever wings and flesh of the Dera he could capture and growled like a dog, 'All that I have touched shall be mine.' His teeth caught the chair leg in the hyena jaw as he drooled and from his eyes, savagery spilled like savagery.

Reshma became numb witnessing the mobbing display of vendetta like she was watching a horror film. She pinched on her flesh to check if she was dead and could see that the mob had railed through the broken walls and captured the wings and flesh of the Dera like infection, 'Gandhi and his passivity, the violence of the violent I can see demonstrating the fury!' Reshma had been kicked aside. Sarita, Laxmi, Nirja and Ram Lal, the mob behind them had spread like infection over the wings and flesh of the poor Dera vandalizing it.

* * * * *

The sky overhead got darkened by the clouds of the bats and birds chasing each other. The jungle had taken the lunatic shape, winds and sounds engaged in the pitch battles. Panic had worn the garb of horror. The dusky sky was picturing the aerial riot in horror. There were cracks in the sky to let angels peep through and report the riot upward to the authorities. The mountain range shrouded in fogs and silence looked drugged as if to swallow pain. The winds had gone thick and the evening had lost its flux to the horizon.

We were face to face with the horror scene awaiting to narrate stories of more horror. Our breath had been choked to the gullet and eyes were seeing the melodrama of the catastrophe ahead. A swarm of the black birds shrieked the scariest war cries and would have swooped upon the fleeting owls but for the change in the scene below.

Sarita, Laxmi, Nirja, Ram Lal and the mob behind them thickened into a ball of fury and blasting like live bombs they attacked the walls of the Martin Dera. They were cannoning the walls with their fists made hammers.They applied their teeth and tongue to infuriate them further as their heads crashed upon the walls of the Bangalow. The rioting fury of the mob stealing breaths of the winds howled till their throats cracked and mouth threw blood.

Sarita, Laxmi, Nirja, Ram Lal and others belched words of hate and vengeance looking monstrous in the falling dusk. The sky suffering from the sickness of horror trembled to witness the fury of human capacity, 'These human mobs, these ugly storming of the human capacity to breed fury out of the belly we wonder the humans are the scariest of the creatures of hate and vengeance.' The sky whispered these words to the stars and the stars carried these words up above to the firmament where God sat aloft.

The drama of fury and vengeance on earth around the Martin Dera peaked when the sky saw the texture of fury turning red. It was figurative and nothing more and the sky preferred to watch the melodrama, 'These human furies in riots anywhere in any shape and volume has one common feature that the rioters get diffused and their identities go buried so that when they act, they act as a mass havoc.' This was the remark of the sky overhead now quite determined not to send down any message of sense to the rioters.

Martin till then held captive by his scare had suddenly turned a warrior, his gun hurling overhead and words of mouth gusting forth violent curses had come out of the hide out, 'Bastard, you the scoundrel,' he leveled the gun to the firing position and the scene of havoc created by the mobbers turned into the scene of scattering bottoms and the backs. The gun of Martin seemed to borrow the power but it was the gun in the hand of Martin now irrelevant in the background of the outstanding freedom.

In one gesture the mobbers looked swamped by fright but it was mis-estimation. Sarita, Laxmi, Nirja, Ram Lal and the mobbers had not turned blank. They had crouched like the pouncing beasts and would hurl the attack, 'Stop you Martin man this your weapon of death pointing to us.' The mouths hurled cries of wars, 'Bonga! Bonga! Our savior, come!' The mouths opened the crater-hole of lava. The mob bound itself into the severe rocket tool to fire.

Martin saw them and guessed that they had gone mad because Delhi had caught the independence. Martin lowered the barrels of the gun and for the first time in life he visioned a Bonga figure lurking about. It was a stark delusion of mind but he said that he faced the Bonga figure in a giant shape, 'Is it their Bonga? The face of the Bonga resembled the tigers he had killed.' The Bonga image shook Martin to the bottom. He mewed the words of compromise. He opened his mouth to pop up the words of appeal. But the Bonga thing had clamped his throat. Martin was trembling, his gun was a limping tool. The mountain range behind the scene was now boiling with energy that monsters carry. The sky overhead had held its breath vigilant, 'Will the mob attack?' This was the humblest query of the sky which the authority above did not clarify.

Martin looked behind him hoping for Sophia to turn up but the lady was lagging behind not confused about herself. She knew that the sudden advent of independence had sparked spark reaction of this magnitude, 'Yes, I know the mob has no commander. Gandhi and fear of the English both have together left the scene. These mobbers are the outcome of the un-diked energy. They will wreak vengeance. They will vent their long-contained anger and fire. We would be the most vulnerable targets.' Sophie forgot that she had been their favorite and never expected anything concessional. She knew that a mad mob acts from the impulse of self-operating hate biz.

She reached the Martin thing. She touched him on the shoulder. She felt that he was a bad soldier in the crisis. She pitied him and said nothing cutting, 'Well sir. Patience! This is the time of crisis. We cannot over-excite us otherwise the mob would react lethally.'

This was the warning from her in the time when Martin was losing his guts. He touched her on the shoulder and patting her said nothing concrete. He was wary and scared and was a picture of the universal defeat in the form he was, 'What to do? Whom to call for help? Shall I call Salim Bahadur? He is the master of these rowdy gangs. He might control them.' Martin finished the line and turned like a storm. He caught Rabbani by collar and pulling him roughly ordered him to rush to Salim Bahadur.

* * * * *

Rabbani who had been out to loot the Bangalow and make Sophia mam his keep was as if bounced into action, 'Sir! Sir ji *saheb*!' he saluted him and stepping five steps back he turned as if he were a military man, 'I shall run to Salim *saheb*.' He obeyed the command and his obedience confirmed his servility. His mind got a den of dark recluse where he hid his dirty plans of loot.

He was running on foot to Hawa Mahal to catch Salim Khan and his wife, 'Sir *saheb* ji,' he checked his breath heaving hugely and delivered the massage like the pregnant bitch littering on the road, 'Sir *ji saheb* this your Martin forester is in troubles. The village mob has gathered before his Dera. He summons you to come to his rescue fast.'

Rabbani was not talking in resonance with the desire to fetch Salim Khan. Rabbani's plan to loot the Dera was foiled so he wished Salim Khan did not comply, 'Okey,' said the Khan, 'Then the daring mob has reached the Bangalow?' he pressed Shall Jaan to accompany him, '*Begum* this Martin is in troubles. We must reach to his rescue.' Shally forgetting that she was a creature without guts to meet the real threats in a hurry punched wrong sandals into her feet and became ready to set out, 'But your sandals did not you check the texture. You have slipped wrongly mine into your feet.'

Shally shook off the sandals and asking him if her face was looking good, she caught a bundle of something eatable, 'What nuisance bunch you have caught? We are not going on a picnic.' She regretted and leaving the eatable on the table said she would fresh herself.

* * * * *

The couple was on the baggy driving in full speed to Martin Dera. The Martin Bangalow was physically the same but the surrounding scene had changed. It was going to prove a captive of the new developments. The Dera was going to take into record the un-foreseen mishaps. The Martins were targeted. Their life was in danger. The couple from Hawa Mahal had rushed to the Martins rescue.

Salim Khan was the same cowering soul, confused about how he would handle the mob, 'You know *begum* this Martin has never been bad to me. This Martin not treating me equal has not been offending to me. He is in a crisis. He needs help. I do not know how I can help him. But I shall reach him for moral support.' Salim Khan did not expect any sharp words of invectives from his wife, 'Sir Khan Bahadur this is no time to spill words of poppy intent. This is the occasion to disburse your best of help.' Shally got charged with compassion.

'Help? No way. The madding mob would not hear me. I wonder how I can control them, these deranged bellicose herd!' Salim sounded weak, 'These fellows have never been treated like human beings. Now that they have occasion they will return with the beastly.'

Salim Khan urged Rabbani to brief what was happening. Rabbani said a lot of things which mismatched the possible mob-reactions, 'Sir Ji *sahab* we have this opportunity now after years to loosen up.We should not help the *pink-face*. He deserves being paid in his coin.' Rabbani wanted Salim Khan not to render real help.

Shally Khan got offended, 'We cannot leave a good family in danger. Then this lady Sophia has been good. The mob retaliation would harm her. We have to see that she is not harmed.' Shally imagined the rioters vandalizing. She was quite baffled, 'We shall go to protect the couple.'

'But madam ji these *pink-monkeys* have been bad to us. The entire race of the English has been so ruthless. These Bongas of the villagers they destroyed them. Then Gandhi and associates I feel they have un-professed hate of them, at least the way they have held us as serfs.' Rabbani was belching hate. But Salim Khan soberly said, 'Matter is not how the Angrez behaved. Matter is how we behave. The Gandhi-grains of forgiveness matter.'

Rabbani held his tongue. He spurred the pony. The baggy was racing fast. The Martin Dera was the same placid and grand building awaiting consequences of the riot.

* * * * *

'Stop you the devils. Just stop vandalizing.' Salim Khan yelled with the might of whatever authority he could muster in his voice. He was facing a rowdy gang. Sarita, Laxmi, Nirja and the following mob were wild with rage. They were powered by the illusion of the surrender of power to the Gandhi-people. Inside them their blood was talking the language of the belligerent nuisances. They were rowdy and vindicative.

Salim's order fell flat. The sizzling mob turned tornado of sort whirling and whirling in the frenzy. The bodies had welded bodies and the mob had turned a solid bloc of fury, 'Shut up you Salim Khan *saheb*. Shut up you and your orders. Do not intervene. We are going to take the land plot for our dear Bonga's shrine.' The howlers were fierce. Salim Khan was shaken to the bottom. He pumped his lungs to voice the loudest order but his lungs gave way. He mewed and mewed and mewed. Shally Khan took guts to address the mob in the poetry of her appeals:

'Anger, rage, the fury you talk, your venging tongue

We are no more than the waiting fools in a bunch

Stop this your mobbing fury

Take note that revenge is not the fair answer to tarry.'

She found herself discounted. The mob was smoldering. It stood in bunches against the Martin Dera. The Martin Dera still the same lofty residence was indifferent to the development. Shally pitied herself for the unwanted poetry. She was shamed too, 'When the mob turns a mob the words of morality fail to affect.' She receded.

The mob had by then spread like an infection on the land plot and was rolling in crocodile death-roll, 'This sacred land piece is ours. Our Bongas have directed us to take it. We shall raise Bonga shrine over here. No power on earth would deter us.' Sarita, Laxmi, Nirja, Ram Lal and behind them the mob made weird dance over the land plot, 'Bonga Raja!

Bonga Raja! We are yours and you are ours. We shall take revenge on the Martins by raising your shrine here in front of the Killers' Dera.'

Shally Khan nervously pressed the hand of Sophia and Sophia nervously pressed the hand of Martin and Salim Khan caught the arm of Martin, 'No use sir appealing to the madding mob. They are gone crazy. Let us sneak back to the safety of the Bangalow,' pleaded Shally. In her eyes the scene of her father being dragged away by the British sepoy clouded her eyes, 'Mob then and mob now has no difference. It remains the same lethal mob!'

Martin not breaking under the threat he took his gun and rushed out furiously yelling swearwords. On the spur of the moment, he levelled his gun upon the mob and fired two shots. It was no criminal firing. The mob received the bullets. Two bodies fell. Three more got injured. A crack appeared in the mob now running helter-skelter. The scene was bloody red. Shally Khan shut her eyes against the scene. Sophia Juliet hooped in horror. Her mouth yelled. On her tongue the phrase hung like leech, '*The Bongas were lies. They remained invalid. They did not come to save lives.*'

The sky overhead froze in horror. The eyes of the time witnessed the massacre and went inimical to Martin. Martin was raving, 'I shall kill more of you if you dared stand the ground.' The scattered mob again began to collect in a martyring gusto. Sarita, Laxmi, Nirja and Ram Lal along with the desperados gathered like storm and rushed in a fury upon the Dera of the Martins.

Shally Jaan was the first to shed off her poetry and run for life. Next Sophie mam was the person who shedding the hope and pride of belonging to the villagers ran for life. Next the main hero: Martin ran for life! In the face of death, the only language that sounded loudest was the scare of it.

The mob had attacked the Bangalow. The inmates of the Dera were staked to death. Salim Khan dragging Martin Julius by collar entered the Dera. Shally clung to Sophia Juliet and hanging from her frame she rolled over and over on the stairs cutting and bruising her nose and arms, 'Run Martin. Run Sophie. Run for dear life.' Shally ran madly into the room.

Martin stumbled around looking for a hide out. The curtain hangings lured him. He slid behind them. But his crime became his nightmare. He was trembling and gathering his limbs together to make them rest. In his eyes horror of death was visible and in his heart the pining to hold dear life safe was dangling precariously. Shally Jaan, Salim Khan and the poor Sophia were racing together to locate the safety hide outs.

Martin was the most miserable of the creatures, desperate in all versions and finding himself forlorn. He knew her madam had deserted him. His hope tugged on the lady Shally, the character in the story without anything reliable, 'Shally ji dear please save me.' The voice of desperation was heard and Salim Khan mis-hearing it for his name felt most un-safe on the wake of the mob attack.

The mob had stormed inside. Rabbani was leading the gang greedily to vandalize everything that belonged to Martin Dera. He became the self-professed ring leader in the ensuing pogrom. His hands had taken the best of what the booty he could hold but his eyes were searching for the fair lady Sophia. In his satanic mind the lustful legs of Sophie Juliet were looking bare, 'Where is my Sophia lady? I shall *take her* down on my bed. The delicious feast!'

He spotted her precariously kneading her body into the fold of Shally khan. Shally glared at the monster but she was no more than a banana thing. She struggled with nails and teeth and failed to save Sophia Begum. Rabbani picked the cowering Sophia like some doll in the hand of a lusting ravager, 'The fair delicious girl I had nothing else but you in the mind.'

The lady Sophia was wriggling in his hands like a butterfly, 'Leave me.' She cried and then she saw the mob filling the Bangalow like the flood of plundering troops. Sarita, Laxmi, Nirja and all were ravaging the articles and securing their shares except the tiny Gobardhan who was un-expectedly biting on the bottom of Rabbani tearing his flesh, 'Bastard leave the lady. She had been to us our Bonga.' The bite violence was too big for being endured.

Sophia fell off the hold and scuttling in horror she hid herself underneath a gigantic table. In her eyes horror ogled the scene of vandalizing. The Rabbani thing was diverted to the looting spree. He forgot Sophia and Sophia remembered the words of warning her husband had been uttering, 'Yes, I am a non-belonging creature in the foreign land, a total outsider.'

She soothed her arms. She shed tears. She sat broken and havocked. She saw Salim Khan folding hands to the vandals. She felt ashamed of herself and her bare convictions as regard the heaven of freedom. Before her eyes the advent of the heaven of freedom was displaying the nightmare. She was trembling like a thwarted hope! Even Shally jaan had secluded her within the pleas of time. She was standing horrified, a witness to the realm of plunder on vogue.

Outside, the sky was hung up dead and the winds and light and the motion of the stars and everything else was only stunned. The mountain range in the background and the Bonga effect if it was something was invalid. No Bonga in any capacity was active to check the mob. The mob inside the Bangalow was looting its wings and flesh and leaving the inmates dazed and decomposed. In the distance the Buddha banyan tree stood stunned and its snake pop-roots hung like dead fingers.

Martin *saheb* had locked himself in the bathroom hoping for some miracle savior to come while Salim Khan was sitting on a chair where he had been fastened loosely by the saree of Shally Khan now standing in horror looking aghast and trying to mean what her idea of the heaven of freedom had sometimes ago floated in her head chamber.

Sophie Julee was broken in spirit and bowing her head in shame was pondering upon her wooly thoughts of the heaven of freedom, 'I was wrong to interpret the heaven of freedom in the terms I interpreted. I was foolish and ignorant of the other ugly truth of it in terms of what vandalism reflects. My folly. My mishap. I regret and upbraid me. I say that any freedom if it comes without check on its flux will turn mean.'

'Freedom, freedom my dear freedom, come sure but with right bridling

Come to the community only who it naturally could take its feeding

We cannot appreciate the freedom that just flings open its wings wildly

And falls upon all and sundry in a flash boom suddenly.'

Sophie's mind filled with the echo of these lines. She was ashamed and penitent and feeling devastated but she was equally sad and calm and hopeful. It was her part of nature to hope for positivity. She had learned it through her encounters with life and its vagaries so she was hopeful. She could see that her man was nowhere but he was safe as the mobbers had busied themselves in the loot of the Bangalow. Shally Jaan was the witness of the loot and in her the ever-vibrant fantasy was getting arrested as she was plied to the reality that had the other face.

Sophia saw Reshma. Reshma did not see her. Shally too saw Reshma but Reshma did not see her either. The ears heard Reshma yelling in fright the dirtiest swear words, 'Stop you all this carnage. Stop vandalizing.'

Reshma was an alive angel of hope. She was operating from the impulse of good-sense and was vibrant with energy of a savior, 'Stop Rabbani! Drop the hand of Sophie. She is sacred, she is Bonga. Do not defile her.' Reshma bit on the bottom of Rabbani. He was grunting like an injured pig. She whirled like a tornado fighting Sarita, Laxmi, Ram Lal to drop the loot. Goberdhan was on her side howling and biting the vandal. The drama of the rescue was as impressive as the drama of plunder and in between the two the phenomenal relief was that Shally Jaan, Salim Khan and Martin had been brought to the forefront of maturity and made ashamed of what they were while Sophie was to decide where and how the heaven of freedom had fulfilled itself or been left unfulfilled.

* * * * *

The mob suddenly ceased and the scene changed. It had been caught red-handed vandalizing. From somewhere the English forces entered the Bangalow. Martin who had locked himself in the bathroom came out nervously tumbling about and he complained to the commander of the troops about Sarita, Laxmi, Nirja and Ram Lal and forgot to mention his crime, 'Who killed the two?' shouted the commander.

Silence shrouded the scene. It was the silence of confession to make and manipulation to make. The bodies of the two *faceless* villagers were in the custody of the commander, 'Who fired the weapon?' demanded the commander. Silence kept the scene shrouded. Sarita, Laxmi, Nirja and Ram Lal stood drooping heads, the looted-articles clinging to their hands. They uttered no name. Martin was standing crucified to the ground, his hands limping and loose.

'Who fried the weapon and took the lives?'

'It was me.' said Sophie Martin, 'I took the gun. I fired the bullets. I killed the villagers.' Sophie made a lie that was no lie but atonement.

Sarita, Laxmi, Nirja and Ram Lal stood stunned hearing the fair lie.

'No sir *saheb*,' the tiny voice of the tiny boy Gobardhan captured the attention, 'Sophia mam is telling a lie.' The mob trembled with fright of arresting and penitence of the same.

Gobardhan who had fetched attention gave a U-turn to the story, 'The weapon was in the hand of the forester. It had fired shots. The Bonga tigers were the illusion! Sophie mam was innocent. Reshma was innocent. Sarita and Laxmi and the like were innocent. Rabbani Shadman, the scoundrel was the leader of the loot gang.' Gobardhan uttered the witness.

The commander of the troops, a pink-face monkey man looking at Martin and the trembling Sophie with stealth concession slanted his neck to the ear of Martin and whispered, '*The weapon had fired in self-defense.*'

* * * * *